PRAISE FOR
AND GOD CREATED WOMAN

"A gripping story about real women. Mika Miller has created a thought-provoking novel that will have you astonished."
—Jason Poole, Co-Author of *Convict's Candy*

"Definitely a page-turner! Witty, thrilling and well-written, *And God Created Woman* will truly have you enthralled."
—Wahida Clark, Author of *Payback is a Mutha*

"An intelligent read. *And God Created Woman* is captivating, moving and enlighting. Mika Miller's debut novel is intense!"
—Dru Noble, Author of *Sonz of Darkness*

"Mika Miller's novel, *And God Created Woman* is a wonderful read. I can't wait for the sequel!"
—Tony Collins, Author of *Games Women Play*

"*And God Created Woman* captivates from start to finish. A brilliant story of Heavenly proportions!"
—Angela Wallace, Author of *Secret Dramas*

"Mika Miller has proven herself as a talented writer with her debut novel, *And God Created Woman*. The story will move you."
—Emlyn DeGannes, Publisher of *That Was Dirty*

"*And God Created Woman* dazzles you with each ~~~~!"
don Reign

"*And God Created Wo*␣ t women.
Takes you on an emotior␣
—Cartel ␣␣␣␣␣n Hustlers

D1293915

"Explosive! Filled with non-stop action, Mika Miller has masterfully written a novel that focuses on real women issues."
—Treasure E. Blue, Author of *Harlem Girl Lost*

1

GHETTOHEAT® PRODUCTIONS

GHETTOHEAT®
CONVICT'S CANDY
HARDER
SONZ OF DARKNESS
LONDON REIGN
GAMES WOMEN PLAY
GHOST TOWN HUSTLERS
BOY-TOY
SKATE ON!
SOME SEXY, ORGASM 1

A GHETTOHEAT® PRODUCTION

AND GOD CREATED WOMAN

Mika Miller

PUBLISHER'S NOTE
This is a work of fiction. Any names to historical events, real people, living and dead, or to real locales are intended only to give the fiction a setting in historic reality. Other names, characters, places, businesses and incidents are either the product of the author's imagination or are used fictitiously, and their resemblance, if any, to real life counterparts is entirely coincidental.

4

ACKNOWLEDGMENTS

To my mother and father for encouraging and nurturing my love of writing. For buying me my first typewriter, a Brother Word Processor (I thought I was a real writer then). This book is the first of many great things to come.

Anissa, you once gave me a present, a magnet with an angel painted on it, that posed the question, *"How you gonna have wings and don't fly?"* My answer is, *"With you by my side...watch me soar."* Love You.

Princess...girl, you can never imagine how much love I have for you! Keep reading, writing and stay focused! T.N.N. for life! I love you, love you, love you...remember that.

Percell, the love of my life. Baby, I know I got on your nerves...*"Read this part, read this part."* Thank you for keeping me grounded and humble during this whole process.

Brenda Palmer, my *Phenomenal Woman,* thanks for finding the manuscript on my coffee table, and saying, *"Girl, you've got to do something with this!"* Thank you for believing in me, even when I didn't think this was possible.

Jacqueline Turner Banks at Best Selling Books. Thank you for your efforts. If you need a great agent, Google this woman...

HICKSON...thank you. Peace and Blessings to the entire GHETTOHEAT® MOVEMENT.

6

Dedicated to the memory of my best friend, Bryan Howard...taken away from me too soon.

AND GOD CREATED
WOMAN

MEKKA

Chapter 1

Some people call me a *hoe* because I strip for niggas and hustle for cash.

Yeah, I turn tricks.

I tell niggas, "If the price is right, then the deal is real." My momma used to say, *"As long as you got a pussy, you sittin' on a goldmine. Never give your shit away for free."*

If that means I'm a hoe, so be it!

None of these *bitches* pays my bills or puts food on my mutha…fuckin' table, so fuck 'em!

God didn't give me the type of brains where I can understand all that "technical" book shit. In elementary school, I was never good at math and, to tell the truth, I was never that good at readin' either.

It's not like I didn't try.

It's just that, when it came to school, nothin' really registered. In high school, I tried to learn the secretarial trade. I figured that if I had some sort of technical skill, that I could at least get a halfway decent gig after I graduated. Well, it turns out that typin' and shorthand was just another thing that I failed at.

So bein' somebody's secretary was out of the question.

With no real education or skill, I had to settle for minimum wage jobs. My first job was workin' as a maid at a five-star hotel. After about two weeks, I got tired of cleanin' after rich bitches that shitted all over the toilet seats, and hid bloody tampons all over the *goddamn* place!

And I wasn't 'bout to work in *nobody's* fast-food restaurant. So I had to come up with a new plan. And that's when I met this f-i-n-e-ass, Puerto Rican *muthafucka* by the name of Ricky.

Ricky was a straight-up thug. He had tattoos all across his chest and stomach like *Tupac* and shit. When I met Ricky, I had two kids. I was single, workin' my ass off as a hostess in a restaurant and braidin' hair on the side.

I was finally maintainin', you know, gettin' money. But I was always workin', so I didn't have no time to enjoy my kids or my money.

Ricky came on the scene and promised me all kinds of shit. He was like, *"Baby, you ain't gotta work that hard, why don't you lemme take care o' you and nem kids."*

Ricky had my head gassed up, for real!

Plus he was layin' the pipe on the regular. Fuckin' me *real* good wit' his fine ass. So one night, after Ricky got finished eatin' my cooch, he was like, *"Baby, I'ma take you to Philadelphia wit' me. You an' the kids can come wit' me, and I'll hook ya'll up wit' errythang."*

Me, bein' naive, I followed his fine ass all the way to Philly and shit, and the nigga started trippin'! Beatin' me up, knockin' me all upside my head, accusin' me of cheatin'...which I wasn't. Ricky started kickin' my ass to the point that I was too ashamed to go to work with black eyes and busted lips, and I eventually got fired.

Long story short. After a while, I finally had enough. I packed me and my kids up and went to a shelter. I didn't know no fuckin' body, I didn't know shit about Philadelphia—all I knew that I was broke and I needed a place to stay for me and my kids.

So I went to the welfare office....

I tried to work within the system. Well, welfare was draggin' they feet, and in the meantime, I needed to make some cash, fast.

That's when Marilyn popped up on the scene. Marilyn was basically a po' white trash version of myself. She was stayin' wit' me at the shelter.

Marilyn told me between puffs of her *Marlboro* cigarette: *"Mekka why don't you strip? You got a beautiful body, and I know you would make plenty of money 'cause you tall, you got them big, perky titties, and you high yellow. You could make some good money and be outta here in no time; you perky titty bitch!"*

I figured what I lacked in the brains department I'd make up for with the "gifts" that God did give me: my pretty face, this small waist and these big ole titties!

So I took Marilyn's advice. I rolled around wit' her, and she took me to some strip clubs. That's how I got this gig where

I'm at now. Strippin' at a hole-in-the-wall called *Dutch Gardens*. *Dutch Gardens* is where "Mekka" was born, but I gotta finish this story another time, I think I hear them callin' my name.

"Hey Mekka, you go on in five," Trish hollers from the entrance of the locker room. Trish is a white bitch who *swears* she's black!

Only fucks Black men....

And she can get away wit' it 'cause, Trish got a ghetto-booty and a body like a sista. And some niggas think that "white is right", but they'll be alright. Trish is kinda cool though, as far as white girls go.

"Hey hoe; Mekka, you hear me?" Trish calls again.

"Bitch wait! I heard your *muthafuckin'* ass!"

I check my face in my magnetic mirror hung on the inside of my locker, spray on a hint of *Bulgari* "Omnia Eau de Toilette" body mist, adjust my g-string and tighten the laces on my thigh-high boots. Other bitches wear them tall shoes, but I'm gettin' old, and my old-ass feet and ankles need a lil' mo' support.

Plus, it's easier to slide them dollar bills in your boots and keep it movin'.

I slam my locker shut and take inventory of my surroundings. There's a room full of beautiful bitches all *hatin'* on me!

They wanna know how I make it-do-what-it-do! How I make all dat dough in the course of three hours, and they been in here all night lettin' niggas suck on they titties and finger their coochies...and still comin' up broke?

FUCK BITCHES!

Like I always say: "Money over niggas; bitches, stick to the script!"

Men call me a *bitch!*

Because when it comes to business, I'm a man-eater. My mind thinks faster than theirs, my competitive edge is sharper than theirs, my will is stronger than theirs.

Men call me a bitch.

Because I am a machine—I seek and destroy the competition. I close the million-dollar deals. I call the shots.

Men call me a bitch.

Because I'm not a traditional woman, I don't fit into their mold. I don't cook, I don't clean and I *don't* take their mess. I go where I want to go, I do what *I* want to do, and I say *whatever* it is that I want say...all without the assistance, or permission, from *any* man. And they can't *stand* it.

So they call me a bitch....

I say, if the best word that men can conjure up to antagonize me with is "bitch", then I'll *be* that...we all know that obedient and docile women are *never* the kind to make history.

I used to take offense to the word "bitch", but now...*humph*...I take it as the highest compliment. Do you know what I tell them? I tell them "bitch" stands for: "*B*eing *I*n *T*otal *C*ontrol of *H*erself." After all, with my high-end, six-figure salary, I can *afford* to be a "bitch"! I can also afford my newly-renovated condominium on *Rittenhouse Square,* my summer home in the Hamptons, my lodge in Namibia, my chauffeur-driven *Bentley,* and my *Gucci,* glitz and glamorous lifestyle.

The stigma of a being labeled a bitch is *clearly* a double standard. Why is it that every time a woman, such as myself, climbs the ladder of success, stands at the top of the financial hierarchy, and makes a name for herself, without taking shit from any man, she has to be considered a bitch?

If the aforementioned attributes is what qualifies someone as being a "bitch", then I must pose this question, is billionaire, real estate developer, *Donald Trump* a bitch? Is rebel and gazillionaire, *Richard Branson,* owner of *Virgin Airlines* a bitch?

Was oil industrialist and investor, *John D. Rockefeller* a bitch? If not, then why me?

Oh well, no sense in losing sleep over it. Que sera sera.

I can only be me.

I have always grabbed life, and men, by the balls. Men may not like me, but they *will* respect me. What men fail to realize is that I didn't always have it like this.

I started out as a stockbroker. I got my Series 7 license while I was at *Harvard Business School.* When I graduated, with an MBA, my first job was at *Merrill Lynch* in Manhattan.

I remember the first day I'd walked onto the *New York Stock Exchange* trading floor. I was meek, skinny, and nervous like a little baby bird, walking out into a sea of vultures and buzzards. The energy was chaotic—men yelling, phones ringing, ticker symbols changing frantically. I was being pushed, poked and prodded, bombarded, elbowed and shoved, until I found myself standing smack dab in the center of the trading room floor.

I felt like the room was spinning.

I felt lost.

And abandoned.

But most of all, I felt powerless.

I went through my first day without making one transaction. At the end of the day, my boss, Donny, took me to dinner. I'll never forget it.

He told me that, *"The trading floor is a 'man's world', maybe you should rethink your role."* Donny also told me, in so many words that, I was too "pretty" for that line of work. He meant it as a compliment, but I'd interpreted his statement as an insult.

What I heard Donny saying was that, I was a woman, and in *his* vocabulary, the word "woman" was synonymous with weak. Donny then looked at me and said, *"Ms. Vincent, I don't think you have what it takes to be a trader. I'll call Human Resources in the morning and see what we may have available in our secretary pool."*

I'd actually began to cry.

The smug bastard handed me a handkerchief, stood up, and walked away. I was dismissed, and the very next day, demoted to the role of executive administrative assistant. I was subjected to typing and filing other broker's reports, and fixing all of the errors that they were too stupid to notice.

It became my main job to make the brokers look good, while they took all the credit and received all of the accolades. Not only was it in my job description to fetch coffee, but I was also forced to endure constant sexual harassment and condescending innuendos.

The whole experience changed my life irrevocably. I'd vowed to recommit myself, and rise above the glass ceiling that *Merrill Lynch* placed above me.

I was a woman on a mission.

I took all of the knowledge, resources and contacts that I'd made along the way, and used them to reinvent myself.

Now, I own venture capital firm, *Capital Appreciation*. I specialize in raising money for high-profile clients who need to close various deals. I associate with a lot of major players, but I prefer being behind the scenes—incognito if you will.

I've never been one to get caught up in the celebrity aspect of the business. I've got enough headaches of my own without dealing with the sensational side of this industry.

My desk intercom buzzes, and the voice of Anissa, my executive assistant, pours into the atmosphere of my corner office suite.

"Ms. Vincent, excuse the interruption, but it's six o' clock, and if there's nothing else you need me to do, I'm heading home for the evening. If I miss the six-fifteen train, I won't get to the daycare to pick up Princess until after seven. And you know when you're late they start charging ten dollars a minute."

I look at the gold hands on my diamond encrusted *Movado* watch, and it's straight up-and-down; six o' clock on the nose.

"Anissa, you're right. I'm sorry. You know how I can get carried away when I'm engrossed. I tell you what, stop by my office so we can brief for tomorrow's agenda, and I'll have my chauffeur take you straight to the daycare, and then take you home. No trains for you tonight; is that a deal?"

"That's what's up! Just let me grab my things and I'll be right there!"

Ever since I first interviewed Anissa, I was impressed by her ability to play both sides. She can be very professional when she needs to be, and at the same time, Anissa's a natural-born street-hustler.

When I first met her, she only had an Associates degree in Business Administration, but Anissa was very driven, resourceful,

15

down to earth and full of life. I respected her vivacity and determination, so I gave Anissa a shot. And so far, I haven't regretted taking a chance on her.

The noisy shuffle of people hastily rushing past my office finally falls to a still, calm silence. Six o'clock is quitting time for the rest of my associates, but not for me. It's usually the only time I can get anything accomplished.

I stuff a stack of contracts into my *Louis Vuitton* attaché case, and slide my *Blackberry* phone into the front compartment. I then pick up a remote from the midst of paperwork on my desk and aim it at the floor, then to ceiling windows overlooking *Liberty Bell Square*. With the push of a button, the vertical blinds whisk shut and the chandelier above my conference desk goes dim.

At that moment, Anissa glides into my office, legal pad in hand, ready to brief me on the course of tomorrow's events. She's wearing a cream-colored jersey top, camel-colored suede pants with a matching suede bag; all by *Chloe'*.

Anissa's hair is styled in a ghetto-fabulous ponytail with long bangs swept across one eye. She's professional, chic and hip, all rolled into one. Anissa then looks at me quizzically after noticing that I have begun to clear my desk off.

"Ms. Vincent, I can't *believe* you're actually leaving at six. That's a bit early for you, isn't it? What's up? You got a hot date?"

"Yeah, I've got a *real* hot date with this stack of contracts, and then I have a booty call with these payroll checks that need my signature," I answer with sarcasm. Anissa rolls her eyes.

"You got jokes. But, if you ask me, I'd say a 'booty call' is just what you need."

I cut my eyes at Anissa. "Well, nobody's *asking* you."

"Naw, seriously, you're beautiful, successful...you could have *any* man you want, but instead, you flee men like you're allergic. You've got that thing where you *act* like you don't need a man."

"Oh, I see, so you think a man is the answer to *all* my problems? Anissa, I didn't get to be where I am in life by running after men. I have *everything* I need and more, no thanks to *anyone* but myself," I answer with firm finality, queuing Anissa that this conversation is over and that I'm ready to leave. I then stand up and pull my classic black *Dolce & Gabbana,* double-breasted,

16

wool blazer from the back of my chair; I ease into the silk lining and fasten the buttons.

Anissa obviously didn't catch my subtle hint.

"See, there you go again. Why is it that every time a Black woman gets ahead they forget how to be feminine? I've been working with you for two years, and not *once* have I seen you go out on a date, or even get excited about a man.

"We all know you can pay your own bills, you got plenty of money and fancy cars, and you hold your own around here with the big dogs. Nobody's questioning that. All I'm saying is that…it must be *awfully* unsatisfying to go home to a big-ass empty condo day-after-day, and sleep in a cold, lonely bed, night-after-night. I don't care what you say, *every* woman needs a man to cuddle up to when it's all said and done."

Anissa then took a calculated pause and stood to face me before delivering the final blow.

"…You know you're one step away from being a lesbian. I'm just keeping it real," she finished with a 'round-the-way girl smirk, before pulling a tube of *Laura Mercier* lip gloss from her purse; applying a layer of shine to her pouty lips, as if the conversation was over.

This little heifer has obviously lost her mind!

Anissa has the *audacity* to come into my office, critique my life, call me a lesbian, and think she's going to get away with it?

OH, HELL NO!

I can feel my temperature rising. But before I commence to give Anissa a verbal beat down, I remind myself to maintain control of the situation. After all, this conversation is really a small thing to a giant, but it's time for me to nip this in the bud.

I lean in close.

I smile venomously and instantaneously, Anissa is thrown off-balance.

"Put the lipstick away and listen to me well, because I *don't* intend to repeat myself. You and I are not friends, you see, so don't get it twisted. I'm your boss. The extent of our conversations should be about business and *that's* the bottom line.

"Your advice is completely unsolicited, unwarranted and without any merit. The name on my door reads 'Tristan Vincent', not 'Anissa McCloud', and I *expect* you to respect those boundaries. Furthermore, whether I have someone to cuddle with at night is none of your concern. All you need to be concerned with is my signature on your check. Is that understood?"

Anissa nods a yes.

"The difference between you and I, Anissa, is...I don't have a man...I don't want a man...and I don't *need* a man. That may be a hard concept for you to wrap your little mind around but, that's just the way *I* am. That's how it is and that's how it's going to be, whether you agree with it or not."

And with that being said, I slide on my *Gucci* shades, grab my attaché case and head towards the door. I stop abruptly at the thresh-hold and look back at Anissa over my shoulder. Her expression is heavy with the weight of her foot in her mouth.

"My chauffeur will be waiting in the *Town Car* for you out front to see that you get to the daycare on time. We'll go over the agenda first thing in the morning. I'll see you tomorrow, *Miss Thing.*"

I then slide my shades to the tip of my nose. I wink at Anissa and disappear down the hall. For the first time in a long time, I am actually leaving the office at a decent hour.

Suddenly I feel invigorated.

I contemplate all the alternatives that are more exciting than going home, ordering Chinese food, and reviewing profit-loss statements in my pajamas. My mind starts to spin.

As my mind calculates the plethora of possibilities, my body goes on auto-pilot. I press the elevator button, call the valet, and instruct them to bring my Bentley around to the front of the building.

As I wait for the elevator, I reflect on the hectic week that I've had, and I am suddenly overcome with a compelling desire for a stiff drink and some jazz music. I try to remember the name of the restaurant my girlfriend, Shawn told me about. She said it had a decent happy hour? If only I could remember the name....

Zanzalia...no, that's not it...Zanizia...no that's not it either. Hmmm, what is the name of that place?

The elevator now dings and opens before me. Two guys who work in the advertising firm on the floor above me are already inside. I see them from time-to-time as I enter or exit the building, but I've never ever said more than "good morning" or "good night" to any one of them; and never much cared to make "small talk".

In my opinion, small talk is for people who need to fill space. Most people don't know how to simply enjoy silence. If the conversation is not productive or conducive to my needs, then there's *no* need for mindless banter.

I step inside the elevator and the two men adjust themselves to accommodate me. I smile and then immediately face forward.

"Hey Larry, you feel like heading over to *Zanzibar Blue* for a drink?" the blonde haired guy asks in a nonchalant tone.

"Can't. I've got to get an early start on this new ad campaign. Gotta pitch an ad in Jersey tomorrow. Maybe we'll do *Zanzibar Blue* on Friday."

As I eavesdrop on their conversation, I hear the name *"Zanzibar Blue "*, and it hits me. That's the name of the spot Shawn was telling me about.

The elevator descends and slows to a halt at the lobby on the ground floor. The lobby is completely empty except for a lone security guard. He barely looks up from the mini television hidden under his desk in order to acknowledge me.

I step onto the glossy marble floor and make my way outside through the revolving glass doors, where my driver, Cornelius, is standing by my *Bentley*. Upon my arrival, he opens the door.

"Hello Cornelius."

"Hello, Ms. Vincent. I've taken the liberty of calling ahead to your favorite Chinese restaurant to pick up dinner on your way home."

His comment stops me dead in my tracks.

"Cornelius, am I *really* that predictable and boring?"

Cornelius now stares at me compassionately, hoping that he hasn't offended me.

"Pardon me, Ms. Vincent I didn't mean to imply that you were predictable or boring. Your usual Friday night routine is Chinese takeout—sesame chicken...wonton soup...and straight home to finish up paperwork."

"Well, Cornelius, that's about to change. I think that it's time that I step out of the same old routine."

"And how exactly do you presume to do that?"

I lean against the car and look out at rush hour traffic on Market Street: "I've been hearing people talk about a place called *Zanzibar Blue.* Have you ever heard it?"

"Yes, ma'am, I have."

"Is it a reputable place?"

"From what I've heard."

"Is it the sort of place where a person of *my* caliber would frequent?" I ask, sounding like a one-hundred percent snob.

"If you mean a place filled with stuffy business people trying to act like they have a life, then yes, you might enjoy it."

Cornelius is the only person that can be sarcastic with me and get away with it. He's been my butler and chauffeur for several years, and has grown into sort of a father figure, in a Morgan Freeman sort of way.

"Point taken. It's just that I haven't gone out in a while and I like to do my research first."

"Good Lord, woman, it's not rocket science. Now, if you want to go to *Zanzibar Blue,* then I'll take you. You're so scared to enjoy life, that you'll talk yourself out of anything that even remotely sounds like fun. Now, get in the car."

I sit inside my *Bentley* and Cornelius closes the door behind me. I can still hear him fussing at me after he shuts the door. Cornelius then positions himself in the driver's seat. He pushes the speakerphone on and calls the *Dynasty Chinese Restaurant* as he pulls away from the curb. He cancels my order.

"Now, that settles it." Cornelius says triumphantly.

MELANIE
Chapter 3

I never cared much for dick.

Pussy has *always* been my thang!

When I was thirteen, there were two dykes that lived on my block. At the time, I didn't know they were dykes; I didn't even know what the word "dyke" meant. All I thought was that, the two ladies, who were "roommates", lived across the street.

One was named Miss Tanya; the other, Miss Gloria. Miss Gloria was the pretty one, not that Miss Tanya wasn't pretty, it's just that, Miss Gloria had a more conventional type beauty: pretty face, pretty smile and long, pretty hair. Tonya, well, she was a bit rough around the edges, but back then, so was I.

Miss Tanya wore baggy clothes, like me. She wore her hair in cornrows, like mine (before I chopped all my hair off), and Miss Tanya had a swagger in the way she walked, like me.

Miss Tanya walked like a man.

And talked like a man.

She was confident, and strutted like a peacock. Miss Tanya always wore *Dickies* work suits and denim coveralls.

Miss Gloria was more dainty and feminine.

She shimmied when she walked, kinda like *Jackee* did on the TV show, *227;* always wearing tight sweaters and painted on *Sassoon* jeans.

Miss Gloria always smelled like fancy perfume.

Miss Tanya always smelled like motor oil.

Miss Gloria hosted *Tupperware* parties.

Miss Tanya worked as a janitor at *Temple University,* who also drank *Pabst Blue Ribbon Beer.*

Miss Gloria liked to drink hot cocoa with marshmallows and eat iced apple pie a la mode. That's the one thing that she and I had in common. Now, come to think of it, that's probably why we bonded so quickly.

When "the dykes" first moved on the block, it was wintertime. I remember because, three weeks after they moved in we had this huge snowstorm, and the block was snowed in. School was closed, so my sister, Tristan and I were stuck at home, while my dad braved the weather and went to work at the hospital.

I got up early that morning, threw on my rainbow-colored snowsuit, and raced outside to make some dough; shoveling out sidewalks, stoops and walkways for the folks on the block. It snowed for two weeks straight, so I made plenty of holiday dough that year; not to mention the fact that I got cool with most of the neighbors, especially with Miss Gloria....

Whenever Miss Tanya was home, she always shoveled her own walkway, but there were those rare occasions that she had to work, and I would step in and "fill her shoes".

On those days, I always saved "the dykes'" house for last, because Miss Gloria tipped the best, and always made me come inside for hot cocoa and apple pie when I was done. We'd also sit in her living room and listen to albums. Miss Gloria and I would dance and lip sync, or play cards until it was time for me to go home for lunch.

I loved those snow days.

Soon, the winter season went away, and spring appeared. Shoveling snow transformed into mowing lawns, and in the fall, mowing lawns turned into raking leaves. It didn't really matter what the season was, Miss Gloria would *always* invite me in....

This went on for three years.

By that time, I was sixteen, she and Miss Tanya had broken up, and Miss Gloria lived in that big old house by herself. She would always find reasons to have me come over.

Miss Gloria would need something fixed, or a picture hung, or her car tuned up. She would always watch me work and tell me how much I reminded her of Miss Tanya.

I didn't think much of it, until that day....

I remember it like it was yesterday. It was back when VCR's first came out. My father was the first one on the block to get a VCR, and I'd bragged on it so much, that Miss Gloria went out and bought one, too. She didn't know how to set her timer, so Miss Gloria called me over and asked me to set it for her, as usual.

"Tanya was always so good at this sort of thing," she would say. *"I don't know what to do without someone handy around the house."* Then, Miss Gloria would smile and shimmy into the kitchen, getting me something to snack on; sometimes even sneaking me a beer.

On this particular day, I was sitting on the floor, Indian style, reading the manual and setting the clock on her VCR, when Miss Gloria asked: *"Did you ever had a boyfriend?"*

I said: *"No."*

"Why not?"

I told her: *"Boys were stupid and immature."*

Miss Gloria said, *"Grown men were immature, too. That's why I only 'like' women."*

By that time, I knew what it meant when a woman said she "liked" another woman, but for some reason, I had never put two-and-two together with she and Miss Tanya; until right at that very moment. It didn't freak me out though, because Miss Gloria was *always* so nice to me.

It didn't matter.

Three beers later, I had her VCR all hooked up and I was enjoying my first buzz. I laid back on the floor while Miss Gloria had grabbed some old photo albums, from when she and Miss Tanya used to be together. She'd then sat down on the floor next to me and reminisced.

And we'd drank some more.

Miss Gloria told me that she'd really missed Tanya, and how Tanya used to make her feel. She'd asked me if I'd ever been kissed.

I said: *"No."*

Miss Gloria then asked if I'd ever been touched.

I said: *"No."*

Then, she'd told me how much I reminded her of Miss Tanya and asked me if she could kiss me.

I liked her.

I had a crush on her.

I told her, *"Yeah."*

Miss Gloria had leaned in and kissed my forehead. Then she kissed my left cheek, my chin, and then kissed my right cheek. Momentarily, Miss Gloria had paused to see if I was okay with everything. I'd closed my eyes, and seconds later, I'd felt her soft lips on my mouth.

Her warm tongue in my mouth.

Miss Gloria tasted sweet.

She smelled like warm vanilla sugar.

From that day forward, I'd sneak over to Miss Gloria's house *every* chance I got. And soon, the kissing turned to fondling.

23

The fondling turned to oral sex. I couldn't get *enough* of her big breasts, full hips, thick legs and plump ass.

Miss Gloria was soft.

She felt good all over.

I was in love....

Miss Gloria had moved away that next summer.

Claimed that my father was "on to us"....

Said that he'd threatened her.

Said that it wasn't safe to see each other anymore.

I'd never felt quite the same way 'bout anyone else.

Until now.

I guess that's how I ended up here, eight years later, sitting at the bar in a strip joint in downtown Philly called *Dutch Gardens*.

"Josh, lemme get a shot of *Tequila* and a *Corona* with lime," I place my order and the house lights go down. I'm the only female in the joint who ain't a dancer. I look around the bar. The so-called ballers and shot-callers sit right up front at the bar.

Then you got the businessmen and college boys who like to sit at the round bar tables. At the head of the bar, you got the straight-up dick heads who like to get drunk and make a lot of ruckus, feeling on the girls and shit; fucking up everybody's good time.

Then you get people like me who like to keep a low profile. We sit at the back of the bar where the lights are low, so when the girls come out, we see everything from the back end.

It's kinda like having bad seats at a concert.

I toss the *Tequila* down my throat in one shot, and the first exotic dancer hits the stage. She's tall, with long, blonde hair down to her ass, but she's boney with no curves, and doesn't hold my attention.

I only come here to see *one* chick!

I shouldn't even call her a chick. She's outta my league, for real. No matter how much money I spend on her, or how many drinks I buy, she won't give me the time of day.

So I keep her on a pedestal.

But trust me, whatever girl I want...I get. It's just gonna take me a lil' longer than I thought. But that's okay, 'cause when I get her, I'm gonna *turn* her out! I'm gonna use every trick I know, and *then* she's gonna be mine.

Josh, the bartender slides me my drink. He has to wear one of those ridiculous-looking, cheap bow ties and cumber bund hook ups, and his tie is always crooked.

"Here you go, Mel. Wanna start a tab?"

"I oughta own stock up in this *bitch*, as much money as I spend in here."

Josh smiles that familiar smile. A smile that tells me he's heard that line a million times.

I catch the guy sitting next to me giving me a funny look. I can see that he's trying to figure out whether I'm a girl or a guy.

It's not easy to tell.

I wear a closely cropped, boyish haircut, bind my breasts until they look flat, and wear baggy men's clothes, tennis shoes and sunglasses. With one glance, you'd probably think I was a dude, but if you look close enough, past the clothes and the short haircut, you can tell I'm really a woman.

I've been coming to *Dutch Gardens* for years. Most of the guys know me, and they treat me just like one of the fellas. The dancers *love* me, because they know that *dykes* always tip better than men do. It's as if we have something to prove.

Or maybe it's because, deep down, we know that if we didn't over tip, they wouldn't pay us any mind. They'd look straight pass us and spend time with all the dicks in the room.

The skinny white chick on stage finishes her dance. Josh hands me another shot of *Tequila* without me having to ask for it. Josh and I have an understanding. He understands that I'm a dyke who tips well, and I understand that he can get me the inside track with that girl I was telling you 'bout.

The chick who's outta my league.

She dances here at *Dutch Gardens*.

Goes by the name o' Mekka.

I'm telling you, she's a *b-a-d* bitch!

SHAWN
Chapter 4

Some people call me desperate. The truth is, I'm a basket case, a borderline alcoholic; I hate being by myself and my luck with men is shitty.

I'm clutching my sleek, silver cell phone in the palm of one hand, and a scotch on the rocks in the other. I want to call Mike, but I'm trying to muster up enough will power to sustain the urge.

What did I do that was so wrong that would make him not want to talk to me anymore?

I scan the room to ensure that none of my colleagues are around to witness my drunken, self-induced pity party. It's happy hour at *Zanzibar Blue,* the premiere venue for world-renowned live jazz music and fine dining, located along the prestigious *Avenue of the Arts.*

It's an upscale restaurant with an intimate atmosphere, where corporate types go to unwind after work.

I sit alone at a table for two, within the semi-private topside dining room, and I wonder what Mike is doing now... *He hasn't answered my chirps since I told him about those dreams I've been having about being pregnant.* Shit, Mike knew that he was taking a chance by sleeping with me without a condom. If he thought that I was a slut, then Mike would have never taken it there.

Right?

...I mean, one minute he was talking marriage, the next minute Mike's acting as if I don't exist, just because I told him about my pregnancy dreams.

He still hasn't called me....

I've even written Mike a letter...or two...or three, and he won't even respond to that.

I don't understand why Mike's tripping.

I cooked breakfast for him, wrote him poetry, and even bought Mike a shit load of clothes.

Why won't he talk to me?

...What did *I* do wrong?

I let Mike fuck me the same day we'd met, and he was sprung! Talking about, I'm so sexy this, I'm so pretty that, blah-blah-blah, now, he won't even talk to me.

I just have to try harder and make Mike realize how much he *needs* me in his life. I have to make him understand that were good together.

Why can't Mike see that?

…All I want is to be happy. I want to be in love, and I want someone to love me the way *Allen Payne* loved *Jada Pinkett* in *Jason's Lyric.* How he took her out on picnics, washed *Jada's* feet, made butt-naked love to her in the grass, and was romantic and gentle—*Allen* worshiped her. I want Mike to want me the same way.

Why does this *always* happen to me?

Why? Why? Why?

I'm a beautiful person.

Right?

…I mean, I deserve to be loved. I'll *make* Mike see. If I'm pregnant, he'll have to take care of his responsibilities. Then Mike will understand that this is a blessing.

Maybe I ought to call him now.

Mike has to answer sooner or later. If I'm pregnant, he's *gonna* have to face me eventually.

Fuck Mike!

Fuck me.

Why does this *always* happen to me?

I dial his number and Mike's machine immediately picks up. His prerecorded message plays: *"Hey, yo, what up? I'm not available at the moment. Leave me a message and I'll holla back. Or hit me up on my two-way. You know the deal."*

B-e-e-e-e-e-e-p!

I whisper into the phone. All the while, I'm checking the door for any signs of someone who could bust me.

"Um, Mike. It's Shawn. I just wanted you to know that I'm fine. I had another dream last night about the baby. It was a boy, and he looked just like you.

"Just because I might be pregnant, doesn't mean you have to treat me this way…I love you…I love you Mike. We may have only known each other for a month, but I *do* love you. You'll see...please call me.

"I, um...wrote you a letter. You should get it tomorrow. I'll be home all day tomorrow because it's Saturday, and I haven't made plans. Stop by if you want to—"

"Shawn, hang up the phone," Tristan commands. When I see her towering over me, I can't believe my eyes. Who in the hell would think Tristan would ever remember me even mentioning this place?

In one swift motion, "Tristan the tyrant" snatches the phone away from me and snaps it shut. She unbuttons her blazer and slides it onto the back of the chair, then glides into the seat across from me.

Every hair in Tristan's neat bun is in place. Her make-up is impeccable. Tristan's suit is so crisp that it looks like it could stand alone. Her white *La Perla* camisole and *Swarovski* crystal necklace seem to glow against Tristan's mocha complexion.

I've got to save face. I don't know how much she may have heard, but obviously, Tristan is *too* through with me. I close my eyes long enough to produce a tear. Trust me, when it comes to turning on the water works, I'm a pro.

As I use a cocktail napkin to dab the corners of my eyes, I notice Tristan's facial expression soften. I begin to rattle on like I always do when I feel cornered: "I know I'm pregnant. I'm four days late. I'm *never* late. I'm pregnant. I can feel it.... He won't even speak to me, girl."

More waterworks follows my barrage of words.

"Slow down a minute, Shawn. Get yourself together. Don't play yourself in the middle of happy hour at *Zanzibar Blue,* girl. Get it together."

Tristan then picks up my scotch and takes a long hard swallow. She leans back in her chair and waits for me to dry my tears before she continues.

"I can't *believe* you let some *trifling* Negro get the best of you. What have I always told you? You have to always have the upper hand with men. The only thing a man respects is power. If you show any signs of weakness, you've lost.

"It's the battle of the sexes and men already have a head start. I can't *believe* you could do something so *asinine* as to give away your pussy, and your power to him. Girl, you're a *fool* if I ever saw one."

At that moment a waiter interrupts us. He's holding a tray, presenting Tristan with a drink. Tristan looks him over as if he'd lost his damn mind.

"Courtesy of the gentleman at the bar, ma'am." The waiter is referring to a fine, chocolate brother sitting alone at the bar; casually dressed in a steel-gray cashmere sweater and slacks— both by *Ralph Lauren*. The handsome man looks our way and smiles the most brilliant smile I've ever seen. Chills run up-and-down my spine, as I watch this well-dressed, attractive stranger subtly flirting with Tristan.

Tristan then gives the man at the bar a half of a second of her attention before she rebuffs the drink: "You tell the gentleman at the bar that I don't *need* him, or any *other* man to buy me anything. I'm very capable of buying my *own* drinks. *That's* why I have a "Black" *American Express Card* with my name on it. He can't buy me *anything* I can't buy for myself; is that understood?"

The waiter nods a yes.

"I'm *not* one of those desperate females waiting for a man to buy me a drink and rescue me." Tristan then pulls out her "Black" *American Express Card* tucked inside of her *Louis Vuitton* monogram wallet, and slaps it on the waiter's tray: "You can also tell him that his drink is on me." The waiter walks away embarrassed.

I now look over at the mysterious stranger at the bar, and judging by his expression, he has clearly heard every word of Tristan's ugly dismissal. The handsome man then turns away from us, pays his bill, and exits. I find myself studying him as he walks away.

I wish he would have offered me that drink.
Why don't men ever approach me like that?
...What's wrong with me?

A tear slides down my cheek. This time, the tears are real.

Sometimes I truly hate Tristan for acting the way she does. Here she is being offered a man on a silver platter, and Tristan kicks him in the nuts.

"Tristan, why do you have to be such a bitch?"

Tristan's perfectly arched eyebrow rises in defense. Her jaws tighten, and she folds her arms across her chest; clearly in defense mode.

"Shawn, dear, I've already had this conversation once today with Anissa. Frankly, I'm beginning to get bored with the whole *'bitch thing'*. Surely there are other topics. I came here tonight to clear my head and relax. Maybe even enjoy myself for *once* in my life, but I bump into *you*, so now *all* my plans are out the window."

"You can be so smug and self-righteous, with your nose stuck up in the air like your *shit* don't stink! Well, I'm sorry if I *spoiled* your good time, but, guess what, 'Ms. Diva'? Contrary to what you believe, it *ain't* always about you!"

With every word my voice rises. I'm clearly making Tristan uncomfortable. And to top it off, I'm so angry with her that I began to cry again.

A look of disdain washes over Tristan's face. Now she's armored up and in full combat mode.

"You can be *such* a juvenile. Whenever you don't get your way you cry. Are you thirty-years-old or a three-year-old child? For Christ sake, it's embarrassing. I wish you would compose yourself—it's pathetic!"

"Well, we can't *all* hide behind a wall of ice like you. Here I am, one of your *closest* friends, one of the *only* friends you still have from college who puts up with your shit, and you don't even have enough consideration to be *compassionate* for a moment."

"You've obviously had too much to drink—"

"Tristan, you drank my scotch before I had a chance to. But that's typical of you…to only think of yourself when a friend is in crisis."

"Crisis my ass! I walk in on you *begging* some fool to take you back, and now you want me to coax you, is that it? I'm supposed to let you lay your burdens down on me? Well, unfortunately that's *not* how I operate.

"This is just another one of your melodramas. Today, you're pregnant, last week, some guy *slapped* you with a restraining order. Every time I turn around you've got a soap opera going on. I swear, you're more hopeless than my sister, Melanie. If I'm not doling out money to her, I'm doling out advice to you!"

"I guess it's easy to give advice when you don't have a *life* of your own!"

At that very moment, the waiter interjects and takes away my empty glass. His timing diffuses what was about to escalate into a heated debate: "Ladies would you care for another drink?" he asks hesitantly.

As if the waiter is beneath her level, Tristan doesn't bother to look at him. She waves the waiter away with a swift motion of her hand.

"Shawn, this pity party of yours, is a party that I'd *rather* not attend. I'm going to leave before this gets ugly." Tristan then stands up and throws her blazer over her arm. "My suggestion to you is, get your *shit* together, girlfriend. Quick!" Tristan now walks away; she doesn't say goodbye.

To hell with her!

BITCH!

Fuck her!

I give what Tristan said about two seconds of further consideration before I shake it off and signal the waiter by tapping him on the shoulder. It's time for me to do what I came here to do: get drunk and hopefully, get laid. The waiter now turns to me.

"Excuse me, sweetie. I'd like to start a tab please. Scotch-on-the-rocks, and a shot of tequila…and keep 'em coming."

MEKKA
Chapter 5

My four-song set just ended, and traces of my theme song, *Erotic City,* still lingers in the air. I always dance to *Prince.* That's my style: sensual and erotic.

I pick up dirty bills from the stage and stuff the money into my boots. All-in-all, I collected about thirty dollars, which averages out to be seven dollars for each three-and-a-half minute song.

Pitiful.

As I round the back of the stage, what do my eyes behold? I see five crisp twenty-dollar bills. Even in pitch-black darkness with the house lights low, I can still differentiate between denominations.

It's a skill that comes along with the trade.

I lean over and pick up the twenties with the swiftness. While I'm at it, I get a good look at my benefactor. At first, I think it's just some shy nigga, but then, when I look more closely, I realize that it's a female with a faded haircut; dressed in a black baggy *Sean John* velour sweat suit.

With her close-cropped hair and masculine clothes, it's easy to mistake her for a man. That's when I notice that it's Melanie. Melanie can't take a hint, but guess what, until she wises up and gets a *fuckin'* clue, her money is a-l-l good.

I push my weave away from my face and throw Melanie a sexy smile. I know how to put it on her, keep her comin' back for the fantasy.

"'Sup, Mel?"

"'Sup, Mekka? You got a dance for me?"

"Hol' up. I gotta freshen up first. Let me make my rounds and I'll meet you for a private dance."

"Damn, girl. Why you make me wait in line behind these nasty niggas? I'm tired o' givin' you my good money and you treatin' me like a second-class, poo-putt trick. What's it gonna be?"

"I *said* hold up a minute. If you tired of waitin', you can tear yo' ass. You know what it is, the shit don't never change."

Melanie's money was long and strong, but every now and then, I gotta let her know who's *really* the boss up in this *mutha fucka!* I know Melanie got it bad for me because the waiter, Josh, told me so. But, as nice as she treats me, it's *strictly* business!

If I let myself get it twisted, I'd be just like the rest of these *broke* hoes dancin' in here. That's why I drive a money-green convertible *Jaquar*, and they pushin' *Altimas,* thinkin' they really gettin' it.

I change my tone. I can't push Melanie too far and blow it.

"Look, baby, I got you. You know I'm gonna take *r-e-a-l* good care of you when I'm done handlin' my business. Feel me?" I now give Josh a nod. "Give her somethin' smooth so she can mellow out; like some *Courvoisier.* I'll be right back."

I sashay off the stage.

Walk the floor.

I see my regulars, the white guys who work at *Dell.* I also see my doctor and lawyer friends, and I spot a couple of drug pushers who take care of me on the regular.

Damn! Like *Nelly* said, *It's gettin' hot in herrre!*

If I play my cards right, I can walk out of here with close to a G. Maybe more!

After I make my lap dance rounds, I feel the need to take a birdbath and wash the sweaty, musty odor of men off of my body. I run to the locker room, cock my leg up on the sink, push my g-string to the side and wash out the coochie juice residue.

I pull my bra top under my tits and quickly suds up— washin' off my breasts and underarm pits. Then, I spritz "Subtil" by *Salvatore Ferragamo* vanilla mist over my body. I also examine my face in the mirror. I pat the sweat from my face and make sure my *Chanel* make-up is holdin' up.

I feel my stomach begin to growl but, I ain't got no time to order dinner, so I run to my locker and devour a rice crispy treat. Anybody whose been in this game knows that as soon as you stop to eat a real meal, that's when another *hoe* has time to push up on one of your tricks, and steal your money right from under you!

I ain't got *no* time to chit-chat either!

I'm out the door!

And back on the floor, headin' *straight* for Melanie!

By this time, the *Courvoisier* has Melanie cooled out. I haven't seen her for a coupla' weeks. I actually find myself wonderin' where Melanie has been, and what she's been up too. Wherever she's been, Melanie came back wit' plenty paper.

I put on my "happy face" and stand next to her.

Melanie looks me over....

Her eyes travel over my body, slowly. First my face, then my neck and shoulder blades. Melanie stops to take in my ample breasts, then my flat belly and firm thighs. She stares hard at my French pedicured toes and my diamond toe ring.

Melanie now licks her lips, *LL Cool J* style, before admittin' her desires: "I gotta get me some o' dat," she says, primed and ready to go.

"Wanna do the "VIP" thang?" I ask.

"Yeah, girl, let's do-the-damn-thang!"

"Josh, lemme get the rest of that bottle of *Courvoisier* to go, for Mel. Looks like we'll be back in the "VIP" for a whole minute, and she might get a lil' thirsty."

I wink at Melanie.

I smile at Josh.

All the players are playin' their part, just the way I like.

When it's done right, it's as *s-m-o-o-t-h* as poetry.

MELANIE
Chapter 6

"She-got-me-in-the-'VIP'-chillin'-like-WHOA!"

Mekka's wearing one of those sexy white bikinis with the fringes hanging down.

I study her from head-to-toe....

Mekka is truly beautiful, with her long black hair parted straight down the center, falling on her soft shoulders....

Chinky eyes....

Full lips....

Double D's....

Legs like *Beyonce!*

Ass like *J-Lo!*

WOO-WEE!!!

Mekka stands in front of me, raises her long leg, slides her pretty manicured toes against my lips, and slowly pours *Courvoisier* down her thigh. The liquor slides over Mekka's kneecap and drains down her leg, directly into my mouth. Then she pours some along her cleavage. Mekka then leans over and lets me lick it off the top of her big tits.

"You the *only* one I let touch me like this, Mel. The *only* one," she whispers.

Mekka got me in the danger zone. I just wanna flip her ass over and lick her from head-to-toe!

It's dangerous to want somebody so much.

Lust is a *muthafucka* for yo ass!

Mekka now kicks game to me: "What we got is on a whole notha level."

"Why? 'Cause you know that I'm 'bout to throw you my whole check?"

"I dunno know if it's because you're a woman and I feel I can trust you, or if it's because you seem so genuine."

That's Mekka's game.

She now pushes her cleavage into my face, and Mekka's soft, silky hair, grazes my face.

"If we on that level, why won't you lemme see you *outside* the club, one-on-one?"

35

Mekka ignores me and continues to rub her bikini-clad titties on my face.

"Oh, I see Mekka. If I ain't paying, I ain't playing."

"It ain't that."

"Okay, then what is it? If I had a *dick* like one of these other niggas, then it woulda been on a long time ago. What? I ain't *good* enough because I'm a woman?

"I treat you better than *any* one of those dudes. I spend more dough on you. Talk nice to you. Offer to take care of you. I'll treat you right, better than *any* man *ever* could. What more do you want? These niggas out here *ain't* gonna do *shit* for you! Trust me on that. Niggas ain't no good!"

"There you go gettin' serious on me again. I got somethin' for that."

Mekka then pulls her right breast out from the confines of her bikini, and I'm staring at that chocolate, silver dollar-sized nipple. Then she pulls out the left breast. Mekka now straddles my lap and grinds in a slow circular motion.

I am eye-to-eye with her erect nipples!

"You start talkin' crazy when you ain't had yo' medicine in a while. Once you had a dose of 'Mekka', you be *a-l-r-i-g-h-t,* won't ya, baby?" Mekka whispers, full of syrupy sweetness. Even though it's all bullshit, she got me in a serious zone.

"Mekka, can I feel your ass?" I whisper in her ear.

Just then, the door slides open, and the muscular silhouette of a bouncer named, Smitty, darkens the doorway. His voice bellows: "Ten minutes are up. Sir, would you like to pay for another dance?" he asks me.

I'm kinda flattered that the bouncer mistakes me for a man. Going another round with Mekka in the "VIP" means another fifty dollars. I hesitate for a minute, trying to calculate how far in the hole I am already.

Bad enough that I'm blowing rent money on her!

The worst part is, I'm gonna have to call my sister, Tristan, and ask her to loan me more cash 'til next payday; which is the *last* thing I wanna do. Tristan is my sister and all, but she's a *bitch!* I *hate* having to ask her uptight ass for anything!

Tristan be trying to play high post, like she don't know nobody, just because she went to college and got a high-profile job; and I earn minimum wage, working for the water department.

But at this point, I'm buzzed, so I *really* don't give-a-fuck! I got my prize piece grinding on my lap, and Mekka's worth all the jaw-jabbing I'll get from Tristan on Monday. Right now, it's Friday night, the mood is right and I'm feeling a-l-r-i-g-h-t.

Mekka senses my hesitation. "Smitty, leave us be." She answers for me, and I don't protest. Smitty takes his cue and exits.

"Now, where were we?" Mekka asks seductively.

"Right 'bout here," I respond, as I slide my hands over her hips and onto each ass cheek. "Right 'bout here."

SPRING FEVER

SHAWN
Chapter 7

First day of Spring. Sunday morning. Mike finally calls: "Hey, I'm on my way. We need to talk."

My heart flutters at the sound of his voice, then it immediately dropped when he said, *"We need to talk."* From my experience, when someone announces the need to talk, it's never ever been a good thing. But I won't jump to any conclusions. Maybe once Mike sees me, he'll have a change of heart.

Maybe.

This is *not* going to turn out good.

I rummage through my closet, trying to find something to wear, but nothing seems appropriate. Everything I own is business-casual. There are a few cute things that Mike has already seen me in. I toss those outfits aside.

Today is *not* the day for a repeat performance.

I have to grab his attention and keep it for as long as I can. If Mike's thinking of breaking up, this outfit has *got* to be good enough to make him reconsider!

The more I thumb through my closet, the more disappointed I become. The clock above my dresser reads "1 PM". Mike will be here in exactly one hour and I still have to shave my legs, take a shower, fix my hair, do my makeup, touch up my toenails and straighten up my apartment!

Beads of sweat form on my forehead.

I've got to calm down. Chill the fuck out.

If I panic now, I'm screwed!

I walk away from the closet and head towards the bedroom window. I pull the curtains aside and take in the view of Philadelphia's skyline. Philly in the springtime is picturesque.

Intoxicating.

Cherry blossoms hang from the trees in *Fairmount Park;* pink buds fall and blanket the perfectly manicured, rich green grass.

Everyone is buzzing! High on the spring vibes, trading in their winter gear for shorts, mini-skirts and sandals. The feeling is contagious! Activity is plentiful.

Roller-blading. Bicycling. People walking dogs. Convertibles whizzing by. Artists sketching by the river. Tourists taking snapshots. Children playing softball. Mothers pushing strollers. Babies licking ice cream. Lovers holding hands.

Lovers....

I turn away and focus back to the matter at hand—my wardrobe. *What am I going to wear?* It's got to be sexy, but not overt. Not too much cleavage. Nothing too tight. Nothing sheer. I don't want to look like I'm trying too hard. It's got to be casual, but enough to make a statement. It's got to be fun and colorful, yet subtle. Classy, but not uptight.

I drag a box full of spring and summer clothes tucked away in my hall closet, hibernating from the harsh winter weather. I sit on the floor and toss everything out until I strike oil! In my hands is just what I need to seal the deal: a silk, spaghetti strap, sundress by *BCBG*, in pastel shades of blue and white.

Inspiration flows through my veins.

I can already picture the shoes, jewelry, hues of makeup, and the hairstyle I need to pull it all together. I look at the clock: sixteen minutes have gone by!

I shower, shave my legs and douche. I pull my henna-colored dreadlocks into a playful knot on the top of my head, apply a little *Clinique* lip-gloss, and pluck a few stray hairs from my brows; spot paint my toenails.

I generously apply *Neutrogena* body oil until my naked body glistens. Then, I don a white, lacy push-up bra and thong from *Victoria's Secret,* slip on a pair of Cole *Haan* "Tia" sandals and carefully pull my sundress over my head. I adorn my ears with silver drop hoops, and my neck with a silver floating heart necklace from *Tiffany's.*

According to the clock, I still have three minutes to spare before Mike arrives. Careful as to not break a sweat, I speed through the house and tidy up my bi-level apartment. One hazard of me being a teacher is, having a tendency to have papers and books strewn all over my office and living room.

I gather all of the books, papers and miscellaneous items lying around, and stuff them all inside the main closet, forcing the door closed. I then run to the kitchen, toss the dishes into the dishwasher, before racing through the apartment spraying *Oust* and lighting "Batchouli" incense sticks.

Next, I head upstairs into the bathroom, wipe the counter with a *Clorox* wipe and pull the shower curtain shut. In the bedroom, I strip and change the bed linens, spray the sheets with lavender scented mist, and light the *Glade* vanilla scented candle on my nightstand.

I immediately kick the box of clothes back inside the closet, and once I am satisfied, I run back into the bathroom, check my appearance and head back downstairs for a glass of *Merlot,* and a hit of the marijuana roach in my ashtray to mellow out.

An hour passes by, and I'm *still* sitting on the couch waiting for this *mother...fucker* to show up! It takes everything in my being not to pick up the phone and blow Mike's two-way up with obscene text messages. Waiting on him, I've managed to finish off the roach and the bottle of *Merlot.*

I can't *b-e-l-i-e-v-e* this asshole has the nerve to stand me up! And I have *nobody* to blame but myself. *Stupid! Stupid! Stupid!* I should have known better than to trust Mike to show up after he hasn't contacted me for a month.

No phone call.

No letter.

No visit.

WELL, FUCK HIM!

If Mike thinks he can just come in-and-out of my life whenever he feels like it, then he's *sadly* mistaken. What does he take me for? Some ghetto-hood rat that he can toss aside like trash?

OH, HELL NO!

No more! Spring is here, and baby, I'm going turn over a new fucking leaf! I've got a *new* attitude: FUCK MIKE!

Fuck him, a-n-d his big dick! Shit, Mike ain't the *only* nigga that's got it going on.

I pick up the bottle of *Merlot,* press it to my lips in a futile attempt to drain the last drop of nectar. When I finally accept that the bottle is empty, I take and *hurl* it to the fireplace! It crashes and shattered glass flies everywhere.

"Fuck me for not being smarter!"

I realize that I've just wasted a total of two-and-a-half hours of my life waiting on this loser. Finally, I decide to give up on his *sorry* ass. I manage to push myself up and stand. I head for the staircase.

As I slowly climb the stairs, the doorbell rings.

TRISTAN
Chapter 8

First day of Spring. Sunday Afternoon. My private pilates session kicked my ass!

It's amazing how muscles you didn't even know you had, ache. Nevertheless, I drag my tired, weary bones outside of the dimly lit gym, and the brilliant sunlight blinds me. I squint and find Cornelius standing by my *Bentley* parked out front.

He greets me with a smile and newspaper in hand, reaches for my gym bag and tosses it in the passenger side; opening up the back passenger side door for me to climb inside. I look past Cornelius, seeing the energetic and lively activities taking place on *Walnut Street.* A couple of blocks westward, Walnut Street intersects with *Rittenhouse Square*—that's where I make my home.

Rittenhouse Square is a private community for the "intellectual bourgeoisie". It's a haven for old money and aristocracy. It has a culture all its own. A tiny microcosm of the elite people who own and run this city. It's the *perfect* environment for a woman like me, who aspires to rule the world...or at least *everything* within my reach.

In the world of *Rittenhouse Square*, everyone is beautiful. Everybody looks like they had a nip-and-tuck: nose jobs, boob jobs, collagen and Botox.

In this world, everyone generally carries *Louis Vuitton* bags. Everyone air-kisses you. Everyone has a maid, a butler, a driver and a nanny.

Everyone sees a shrink.

Everyone is manic depressive.

Most kids from *Rittenhouse Square* usually have Attention Deficit Disorder, and/or suffer from eating disorders.

Here, everyone is rich and loves to be miserable. Rich people have a flair for melodrama. It's such an oxymoron to me.

Yet, *Rittenhouse Square* is alive: older married couples feeding pigeons gourmet breadcrumbs. Lovers taking long, intimate strolls through the park. People power-walking and window shopping. Sophisticated, stylish women with arms full of

42

shopping bags from the finest boutiques. People eating and reading books at sidewalk cafes.

"Good afternoon, Ms. Vincent," Cornelius says in a singsong manner. The nice weather seems to have an affect on him, also.

"Good afternoon, Cornelius."

"Ms. Vincent, I already have your unfinished paperwork laid out in the study for you. Shall I call ahead and have a massage and private sauna reserved?"

"You know, Cornelius, as tempting as that sounds, and I know that's my normal mode of operation, today, I'm going to try something new."

"Oh?"

"Take me home to change. Afterwards, I intend to come back out and do a little shopping, and enjoy the day."

Cornelius seems pleased. He helps me into the car, then gently closes the car door behind me. Cornelius is the only Black driver/butler in my neighborhood, and I am *Rittenhouse Square's* only Black resident, which makes Cornelius very protective of me; especially of my image—in a father like manner.

He makes sure that *everyone* around here knows that I am a force to be reckoned with! I am thankful for Cornelius being there to remind me to never forget where I am, and that I am constantly being watched by the "Caucasian persuasion".

The other residents, being rich from old money, would just love for me to give them something to talk about. Thus far, all they've been able to say is that I'm a work-aholic. And I'm fine with that; there are a lot of other "names" they could call me.

We drive down *Walnut Street,* pass flower vendors, antique book stores, consignment shops, art galleries, bakeries, coffee and chocolate shops. Old world charm. Nouveau chic.

It takes about five minutes for us to reach the semi-circle driveway to the *Rittenhouse Hotel and Condominiums.* Cornelius valets the car, then he and I ride the elevator up to my condo. The ride is quiet. Cornelius keeps looking at me furtively, and when I look back at him, he quickly averts his eyes.

Once we arrive at my floor, entering the modern-industrial style condo, I confront Cornelius. We stand in the center of the spacious, open-floor designed living room. The walls are sparsely painted with tones of brown, beige, gray and chrome.

The space is divided with modular furniture: cube armchairs, tubular steel and black leather sofas, and low bookcases and partial walls. The only punch of color comes from abstract paintings and pop art.

I can no longer withstand the cloud of awkwardness dangling in the air: "What is it, Cornelius?" I ask in a no nonsense tone. "All the way up here you've been looking at me funny, and it's beginning to make me feel uncomfortable. So out with whatever it is you have to say."

"Ms. Vincent, I have no idea what you're talking about," Cornelius says, in an attempt to throw me off.

"So, I guess it's just my imagination?" I throw my hands up in frustration, storm into the living room and toss the newspaper onto the coffee table. Cornelius heads to the bathroom and draws me a bath. When he returns, Cornelius still has the look of someone who's bursting at the seams. I try to ignore him.

Whatever is on Cornelius' mind, he obviously wants to keep it to himself until the time is right. Cornelius now walks pass me, and heads to the kitchen to fix herbal tea with peppermint licorice. I sit on the couch while my bath water is running, thumbing through the *New York Times*. Every now and then, I look over at Cornelius, and he tries to appear engrossed in what he's doing. *Fine. If he wants to play this game, then so shall I.*

I toss the newspaper back down and head for my walk-in closet, which I had remodeled after I saw an episode of *Oprah*. Now my closet mirrors hers. It has clean lines, plenty of shelving and storage space, and everything is hung according to season, color, fabric and style.

I pull out a crisp, white button down oxford shirt and an A-line black skirt, both by *Calvin Klein*. I select a pair of black satin *Elie Tahari* ballerina flats, and arrange everything on a mahogany and brass valet.

I then undo my ponytail, and my bone-straight, freshly permed brown hair with golden highlights, falls against my shoulders.

The aroma of the peppermint tea filters from the bathroom suite. Cornelius has readied my bath and sat my tea on the vanity table. All this without saying a word. *Something is definitely up.*

I walk into the bathroom, brushing my hair, following the scent of the tea. When I reach the vanity, there's the teacup, but there's also a beige linen envelope with a shiny gold seal. My name is nicely handwritten in calligraphy, and there's no return address, which means that it was hand delivered.

I throw on my white, plush *Ralph Lauren* bathrobe, and make route to the reading room, where I find Cornelius sitting at my desk sorting the mail. Arms at my side, I confront him.

"So, is the note on my vanity the reason you've been walking around here suspiciously?"

"Maybe," Cornelius answers without looking up at me. He continues to sort the mail.

"So how did it get here?"

"It was hand delivered by a gentleman this morning. Quite a handsome fellow if you ask me."

"What does his looks have to do with anything?"

Cornelius chooses to ignore me.

"Well, *what* did he want?" I then demand.

He looks me squarely in the eye and replies, "Why ask me when you can simply read the note."

I storm out of the room determined to put an end to this charade. I snatch the envelope from the vanity and tear it open. The delicate handmade paper inside the envelope falls out and floats to the floor. I kneel to pick it up. After I see the words, I can't move. The letter reads:

"I hope that 'Black' American Express Card can buy you warm smiles and intriguing conversations. I hope it can buy long walks through the park and moonlit strolls along the beach. I hope it can buy you the feeling that there is no other woman in the world as amazing as you.

And, I hope it whispers in your ear, all the beautiful words you never gave me the chance to utter that night at Zanzibar Blue. If your 'Black' American Express Card can buy you all these things, then I truly apologize for the interruption. For with a credit card like that, who needs a man like me?"

MEKKA

Chapter 9

First day of Spring. Sunday Afternoon. I'm hung over....
I'm tired...worn out from bein' on my feet dancin' all night, and
my kids...refuse...to...SHUT...THE FUCK...UP! Even though
I'm buried under my *Croscill* comforter, and my bedroom door is
closed, I can *still* hear freakin' *Sponge Bob,* blastin' from the TV
in the livin' room downstairs.

I unbury myself, and although my head is poundin', I yell:
"SHEKA AND MAN-MAN, TURN THE *DAMN* TV DOWN!"

They respond in unison, "Huh, mama?"

Now I'm *pissed* because a jackhammer is diggin' through
my brain, and these little *bastards* are makin' me repeat myself, "I
s-a-i-d, turn the *damn* TV down! Mama's tryna sleep."

A minute later, my door bursts open, and five-year-old,
Sheka, races to my bed and jumps on top of the covers.

"A-u-g-g-g-h," I moan upon her impact. Sheka crawls
towards me and pulls the covers from my face.

"Mama," she whispers.

"Yes, Sheka," I groan.

"Are you awake?"

"I am now, Sheka."

"Mama?"

"Yes, Sheka!"

"I'm hungry."

I turn over. I slide the gel-filled sleepin' mask from my
eyes and look at her...My baby...She is so cute! Cocoa-brown
skin. Dimples and afro puffs.

I fall in love with Sheka all over again.

"Mama?" Sheka softly whispers again.

"Yes, Sheka."

"I'm h-u-n-g-r-y."

"Get Man-Man to make you some cereal."

"Man-Man ate all the cereal."

"Shit!" There goes my easy way out. "What about the
French toast sticks that you like?"

"Man-Man ate those last night."

6

I pull the sleepin' mask back over my eyes, then the covers back over my head. Sheka sits there for a minute...Quiet. Before she grabs the covers back down and pats my cheek.

"Mama," Sheka whispers.

"Yes, Sheka."

"Man-Man ate all the *Pop Tarts,* too." Sheka then gets up, hops off the bed and walk away on her tip-toes. I guess that's my cue to get up and feed my child.

"Sheka, stop walkin' on your tip-toes!"

"Okay, mama."

*   *   *   *   *

A half-hour later, I've showered, and I'm amongst the livin'. I pick up my white *Louis Vuitton* duffel bag with the multi-colored "LV" print, filled with my exotic dance costumes and high-heeled stiletto boots, and shove it under the bed. I throw on my purple, silk penior robe, and take a long look at my face in the mirror.

I got bags under my eyes....

My skin is startin' to breakout from fallin' asleep with my make-up on, I got new growth comin' in, and this *damn* weave glue is startin' to cake up and itch my scalp. And to top it off, I think my period is tryna come on. I tie my pink *Pucci* silk scarf around my head and trudge out of my bedroom.

Man-Man is parked on the floor two inches away from the TV. He's an eight-year-old terrorist. The splittin' image of his no-good father! Man-Man's at that age where he's gettin' tall and thinnin' out. His knees and elbows are bony, and his head looks big, but Man-Man's still handsome to me.

I look him over...Man-Man needs a haircut and he's outgrowin' his pajamas. I call to him: "Man-Man! Back up from the TV! Matter fact, get up, and get Mama's headache pills from the kitchen counter."

He doesn't budge.

"Boy, get ya *ass* up! *Sponge Bob* ain't goin' nowhere."

"Dang, mom," Man-Man complains and sulkily gets up, while headin' towards the kitchen.

"While you're in there, clean up that *mess* you made! Cereal and *shit* everywhere! Sheka told me you ate up everything."

Man-Man turns to Sheka and glares at her, "Sheka, you make me sick. You got a big mouth."

"So what," Sheka responds.

"Man-Man, shut up fussin' at your sister and *hand* me my pills. I got a headache and you're makin' it worse."

"Yes, ma'am."

"Sheka wasn't rattin' on you," I inform him, "she's just hungry."

Sheka then sticks her tongue out at Man-Man and taunts him.

"Quit it!" I warn her. "Before you get in trouble, too."

"Yes, ma'am," Sheka quietly whispers.

Man-Man hands me my pills, and I pick up a warm bottle of *Schweppes* raspberry ginger ale I left on the table from the night before. I take two horse pills and chase it with the soda. Then, I walk over to the cupboard and pull out a box of maple flavored oatmeal for Sheka.

I sit a pot of water on the stove and turn the burner up full blast. Sheka pulls her favorite *Lion King* bowl from the dishwasher. I turn my back, lean on the counter and watch Man-Man wipe crumbs from the kitchen counter. Sheka is now parked in front of the TV, watchin' re-runs of *The Cosby Show*. She loves little "Olivia".

The water bubbles into a boil. I stir in the flakes and season it with a little cinnamon and sugar. I then pour the steamin', hot oatmeal into the *Lion King* bowl, and fix Sheka a glass of orange juice. On cue, she springs up from the floor and tip-toes over to the kitchen table.

"No tip-toes, Sheka, remember?"

"Okay, mama."

Sheka sits down at the table, and I rub the soft hair atop of her head.

"Let it cool down first. Blow on it before you take a spoonful. When I get done lookin' over these bills, I want you both dressed, faces washed, and teeth brushed. Ya hear me?"

My kids say "yes" in unison, and I then look at the stack of bills on the kitchen counter. I grab them and head over to the slate-toned, glass and steel L-shape desk in the den. I reach for my blue and white *Christian Dior* monogram purse, which is so overstuffed with money, that the clutch won't snap shut, then walk away into the den.

48

The shutters are open and I am greeted by the warm sunlight. If I didn't have such a headache, I think I'd enjoy it. Man-Man and Sheka's friends are already out on the block playin' street ball, hopscotch, double-dutch, and all those other games I used to play as a child.

Amazin' how some things change and some things stay the same. The only difference is that, I've moved out of the projects, and into a nice family-oriented neighborhood in *Mount Airy*. The homes here are a little over priced, but it's worth *every* penny to keep my kids away from the gunfire and drug pushers in the neighborhood that I grew up in.

For most of the residents, *Mount Airy* represents upward mobility. As children, most of us grew up in *North Philadelphia*. As workin' adults, we escaped to *Mount Airy*, leavin' behind the harsh realities of ghetto-livin'. We left behind the dilapidated homes. Roamin' crack heads and crack vials all over the place. Liquor stores next to churches on every other corner. Violent street fights and gun fights, loud yellin', filthy litter, and graffiti.

We traded all of that in for beautiful front lawns and swimmin' pools. Clean playgrounds, better schools, crossin' guards and friendly neighbors. To us, *Mount Airy* was a little piece of suburbia.

A little peace of mind.

An hour goes by, and I have finally sorted and counted all of my tips from last night. I made a total of seven-hundred and seventy-eight dollars. Not bad, but not good either. A couple of years ago, I used to come home with a thousand dollars or more. But, I'm older now, and a lot of the newer *hoes* are movin' in on my territory. You know how the game goes—men are always lookin' for the "new face".

It used to be that way for me.

I *never* used to have to work hard to make this kinda money. Money seemed to flow in my direction. Now it seems that the tides are turnin', and the currency is flowin' in the other direction.

I begin to write checks to cover the bills: car note, mortgage, Catholic school tuition, dental bills, daycare, and the list goes on-and-on. By the time I'm done payin' bills, I'm already thinkin' of the week ahead, and how much money I need to hustle up.

Lately, I've been thinkin' about investin' my money, but I dunno know where to begin.... I've never been good at math, I've never understood how the stock market and all that investment stuff works, but I know I can't keep at this dancin' thing for too much longer. A *bitch* is gettin' tired, and I owe it to my kids and myself to get out!

But where do I go from here?

I dunno how to do anything else.

Hidin' at the bottom of the list of bills is a brochure advertisin' vacation packages. *That's exactly what I need. To take a fuckin' vacation and broaden my horizons.* I toss the brochure in the trash. *I can't be frivolous right now. I've got to stay focused!*

If I plan to get out of the game, then I've got to stack as much money as possible, as *quickly* as possible. Right now, a vacation doesn't fit into the equation!

What I will do today? ...Since it turned out to be such a gorgeous afternoon, I'll take the kids shoppin', buy 'em some new clothes, and get Man-Man some new pajamas. I'll take 'em to the bookstore. Go to *Target* and buy some things for the house. Also, we'll go to *TGI Friday's* for dinner and I'll rent a coupla of movies; then take a bubble bath, undo my weave and get to bed early, for a change. Yeah, I'd like that!

My cell phone now rings. I read the caller ID. It's the phone number of one of my White tricks, Drew. What the *fuck* does he want on a Sunday afternoon? I pop the flip phone open and answer, "What's up, Drew?"

"You baby," he says panting. I can tell he's jerking off.

"What do you want?" I ask in a frustrated tone.

"I want some of that brown sugar, baby. Can you squeeze me in this afternoon? Baby, I need you. I got it bad! I need those big, sweet lips wrapped around my cock, baby," Drew replies; still panting.

I swear, White men are *so* corny! That can't even talk dirty without soundin' like little fuckin' wimps.

"Now, Drew, you know Sundays are off limits." Just then, Man-Man runs into the den. I cover the receiver. I can still hear Drew panting as I motion for Man-Man to get out. "Boy, what did I tell you 'bout runnin' in here while mama is handlin' business?"

"You told me to knock first."

"So? Why didn't you?"

"'Cause I forgot."

"Well, don't forget! Now get out until I'm done on the phone!"

Man-Man leaves the room, and I shut the door behind him. I put the phone back up to my ear and Drew is still begging.

"Can you meet me here? Mekka, I promise I won't take long. I'm burning for you, baby," he pleads.

"No, Drew. I'm tryna chill today. Get wit' me Monday night."

"But I'm working late Monday night, and I *can't* wait that long. If you come over today, I'll make it worth your while."

My eyes find their way to the wastebasket, and the vacation brochure is starin' me right in the face. I stare at the picture of the fancy hotel on the cover.

"Mekka, I just need some head."

I pull the brochure from the trash, and open it to the *"Jamaican Weekend Get-Away"*. Five-star hotel beach resort. Sunshine. White sand. Blue water.

Drew is still panting in my ear. It sounds like he's having an asthma attack. There's a knock on the den room's door: *BOOMP-BOOMP-BOOMP!* I cover the receiver, "Come in."

"Mommy, can I go outside," Man-Man asks.

"No! Get dressed. I'm takin' you and Sheka to *Target* at the *Cherry Hill Mall*." I then shoo Man-Man away.

"A-w-w-w man!" he whines. "I *never* get to do nothin'!" Man-Man states before slamming the door shut.

Man-Man's lucky I can't get to his ass right now. Right now, I have to deal with beggin'-ass Drew: "Look, Drew. I got things to do. If I fit you in my schedule, it's gonna cost! And I mean cost!"

"Whatever you want. Just bring your fine self to me, ASAP."

Jamaica calls my name!

No kids. No nasty tricks *beggin'* for sex.

No drama.

I weigh all my options and Jamaica wins.

"Five-hundred dollars, Drew. Just head, no sex! Got it?"

"Do I get to spank you?"

"Don't push it!"

"Just a little paddle to that big, round ass of yours...and some head."

I pause.

"A thousand dollars," he says. "Now get your ass over here before I spend my money somewhere else."

I know Drew's money is good. He always pays cash.

"Give me an hour, I'm on my way."

I hang up on Drew and speed-dial my neighbor, Maria. Maria's answering machine picks up, but then she answers in the middle of the recording.

"Praise the Lord," Maria answers in her usual cheery Spanglish dialect.

"Hey, Maria."

"Aye, Mekka. What's up?" she asks. I can hear her Sunday morning gospel playing in the background.

"Hey, look, Maria. I need a huge favor. Can you watch the kids for about two hours? I gotta make a quick run."

MELANIE
Chapter 10

First Day of Spring. Sunday afternoon. Someone's banging and kicking my front door like they the *goddamn* po-lice!

I instinctively jump up outta bed, pull on my masculine *Joe Boxer* boxer shorts and "wife beater" tank top, and re-adjust my wave "Du Rag" cap. The banging at my door gets louder. More urgent. My whole apartment seems to shake and rattle with each thrust.

I'm *not* in the mood!

I'm tired of putting up with the drama that goes on around here. But, this is *exactly* the kinda *bullshit* you have to deal with when you live in *North Philly's* Section 8 housing.

Someone's *always* fighting. The cops stay raiding some drug dealer's hideout. Constant domestic violence. Yelling and screaming. Babies crying a-l-l…night…long. Loud, vibrating music. Stink, pissy walkways. Crack heads everywhere.

I swear, as s-o-o-n as I get some real dough, I'm moving the *fuck* outta triflin', ghetto-ass *North Philly!*

My doorknob rattles.

Somebody's gonna *catch* it!

I reach under my pillow and grab my tiny, bitch-ass .22 handgun. I slowly creep towards the door, careful as to not make a sound.

The banging continues!

The weak hinges on my front door rattles, as they loosen under the force of the kicking and banging.

The thumping noise stops for a moment….

The brief silence is followed by a loud hard thud against the door. It sounds as if someone is throwing their body up against the door, trying to force it open.

I click off the hall light and crouch down, raising the .22 in front of me, aiming it straight for the door. My hand nervously trembles, 'cause I ain't never shot nobody before; and I ain't ready to start now.

"THERESA!" A deep man's voice calls out from the other side of the door. "THERESA, GET YOUR *MUTHAFUCKIN'*, HOE-ASS OUT HERE, NOW!"

Suddenly, it hits me. He's lookin' for Theresa, one of my hoes. She came by last night, and we got our freak on!

I run back into the bedroom, close the door behind me, click on the light, and see there's a lump on one side of my bed, covered in blankets. I kick the bed, but the lump doesn't move.

The yelling and kicking at my door continues!

It won't be long before whoever is on the other side of the threshold, come crashing through, and commence to whoop some ass!

"Theresa! Wake the fuck up!" I demand frantically. I'm shaking her, but the *bitch* sleeps like a log! "Theresa, will you puh-l-e-a-s-e wake up."

She still doesn't respond.

I sit the gun on the nightstand, grab Theresa's feet and pull her outta the bed. Her skinny, butt-naked body falls onto the floor. Theresa now wakes up like someone shocked her back to life with a defibrillator.

"Mel, what the *fuck* is wrong with you! Bitch, have you lost your *goddamn* mind?" Theresa is furious. She jumps up and is 'bout to swing at me, just as the front door crashes open. We both jump at the sound.

"T-H-E-R-E-S-A!" He screams and whines her name at the top of his lungs. I can't *believe* my eyes or my ears. I've got a butt-naked, crazy woman in my bedroom, and a hysterical mad man destroying my living room!

Theresa's eyes bug out in horror: "Oh shit, Mel, it's Marvin. He'll kill me if he finds out I'm screwing around with you again." In a frenzy, Theresa now scours the floor for her clothing.

"What? Theresa, you told me you and Marvin broke up— you're on your own!"

We now can hear Marvin quickly searching the living room like a raging lunatic. He turns over the couch, yanks my closet doors open, slams open my sliding glass door, and the glass cracks and shatters under the force of the impact.

Theresa then grabs my arm and squeezes with all her might: "Mel, please, hide me," she whispers. Her pretty face is streaming with tears. Her petite, naked body is shaking uncontrollably with fear.

54

I quickly scan the room, searching for a hiding place for Theresa. *Under the bed? No, too obvious. The closet? No, still too obvious.*

I can hear Marvin's heavy footsteps drawing nearer.

"Quick, in here." I immediately pull Theresa towards the oversized wicker hamper, over flowing with dirty clothes, and we start tossing dirty clothes out onto the floor.

Marvin's footsteps pause outside my bedroom door at the hallway closet. I hear him pull open the closet door and step inside. Meanwhile, Theresa's climbing inside the hamper. I help shove her tiny frame into the wicker basket, then I throw the dirty clothes back on top. Just as I finish, my doorknob slowly turns and the door opens. Marvin enters the room.

Marvin looks like "Dibo" from the movie *Friday.* He's 'bout 6'3", two-hundred and eighty pounds, and mad ugly.

He towers above me.

Marvin's massive chest rises and falls quickly with each breath.

I freeze....

Then, I reach for my gun, before realizing that I sat it on the nightstand on the other side of the room. Marvin then reaches for me, and wraps his huge, thick fingers around my neck.

"BITCH, WHERE'S THERESA?"

In my terrorized state, I manage to whimper, "Who?" Marvin squeezes my throat tighter. I gag. My face gets hot.

"Look you dyke, I ain't *playin'* wit' you!" his deep voice bellows. "I know you're fuckin' her, and I know she's in here somewhere. Now, if you don't open that big, fat, *pussy-eatin'* mouth of yours and tell me where Theresa is, I'm gonna choke the *shit* outta you!"

"What are you talking 'bout?" I muster. Marvin still has my throat locked between his two hands. My evasiveness only infuriates him more. With one hand still clutching my neck, Marvin slowly lifts me until only the tip of my toes are touching the floor.

The pressure cuts off the circulation to my brain.

The lack of oxygen blurs my vision.

My eyes burn.

Tears stream slowly down my face.

In desperation, I hold up a peace sign and chirp out: "Let go."

Marvin loosens his grip and I gasp for air. As air enters my lungs, I begin to cough. He lets me go, and I fall onto the bed like a rag doll.

"Start talking!"

"Theresa...was...here," I gasp.

Marvin's face darkens, and he steps toward me, ready to choke me again. I throw my hands up.

"Wait...hold on...lemme finish," I plea, before taking a deep breath. "Yeah, she was here."

"AND?" Marvin asks, giving me a few seconds to conjure up a lie.

"...I had a party, a few friends dropped by. We all kicked it 'til 'bout 3 AM. Then she left with some dude."

"SOME DUDE?"

Marvin was beginning to buy my lie, so I kept pouring it on: "Yeah, some dude."

"Bitch, you better not be lyin' to cover your ass."

"Well, as you can see, she ain't here."

Marvin glances around the room. Then, he pulls open the closet doors and looks under the bed, before giving up.

"You said she left with some dude?" He rubs his chin. "What's his name?"

"Look man, I don't know all that. All I know is that he was in her ear all night. Then 'bout three, they left together."

Marvin now stares at my face. Tries to gage whether I am lying or not.

"Yo, Theresa ain't even my type. She's too skinny. I like my girls thick."

Marvin concedes to that. Besides, I wasn't lying 'bout Theresa being skinny.

I take a deep breath.

A moment of silence elapses, as we collect our thoughts and reflect on the disastrous, ugly side of love and betrayal.

I think 'bout the woman hiding in my hamper.

Wonder what Theresa would've done if Marvin would have actually succeeded in killing me. I decide this skinny, little tramp isn't worth all the trouble.

As I look at Marvin, I realize that he isn't a monster. He's a man. And though he overacted, Marvin had every right to come in here to confront the person who's sleeping with *his* woman.

It's hard enough to lose your woman to another man. I *can't* imagine the feeling of knowing that your woman sleeps with other women, and there's no way to compete.

Feeling the need to get rid of both Theresa and Marvin, I stand and clear my throat to break the silence. He speaks first.

"Didn't mean to call you a dyke."

"Yes, you did. But it's okay."

"My bad about tearin' up your house. Guess I just lost it when my homeboys told me they saw Theresa at your door last night."

The hamper shifts a little. Marvin doesn't notice.

"Yeah, speaking of tearing the house up, my neighbors probably called 5-O by now. You better go."

Marvin looks at me with a nervous and dumbfounded expression. "When 5-O gets here, whachu gonna say?"

"I'm gonna tell them the truth...somebody robbed me and wrecked the place. Don't worry, I'm not gonna say anything 'bout you being here. If it was my girl, I probably would have done the same thing. So are we cool?" I ask, smiling a weak smile. Marvin smiles back, and for a brief moment, we understand each other.

After Marvin left, followed by Theresa, I have a quiet moment of introspection. I rehearse the whole "robbery scenario" in my head before the cops actually arrive, but the reality of it was that, the *only* person who got robbed today...was Marvin.

SHAWN

Chapter 11

Mike stands in the doorway. I block the entrance like a military guard standing post. He stands on the steps, staring like a dog in heat.

"Damn, girl you look good."

"Well, I was just about to leave out," I lied.

Mike's eyes continue to travel slowly up-and-down my body. His eyes are lit with excitement. "Damn, girl you...look...good."

"What are you, a parrot? Is that *all* you can say after you haven't returned my calls for over a month?" I ask, folding my arms across my chest

"Naw, shorty, I ain't no parrot. It's just...I guess I forgot how *good* you look, baby."

Oh, so now I'm his baby again. It's amazing how when the weather turns to spring, niggas crawl out of the woodworks like roaches, when the lights come on. "Well, I guess you should have *thought* about that before you went AWOL."

I try hard to be strong and stand my ground, but the sight of this man makes me moist. I take a step back to collect myself. I look Mike over.

He's dressed like he just stepped out of a rap video: *76er's* red, white and blue throwback jersey with matching baseball cap, baggy blue jeans by *Enyce,* white "Iverson's" *Reeboks* and a *Marc Jacobs* watch. Not to mention that the diamonds in Mike's ears were larger than mine.

He leans in to give me a kiss on the cheek. I lean back.

"So it's like that, yo?"

"Guess so."

"Can I at least come in?"

"Not sure yet."

"Okay, we'll play it your way," Mike replies, as he shrugs his shoulders and leans back on the railing.

"No other way to play. Especially when you show up two hours late? My time is very precious."

"So is mine. I ain't trying to stand out here on your steps all day. That shit is for the birds," Mike retorts in his usual thuggish tone.

I'm immediately turned on by his rawness! I have always been attracted to bad boys. Their attitude. The way they dress. Their rugged sex. And it seems like thugs have always been attracted to me: the good girl. The smart, sexy, preacher's daughter type. We are each other's addiction. Opposites attracting, doing the Ying and Yang thing.

But our balance is always a little off. Mike continually maintains the upper hand. He draws an emotional line, and *never* crosses it. Mike acts rationally. I act emotionally. I'm the one constantly getting caught up. And in the end, I am a-l-w-a-y-s the one getting hurt. And Mike? Mike is always cool. Cool-ass Mike!

"If I let you in, do you promise to be on your best behavior?"

Mike smiles slyly before answering, "Mos' def."

"You sure?"

"My word."

I lead him inside my Afro-Caribbean inspired apartment; decorated with an eclectic mix of cool tropical colors, African tribal wall hangings, heavy wood and leather furnishings, and animal-patterned accent pieces and area rugs.

I make certain to walk ahead of Mike. My hips seductively sway from side-to-side. My booty bounces beneath the thin fabric of my silk dress.

Mike then takes a seat and on the couch and continues to observe me, as I make my way into the kitchen to grab another bottle of wine and to prepare some fruit. As I wash and slice the mangos, kiwi, pineapples and strawberries, we make light conversation from a distance.

He speaks of the tour he is on, to promote his hip-hop CD scheduled to drop this summer. Mike tells me about all the cities he has traveled to and, the various celebrities he's met. Mike seems very excited about it all. I tell him funny anecdotes about the students in my fourth grade class. How one of my students won the national spelling bee.

We then reminisce about our brief one-month interlude. Mike and I joke about how we first met at *X's and O's,* a cafe bar where intellectual, artistic types meet to network. We were introduced there by a mutual friend. That night, Mike and I discussed politics, and we ended up in a heated debate about the war in *Iraq*. The debate was the preface to us passionately making out in the cab we shared later that evening.

When the cab pulled up in front of my building, Mike walked me to my door and kicked a freestyle rhyme for me. He also kissed my hand. Said he'd write a rhyme for me, took my digits, got back in the cab and drove away. The next day, Mike kicked a freestyle rhyme—an ode to me, on my answering machine. We'd made plans to meet that same night, and ended up fucking on my custom-made chenille sofa.

I now serve the fruit and wine. Mike and I eat and drink—even share a few laughs. The conversation flows with ease. All the while, I wonder what he really came here to talk about.

Mike soon places his hand on my thigh, and the feeling of his warm palm on my bare skin, sends a soft shiver through me. Flashbacks of the last time we'd made love, on the very couch we're sitting on, play inside my head like an erotic slide show.

Being vulnerable, lonely and extremely horny after a two-month drought, I am apprehensive about sitting next to him and going down that road again. I then place my hand on top of Mike's and gently slide it away from my thigh.

"My bad. Guess I got carried away with all the reminiscing going on."

"Let's not get *too* carried away, okay, Mike?"

He looks me over and admits, "Shawn, it's kinda hard for me to keep it together with you looking all good, and smelling like...what is that?"

"Its eucalyptus and peppermint oil. And for your information, I've looked and smelled this good for the past two months! Where were you?"

Mike sits his drink down and gives me a here-we-go-again look. I could kick myself for coming on too strong. I've never been good at playing it smooth. I always end up erupting and getting all motherly—smothering.

"Look, forget I asked," I say, as I stand and turn away, ready to forget Mike and the horse he rode in on.

Mike responds by standing behind me, wrapping his arms around my shoulders. He kisses my shoulder blade and whispers softly in my ear, "Girl, quit actin' like that, you know I been on tour. You know how it is." Mike continues to murmur excuses about his hectic schedule, and his publicist telling him to keep a low profile.

I know it is *a-l-l* bullshit! But to have this gorgeous man next to me again, is worth all the lies and deception.

Mike's lips now graze my earlobe. His chest is pressed firmly against my back, I begin to soften in his embrace.

"They don't have phones on tour? Email...snail mail, what's up?" I ask, trying to push Mike's arms away from me. He holds me tighter and chuckles. Excitement grows in his eyes.

"I love your fire."

"I can't tell. You *never* stay around long enough to show me that you love *anything* about me."

I turn to face Mike. His piercing eyes meet mine, and reciprocate my intensity. I study the rest of Mike's ruggedly handsome face. His bald head. Deep-set dark eyes. Mike's square chin and sexy goatee. His look is, at once, devious and sophisticated, while I'm so earthy and plain.

Mike's a famous rapper, having his pick of any woman in the world, and he chose to spend the day with me.

How could I trip on him?

I now lower my gaze. Mike pulls me in closer, and I rest my head on his firm chest. He unravels my loosely-knotted dreadlocks free. My locks cascade and frame my face. Mike now rubs my back. *I can't believe that I am in his arms again!*

...This feeling is a lie.

It's the thin thread that I base my hopes on.

I dangle from this thread.

The thread gets thinner...

...And thinner...

...And thinner....

Until it is a single strand and can longer take the pressure. The thread of my hopes breaks free, and I am, once again, falling.

Mike then assures me, "Shawn, I wanted to call, but when I'm doing my music thing, I need to stay focused. I can't have distractions."

"Oh, so *now* I'm a distraction?"

Mike soon soothingly strokes my back, I start to wonder:

Maybe he's changed.

Maybe this time things will be different.

Maybe this time it's for real.

God, let this be real, this time.

"Don't take it personal. When it comes to my music, everything is a distraction. When you thought you might've been pregnant, I made some calls. I had folks keeping an eye on you."

"That's not the same thing, Mike! It's not the same thing as you *being* here!" I throw words at Mike and abruptly pull away from him.

"Dammit, girl. I can't be here!"

"Will you stop with the excuses and just admit that you want to get rid of me! Isn't that what you came here to talk about? Why don't we just skip the wine and fruit, and all of the niceties, and get *straight* to the point! You haven't made any attempt to stay in contact with me, and you blame it all on the tour. Why don't you take responsibility for how you feel, and stop making excuses?" I demand. I then wait for a response, but Mike doesn't say a word. He stands still.

I now want to be angry!

I want to fight the affect that Mike has on me!

I want to make him feel the hurt that I am feeling!

"Mike, if you need to move around and be free, then move on! Go on!"

I start to walk towards the door. Mike reaches for me, grabs my arm and pulls me back to him. We are now face-to-face. The anger and hurt in my eyes meet all the lies and deceit in his. My heart wants to *detest* Mike, but my body has an insatiable appetite for this man.

I feel foolish and afraid.

Yet, I have never felt so alive!

My soul is in distress....

Mike's hands grip my arms, and he pulls me closer to his warmth. Mike smells like Egyptian musk. His heart beats a rapid staccato. If I continue to stand so close to Mike, I will surrender. So I close my eyes and try to will myself away from him.

Instead, I feel the moistness of Mike's soft full lips touch mine. His kiss is slow and hesitant. Mike's tongue soon grazes my lips smoothly, then brushes along my cheek—he now nibbles on my earlobe. I immediately search for his lips and return the kiss.

Our tongues dance!

The taste of wine on his tongue, and the urgency of the kiss has my head is spinning!

Our hands travel...we explore....

Legs intertwine. Mike and I lose our balance and we fall onto the couch. He's now on top of me. The weight of Mike's body pins me to the couch. The fall stuns me for a second and logic creeps back into the picture, telling me there's still time to stop; make a strong stand and not give in.

I immediately open my mouth and try to beg Mike to stop, but he pushes my dress hem around my waist...spreads my legs. Mikes fingers are now strumming me like guitar string.

I tug at his jeans.

Pull down Mike's zipper.

Reach inside and take a-l-l of him in my hand.

He then lifts my thigh and places my leg over his muscular shoulder. Mike's pelvis connects with mine and he pushes against me, until my wetness guides him inside.

Mike eagerly enters me...

...Pushes deep and long inside of me until it hurts...

...And I receive the pain....

TRISTAN

I'm now at the mall trying on my fifth pair of *Christian Louboutin* shoes. *That's* what I do when I'm *pissed* off! Shop!

I left Cornelius at the condo, as I could not bring myself to look at him after the incident with the "anonymous" note. Cornelius wouldn't give me any information on the identity of the mysterious author of the note, nor would the concierge, so I hopped into a cab, prepared to do some serious cathartic shopping.

Three-thousand dollars later, I leave *Neiman Marcus,* shopping bags in tow, walking through *King of Prussia Mall,* now heading towards *Gucci.*

Not ten seconds after I enter the store, and the commissioned sales associates are kissing my ass, my *Blackberry* rings. Melanie's phone number registers on the caller ID.

"This *better* be an emergency, Mel. I'm *not* in the mood for *any* more drama today!" I bark.

"Hello to you, too, sis."

"Yeah, yeah. What do you want?" I ask, as I make my way to the handbag and accessories counter.

"I need to borrow some money."

"Borrow?" I say, before laughing at Melanie like she'd told me a joke. It was my first good laugh of the day. "Who do you think you're fooling? You know you can't *afford* to pay me back." I turn to the sales lady, dangling a black patent leather *Gucci* "Romy" tote on my arm and ask: "Does this bag come in any other color?"

"Are you shopping?" Melanie asks.

"I was trying to before you *rudely* interrupted me."

The sales lady now informs me that tote only comes in black, I nod my head yes, and pick up the conversation with Melanie. "So what happened now? Did you *lose* your job?"

"No, I still got my job."

I walk over to the belts, "Does this one come with a smaller buckle?"

"Tristan, can you stop shopping for a second and pay me some attention?"

"No," I answer nonchalantly. The sales lady then shows me several selections of belts with smaller buckles. "I can talk to you and shop at the same time; it's called multi-tasking." I proceed to check out the belt display. "I'll take that one," I say, pointing to a thin, black leather belt with the small, signature intertwining "G" gold buckle. "Mel, if you haven't lost your job, then why do you need *my* money? Have you wasted yours away on your little girlfriend at the strip club again?" I ask in a motherly tone.

The sales associate overhears my last comment and blushes. I instantly turn my back to her.

"My apartment got...robbed."

"Robbed? Oh my God. Are you okay?"

"I'm fine, but I need to replace a few things."

After Melanie assures me that she's fine, I decide that it's okay to resume shopping. I turn back around and ask the sales lady where the silk scarves are located. She leads the way and I follow.

"How much money do you think you'll need to replace your stolen items?"

"I don't know, maybe four or five-hundred."

I sigh. "Meet me at my office tomorrow morning. I'll write you a check."

"Yo, good lookin' out."

"You just caught me at the right moment."

I then point to a blue and white striped neckerchief with a run on print of the *Gucci* logo. The sales associate hands it to me and I try it on.

"Where are you?" Mel asks.

"Doing damage at *Gucci*. I'm spending w-a-y too much money. I ought to be ashamed"

"Shopping spree?"

"Something like that. Just blowing off a little steam?"

"Who pissed you off now? It's Sunday, so it can't be work, and I know it *ain't* no man 'cause you ain't got one; which is the only thing we got in common."

I laugh again. Although we are entirely different, my sister knows me better than anybody else.

"Melanie, you ought to be a comedian. And no, I'm not pissed off about work."

The sales lady rings me up and gives me my total: fifty-five-hundred dollars. I whip out my "Black" *American Express card,* and I suddenly feel nauseous at the sight of it. I immediately think of the "anonymous" note, remembering the gentleman who attempted to buy me a drink that night at *Zanzibar Blue.*

The sales associate looks at me curiously: "Ma'am, are you okay?" she asks sincerely.

"I'm fine!" I snap. I push the *American Express Card* back inside of my *Louis Vuitton* billfold, and pull out my corporate "Platinum" *Visa.*

"If you're not pissed off 'bout work—" Melanie interjects before she pauses. "...Hold up. Tristan, you mean to tell me that some *thing* with a *ding-a-ling,* has got you all bent outta shape?" Melanie exclaims. I can picture her mouth wide open in shock.

"He's just a *stupid* man." I don't want to give my sister the impression that a man has gotten under my skin, so I switch gears. "He's a client that's being intolerable, that's all it is."

"Yeah right. Who is he?"

"A client, like I said." I now walk out of *Gucci* and into *Chanel.* "Now off of me and on to you. Nobody would be robbing you if you'd stop *wasting* your money on hopeless strippers, and move out of that God-forsaken project. I bet you that worthless stripper you spend *all* that money on, lives in a nice house somewhere."

"I don't live in the *projects,* I live in Section 8."

"Same difference!"

"And she's *not* a hopeless stripper...she's smart and beautiful...talented ...sexy—"

"Let's skip the details, you're grossing me out. The point is that you *need* to get your life together. If you get serious and go back to school, then I'll help you out financially. You could move into a better apartment, get a better job and stop *mooching* off of me!"

"Thanks, but no thanks. School ain't for me?"

"Whatever. I can't help those who don't want to be helped," I say, full of exasperation.

"Cool. See ya tomorrow," Melanie chimed and hung up quickly. Classic Melanie. She'll call and beg for money, then hang up on me to avoid being lectured.

Soon after, I reach for a pair of *"Jackie O"* inspired black *Chanel* sunglasses. I slide them on, and almost orgasm at the stunning reflection in the mirror.

Shopping *definitely* gets my endorphins going.

When it comes time to fork over the four-hundred dollars for the sunglasses, the infamous "Black" *American Express Card* once again, confronts me. I decide to stop being ridiculous and slap the credit card on the counter triumphantly. The credit card slip prints out and I smile victoriously, as I sign my name.

I am overcome with sheer satisfaction at the thought that I have, once again, defeating a man who tried to put me down. I am instantly elated, and for some strange reason, I feel like sharing; so I dial Shawn's number.

After several rings she answers huskily: "Hello."

"What's up with the *Toni Braxton* voice? Did I wake you?"

"Tristan, can I call you back? I'm kind of busy right now, if you know what I mean," Shawn whispers.

"Oh..." I put two and two together. "...Are you? ...You know...did I catch you at a bad time?"

"Just got done. I'm recovering from my re-enactment of *Halle Berry* and *Billy Bob Thornton* in *Monster's Ball.* Mike's in the bathroom."

"Mike? Do you *ever* exercise a *little* judgment when it comes to that man...or any man for that matter? I think you've about lost your mind."

"When you have a man that fucks you r-e-a-l good, then you'll see how easy it is for some of us to lose our minds. I don't need to hear any bullshit from you, right now, what I need is a joint and a bubble bath," Shawn chuckles mischievously. "Can I call you back?"

"Don't worry about it. I'm at the mall single-handedly destroying my bank account. I didn't really want anything. Just called to say hello."

"You need to stop shopping so much and start fucking. It'll save you a lot of dough."

"Yeah, but I'd rather be bankrupt than broken-hearted."

"Whatever you need to tell yourself, sweetie. Right about now, I'm feeling like round two might be popping off—gotta go."

Click.

I hang up, wondering why I even bother with Shawn. She was just as pathetic in college, and now, Shawn's only getting worse. She's always had bad luck with men, because she's undiscriminating. Shawn will settle for *any* man that comes her way.

Unlike me.

I've *always* been very selective, and I prefer to keep it strictly business with men; *even* in the bedroom. I treat them as an acquisition, to be used for the sole purpose of sex.

Nothing more.

Nothing less.

No strings attached, and no emotions involved.

MEKKA

Chapter 13

Drew swings the wooden paddle: *WHAP!* He's gettin' his
rocks off by paddlin' my naked ass—Drew's *sick* idea of slave
fantasy. He's pretendin' to be the slave master, and I'm supposed
to be the "runaway slave" who got caught; who's now bein'
punished.

I'm faced down, ass up, wit' my head buried deep into the
pillow; keepin' myself from *cursin'* Drew's white ass out! Images
of Sheka and Man-Man flash through my mind. Why did I ever
decide to leave my kids wit' Maria and subject myself to this
degradin' *bullshit?*

I'd promised to take 'em shoppin' at *Target,* then to *TGI
Fridays*, and I was gonna rent 'em some movies; as we were to sit
around and eat popcorn like one big happy family. I never spend
enough time wit' 'em, and that always makes me feel guilty.
Either I'm out strippin', doin' bachelor parties on the side, or
turnin' tricks.

Sheka and Man-Man *begged* me not to leave 'em today.
But all I could think about was the extra money I was gon' make.
I keep tellin' myself that once the balance of my bank account had
enough zeros attached, that I'll settle down, and eventually quit
this lifestyle. I'm gettin' close to where I wanna be, but the closer
I get, the worse I feel.

Sometimes I wonder if my kids will still want to be wit'
me whenever I decide to make time for them. Or will they be so
used to bein' looked after by someone else, that they'll eventually
grow numb, and I won't even matter to them anymore?

WHAP!

Drew swings the paddle with his left hand and jerks off
with his right: "NIGGA-BITCH!" He roars. "Take this paddle,
you *nasty,* black whore." *WHAP!*

I try to think pleasant thoughts. The image of the five-
hundred dollars Drew's paying me to submit myself to this
perverted torture, makes me feel a little better, but does little to

ease the pain. I conjure up visions of Jamaica inside my mind. I imagine the fancy, five-star hotel room overlooking sandy beaches. Yet, my fantasy is abruptly interrupted by the smack of the wooden paddle, as it connects to my ass.

WHAP!

"I want you to say, 'I'm a *nasty* black whore'," Drew commands. I refuse to say those words, and he makes me pay for it. Drew swings the paddle like *Barry Bonds* hittin' a home run out of Yankee Stadium: *WHAP!*
"SAY IT!"
My ass is burnin' like an inferno searin' through my flesh.

WHAP!

"SAY IT!"
I twist my face to the side, freein' it from the pillow, and my eyes well up wit' tears.

WHAP!

"Didn't I *tell* you to say something?"
I fight through the pain, and prop myself up on my elbows: "I'm a ...nasty...black...whore."
Drew strokes his penis faster. His face is twisted in agonizin' ecstasy. "What else?" *WHAP!*
"I'm a slut!" I holler back.

WHAP! ...WHAP! ...WHAP!

Drew pulls at his tiny dick, which is swollen and just about ready to explode.
"All nigger-bitches *love* to get paddled, don't they?" *WHAP!* "Don't they?" he pants and sweats.
I cry out through the excruciatin' pain: "I *love* it, you pasty...white...shriveled dick...stringy-haired...dog-smellin'...punk-ass...piece-of-shit!"
"A-W-W-W, Y-E-A-H, BABY," Drew now jerks off feverishly, and suddenly, his head falls back—Drew's body shakin' while semen shoots out of his penis. He now collapses onto the bed.

70

I slowly stand up. I wince as I pull my pink panties and *Diesel* denim skirt over my burnin' ass cheeks. I have *no* idea how I'm goin' to drive home wit' my butt cheeks on fire, but I am determined to get the *fuck* out of here quickly!

I'll just have to grin and bear it.

I walk over to the dresser where five, crisp one-hundred dollar bills are waitin' for me. Next to my payment is a picture of Drew's wife in a silver *Mikasa* frame. She's an average lookin' woman wit' short, curly brown hair.

In the picture, Drew's wife is wearing one of those stupid, gaudy, cheap Christmas sweaters, embroidered wit' Santas and snowmen. Next to her picture is a silver tray, filled wit' perfumes, a hairbrush and lipstick cases.

The closet door is open, and hangin' inside are various nurses' scrubs, decorated wit' flower patterns, and festive holiday designs. Drew's wife's white nurse shoes are lined neatly on the floor under the bed skirt. I imagine her in some hospital room saving lives, while her *perverted* husband is at home *jackin'* off to his "jungle fever" fantasies.

For a brief moment, I feel sorry for Drew's wife…

Then I *quickly* come back to my senses!

Shit, he ain't *my* man, so why should *I* worry about it? I then *snatch* the money and throw it inside my *Prada* purse. Drew is sittin' on the edge of the bed butt-naked, smokin' a cigar.

"Drew, do you mind if I use ya bathroom to freshen up before I hit the road?"

He shakes his head no.

I walk into the master bathroom and check my reflection. My hair looks a little tussled, my face is slightly puffy and my *Chanel* lipstick is smeared, other than that, I look like the same ol' Mekka.

I wipe my lipstick off and replace it wit' shimmerin', rose-colored *MAC* "Lipglass" lip gloss. I can now hear Drew movin' around in the bedroom, then his footsteps move out into the hall. When I finish, I find Drew in the kitchen standin' in front of the refrigerator. He's barefoot, wearin' a pair of faded and torn *Rustler* jeans.

"Want a soda?" Drew asks; avoidin' eye contact. "*Pepsi* or *Sprite?*"

"No thanks. I'm headin' out."

"Beer?"

"No thanks."

"Find the money?"

"Yeah, I got it."

"Good."

Drew now looks me in the eyes.

Then at my breasts...

Observes my hips and my legs.

"Brown sugar, you look nice in that skirt. You got nice legs."

"Thanks."

...There is a moment of uncomfortable silence. More uncomfortable for Drew than me. I really don't give a *fuck*, now that the whole spankin' ordeal is over.

"I'll walk you to the door," Drew says, as he slides his hands inside of his pockets and walks ahead of me. "Like I said before, I'll be working late the next few days. Can I call you in a couple of days when I get some free time?"

"Let's play it by ear, okay?"

Drew then opens the side door leadin' into the garage. I walk quickly over to my *Jaguar* and climb inside.

"Drew," I call to him before I pull off.

"Yeah."

"Next time, I'll spank you." I say. "How 'bout that?"

He smiles and jokin'ly asks, "Can I call you 'mommy'?"

"White boy, you can call me whatever the *fuck* you want to, as long as you got my money; ya hear me, baby?"

Drew turns to walk away.

"Oh, Drew."

He looks over his shoulder: "Yes?"

"Tell the *wife* I said, 'hello'."

I burn off leavin' deep skid marks in his driveway.

SHAWN
Chapter 14

"That was incredible," I say, straddling Mike's waist, as he lays flat on the bed. I wipe the sweat from Mike's brow with my fingertips, then trace and study his facial features, as he stares up at me.

"They say the second time is better than the first."

"Most definitely," I agree, leaning over to kiss Mike on the lips. As we kiss, I gently pull my dreadlocks away from my face, and tie them into a knot at the nape of my neck. Mike then soothingly strokes my back, and nibbles on my right shoulder.

"Girl, I'm gonna miss you," he murmurs in my ear.

"Well, next time you go on tour, don't be a stranger. You can always make a pit stop here."

"I wish it was that easy."

"It can be, if you let it."

"Naw, baby," Mike says, turning his face away. "It's not easy at all. In all actuality, it's very complex."

"What are you *talking* about, Mike?" I slide off of him so that we're lying side-by-side. I can feel the conversation taking a turn for the worst, and I want to ground myself.

"Look, shorty, this is it. When I leave here today, I'm gone for good. That's what I came here to talk to you about. "

"What do you mean, *'that's it'*? What the *fuck* was this afternoon all about?" I could have slapped myself! In all of my horniness, I had forgotten that Mike said *'we need to talk'*.

"This afternoon was about closure. I came here to tell you that it's over, basically."

"BASICALLY, MY ASS! If you *came* here to break the bad news, then you could have said that *bullshit* on the front steps and *kept* on moving! Why'd you have to come *a-l-l* up in my space?" I then sit up and reach for my wrinkled silk dress on the floor by the coffee table. Mike grabs his jeans and begins to pull them on.

"Look, Shawn, don't play innocent. You wore that sexy dress and kept the wine flowing. You *wanted* a nigga to bite, so I bit. Don't get mad at me."

"You came here to break up with me because of the tour? Performers travel all the time and still maintain relationships! It's how they stay grounded."

"And I plan to stay grounded. I made roots, just not with you."

"WHAT IS THAT SUPPOSED TO MEAN?"

"It means that I've met someone else. Before I went on tour, I met another woman, and I dig her a lot. We talked and hooked up off-and-on, and now it's getting pretty serious."

It takes a minute for Mike's words to settle in.

"...*Surely* she can't *make* you feel the way that *I* do! After what just happened between us, I can tell that you *still* want me!"

"That was only sex. It doesn't really mean anything. I wanted you...you wanted me. But now it's over. This is *it* for me! I plan on marrying this woman. Shawn, I'm getting married."

I want to wild-out on him, but I can't. I play Mike's last words over-and-over inside of my head: "*I met another woman.*" "*That was only sex.*" "*I plan on marrying this woman.*"

All the while, I was just, "something on the side".

A convenience.

I can't blame him. Mike was only doing what I *allowed* him to do to me. I let Mike use me, and now I have to face the facts that it's come to an end.

Game over.

I am silent...

"Shawn, you cool?"

"HELL NO, I'M NOT COOL, ASSHOLE! You *waltz* in here, *fuck* me, and then drop a *bomb* on me? I'm supposed to do what, throw you a *fucking* wedding shower?"

"I didn't plan on this."

"You just slipped and fell into my pussy! Okay, now *who's* playing innocent?"

I storm past Mike and walk towards the living room closet. I pull out a small box from the top shelf, and carry it back to the coffee table. The box contains my secret stash of "hydro" weed.

I then sit on the couch and separate the seeds from the marijuana. I crumble the weed up, sprinkle it into *Zig-Zag* cigarette paper, then roll it and lick it. This methodical process calms me down a little. My calmness makes Mike feel less uneasy.

He watches me roll and lick like a pro. I can feel Mike analyzing me, judging me; a fourth-grade school teacher...pot head!

"It calms my nerves," I explain.

Mike shrugs his shoulders: "To each his own."

I flip the script: "So, were you seeing her the whole time?"

"I hate to admit it, but yes, I was seeing her while I was still kickin' it with you."

"And what happened?"

"I don't know. I guess I was being selfish and I wanted both of you. I didn't want to choose."

I reach for my lighter and spark up the weed. I take a long drag, inhale, and hold it in, until I feel like my head is floating amongst the clouds. I then exhale slowly, before taking another tote and passing it to Mike. He looks surprised at first, then Mike accepts the joint and takes a hit.

For the next few minutes, Mike and I sit in silence, passing the joint back-and-forth.

We become mellow.

I break the silence: "I got to ask you a few questions. Call it jealousy, call it insecurity, but, I got to know about the woman who snatched my man, right from underneath me."

"Yo, don't go there"

"No, I'm *going* there. Mike, I need to know. You at least *owe* me that; don't you think?"

Mike doesn't disagree.

"Why did you choose her?"

"It's no pressure with her. She's just cool and laid back; let's me do my thang."

"And that makes me?"

"To be quite honest, you're a little high-strung and kinda insecure."

His choice of adjectives hits me like a ton of bricks, but I keep going: "So why'd you stick around?"

"Because I like your passion. I like your fire, but it's not good for me."

"And she's safe."

"Safe? I guess that's a good word."

I take another long drag and pass it back.

"What does *she* do for a living?"

"A & R for my record label?"

Mike takes two puffs and passes it back.

"Is she built like me?"

"Not really. You got that ghetto-booty. She's more petite and athletic."

"Is she as fine as me?"

"Y'all don't look nothing alike."

"How do we differ? What, is she light and bright?" I take a drag and close my eyes.

"She's about as light as you can get. She's white."

I choke.

Hard.

I double over and gasp for air. Mike fans me and rubs my back until I'm cool.

"Mike, don't tell me you sold out. How can you rap about your culture and street life, but when you get a little fame, you dis the sisters?"

"You see me as a sell out?"

"That's what it looks like. She's your blonde, blue-eyed showpiece, and I'm your nappy-headed dread that you *fuck* and keep tucked inside the closet. She's calm and quiet, and I'm high-strung and passionate. Don't you get it? ...That's *exactly* how we got treated during slavery. The White women got put up on pedestals, and the Black slave women were treated like concubines."

"That's bullshit!"

"If the shoe fits."

"The shoe doesn't *fuckin'* fit! If she wasn't White, I don't think that this would be that big of an issue!" Mike gets up from the couch and pulls his throwback jersey back over his head. He's preparing to leave.

"Don't get it twisted. I don't *care* if she's White, Black, purple or blue. It's not about race. It's about you coming in here, *fucking* me, twice, then *telling* me you're getting married!"

"Shawn—" Mike then makes an attempt to explain himself, but I hold up my hands and cut him off. I have *no* interest in *whatever* Mike has to say. The more I look at him, the more I want to smack Mike.

"Mike, don't speak. Don't apologize. Don't *make* excuses. Just leave."

"But Shawn—"

"Just leave! Seriously. You're blowing my high."

BLUE MONDAY

TRISTAN
Chapter 15

There are 117 unread e-mails and 19 voicemail messages waiting for me, when I enter my office suite at 6:45 AM. It feels good to be back in the office Monday morning. Being back at work forces me to focus on other things, other than my own personal life, or lack thereof. I snatch up the phone and dial into my mailbox, fielding through each missed call.

The first message is from my hairstylist, Quincy:

"D-a-r-l-i-n-g, I haven't seen you in a-g-e-s. I know those black roots are starting to show. There's a new style I want to try on you. Saw it on Beyonce's latest video, Miss Thing was looking fierce! I'll expect you in my chair Saturday morning, 10 AM, and don't even think about being late, dearest. Ciao!"

The second message is from my most influential client, Morgan Baxter. He's trying to raise capital to finance a bank in the city. If I manage to close this deal, it will make Mr. Baxter CEO of the first Black-owned and independently-operated financial Institution in Philadelphia.

I listen to Mr. Baxter's message; he sounds furious:

"Ms. Vincent, I still haven't received the contracts that I need to sign. I need to get those documents as soon as possible, so they can be reviewed and finalized. You promised me that they would be sent by Fed Ex and on my desk no later than Friday afternoon. It is now Monday morning, and there is still no sign of the Letter of Intent. Please quit dragging your feet, as I am very anxious to seal this deal. If you can't handle this, then maybe we'll have to find someone who is more competent."

I listen to the message for a second time before pressing "delete". I hang up the phone, feeling embarrassed, humiliated, and most of all, confused. Anissa assured me that she'd dropped it off at *Fed Ex* on Friday.

I can't understand what is happening, and I won't have the opportunity to question Anissa until she arrives at eight o' clock. I decide to give Mr. Baxter a call to apologize, and assure him that I would get to the bottom of this. I *have* to regain his confidence in me.

I reach for my *Rolodex,* but it isn't there. I push papers around and look in places that I knew it would never be, and still come up empty. *What in the hell is going on around here?*

I have to remind myself that it's Monday morning, and nothing ever goes right until I've had my first cup of coffee. I grab the *Starbucks* cup filled with caramel macchiato coffee, and walk towards the floor-to-ceiling windows over looking *Olde City.* I decide to take a moment to indulge myself and hopefully, afterwards everything will be back to normal.

The sky is overcast. Traffic on *Market Street* is pretty light this time of morning. Yellow taxicabs are lining up at their respective stations, preparing for the early morning commuters. Everything outside looks the same as it always does, while everything in my world seems to be in complete disarray.

I take a sip of the coffee and savor the sweet, creamy flavor. The aroma fills the air. When I finish my coffee, I sit back down at my desk, feeling a bit more relaxed and focused.

I begin to sort through the files in my attaché case. One of the files is labeled with Morgan Baxter's name. Enclosed is a rough draft, redlined copy of his Letter of Intent. *I specifically remember asking Anissa to print out an additional copy and overnight it to Baxter.* As soon as she walks into my office this morning, and I see the whites of her eyes, girlfriend will have some *explaining* to do!

The one thing that I pride myself on is my reputation. My hard-hitting, take-no-prisoners approach to doing business is what catapulted me to the level I have risen to, and I can't *afford* to screw that up by blowing this deal.

I stare at Mr. Baxter's name on the file. His voicemail message replays itself inside my head. I can still hear Mr. Baxter's curt, authoritative voice chastising me—making me sound like some incompetent woman.

Anissa startles me back to the present by knocking at the stately, mahogany doors to my office. The clock on my desk reads "7:30 AM". She's thirty minutes early. Anissa enters dressed in a black tailored *Badgley Mischka* power suit, with a pair of leopard print, slingback *Manolo Blahnik* pumps, with her hair pulled into a neat bun, just like my own.

"My, my, my. Don't you look professional?" I say, taken aback by Anissa's new look.

She gives me a twirl: "Like it."

"Where's the big hoop earrings and sassy hair?"

"Gone. This is the new me," Anissa beams. She has a glow that exudes self-confidence.

"It looks good on you. It'll just take me time to get used to you this way."

"Well, the new me is here to stay. It took me some time to realize that, if you want people to take you seriously, you have to dress the part. It's *all* about the image."

"That's a step in the right direction," I motion for Anissa to take a seat in the chair positioned across from me. She grabs her pen and pad, and postures herself to take notes.

"Anissa, before we get started, let me ask you, have you seen my *Rolodex?*"

Anissa ponders for a moment, and then she musters: "Oh, yeah. It's on my desk. I was updating your Rolodex on Friday and I guess I forgot to put it back. I'll go get it as soon as we're finished briefing each other."

"That will be fine. I just need to call Morgan Baxter. I got a disturbing call from him this morning. Mr. Baxter said he never got the Letter of Intent that I asked you to *Fed Ex*. Did you forget?"

A look of confusion washes over Anissa's face. "I took it to the *Fed Ex* station myself."

"Anissa, if you *dropped* the ball on this, I wish you would just admit it. You've made this firm look *very* incompetent."

"Ms. Vincent, I assure you, to the best of my knowledge the Letter of Intent was delivered to Mr. Baxter's office. Would you like me to call his office and try to track it down?"

"No Anissa, that *won't* be necessary. I'll handle this *solely* on my own. I thought I could trust you to take on more responsibility, but I guess I'll *have* to rethink that. You've embarrassed this firm and you've embarrassed me. I just hope it's *not* too late to turn this situation around.

"I am *very* disappointed in you…Just because you change your outer appearance, doesn't mean you can *play* on my level. After all, you *only* have an Associate's degree. Now, if you will, get Mr. Baxter on the line so that I can get down to the bottom of this. Please remove yourself from my office, and don't do *anything* else without my expressed permission."

A minute later my intercom buzzes: "Ms. Vincent, I have Drew Cunningham on the line for you," Anissa informs me that it's Morgan Baxter's Chief Operating Officer.

"Mr. Cunningham, this is Tristan Vincent, how are you?"

"I'm overpaid for what I actually get done around here," he jokes.

"Well in that case, I'm underpaid."

Mr. Cunningham laughs.

Nice to hear that somebody in Mr. Baxter's office has a sense of humor. "Mr. Cunningham, I'll just get straight to the point. I got a call from Mr. Baxter this morning saying that he never got the Letter of Intent we sent by *Fed Ex.*"

"That's right. As a matter of fact, I was here all day Friday and I never saw it come in. I wanted to review it before I gave it to Baxter."

"My assistant, Anissa, said that it should have been delivered to your office this morning."

"Looks like there's been some sort of mistake. But these things happen," Drew says. To my surprise, he's being very understanding.

"What we need to do is move forward and rectify this situation. I'll e-mail you a copy of the Letter of Intent right away so that you can review it, then I'll have a courier personally hand deliver it to you. Let me connect you to Anissa and have her verify your address."

"Sounds like a plan. The sooner Baxter gets these papers, the better."

"I agree. Just give me a call and confirm that you got the delivery. You'll receive my e-mail momentarily."

I then intercom Anissa: "Please have the courier service swing by and pick up the Letter of Intent, ASAP. I *refuse* to have Mr. Baxter thinking that we are incompetent. Somehow, things got screwed up, and we've made a bad impression."

"Ms. Vincent, if you don't mind, I'd like to offer a suggestion."

"And that would be?" I ask, trying to hide my frustration. Anissa hesitates before answering.

"Wouldn't you feel more confident if I delivered it personally? That way there's no middleman to screw this up again. I can take it to Drew, and apologize for the discrepancy in person."

I can't argue with her logic. "That might not be such a bad idea. I'll arrange for my car to take you to Mr. Baxter's office," I continue with a tinge of reservation in my gut, "Okay, Anissa...I'm trusting you."

"Yes, ma'am...and Ms. Vincent, don't worry, I'll make sure that nothing goes wrong...I just want you to know that, you have been a *wonderful* mentor to me. You've taught me so much. One day, you'll see just how instrumental you've been in my development...I promise you that."

Fifteen minutes later, my door swings open, and my sister, Melanie, struts in dressed in an oversized fleece hoodie and baggy jeans, both by *Akademiks*, with *Timberland* boots.

"What's up, sis?" she asks, before plopping down in the leather, executive lounge chair beside the mini conference table. "I passed by your assistant on my way in. What's up with her new look? She looks like your clone. As if one of you isn't scary enough."

"Ha, ha, what do you want?" I ask, not wasting any time.

"Remember yesterday you told me to come by and pick up some dough?"

"That's right," I snap my fingers sarcastically. "You need money, as usual, and lucky for you, the 'Bank of Tristan Savings and Loans' is open this morning," I snatch my checkbook from my sky-blue *Hermes* "Birkin" bag, and begin writing Melanie a check for five-hundred dollars. I pass the check to her: "I believe this should cover your expenses. Now, if you *don't* mind, close the door behind you. *Some* of us have work to do. Not *all* of us can call on other people when we *need* something."

"You know, sometimes, Tristan you are so selfish; just like mom."

I freeze at Melanie's comment.

"Mel, I am *nothing* like our mother."

"Yes you are. You're cold. You never have a kind word to say. You don't even talk to me like I'm your sister."

"What do you expect? You come into my office with your hand held out, *begging* as usual, and just because I don't greet you with a sisterly hug and smile, you accuse me of being like '*that woman*'."

"'*That woman*' is our mother!"

"I *never* had a mother. Now, if you'll excuse me, I have *work* to finish."

"Whatever. Go ahead and hide behind your wall of work. You can't hide from your life forever. Sooner or later, you're gonna have to come from behind that wall, and face how *fucked* up your life really is," Melanie stands, prepared to leave. "You know what? You and I have a whole lot in common."

Melanie's last comment forces me to look at her.

"Melanie, what could you and I *possibly* have in common?" I ask with a chuckle.

With her Caesar fade haircut, Melanie looks just like our father. She has his deep-set eyes, pug nose and full lips. Even Melanie's intense expression mirrors our father's.

A chill runs down my spine.

I stand up and walk towards Melanie from behind my desk. "Look at me," I say, pointing to my black and white, hounds tooth *Michael Kors* jacket and skirt. "Now, look at *you*," I retort, pointing at her athletic attire. "We have *nothing* in common. Mel, you *walk* like a man, *talk* like a man, *dress* like a man, and chase after women…just like a man!"

"And look at you, Tristan! You dress uptight. *Everything* has to be perfect. *Nothing* is *ever* good enough…not even your *own* family! Now, you tell me, who do *you* sound like? …Mom!"

"That's absurd!"

"Take a good, hard look at us. Mom and Dad really screwed us up pretty bad. I never noticed it, until just now."

"Okay, so now that you've had your epiphany, I'd *appreciate* it if you'd let me get back to my job," I sit back down, put on my *Giorgio Armani* reading glasses, and begin to prepare a marketing kit for a prospective client. "Close the door on your way out."

I then focus on the press release and pretend that Melanie isn't in the room. It's the same technique my "mother" used on me, whenever I wanted her attention. Eventually, I would get tired of watching her read fashion magazines, or stare at the TV, and I would just walk away. I was *hoping* that Melanie would get frustrated, and walk away, too!

After a few minutes, Melanie *still* hasn't walked away. She hasn't budged. I can feel Melanie's eyes staring at the top of my head, waiting for me to look up and acknowledge her presence. That's when my telephone rings, and since Anissa is away from her desk, I have to answer it myself. I don't mind answering it, it gives me a reason to further ignore Melanie.

I *snatch* the phone from the cradle: "Thank you for calling *Capital Appreciation,* Tristan Vincent speaking," I speak in a pleasant, professional tone. The caller on the other end is a reporter from *The Wall Street Journal.* I'm scheduled to speak at a financial conference for the *Securities and Exchange Commission* in New York next Monday, and their office is calling to confirm the appearance date.

I then cover the phone receiver and whisper to Melanie, "I *really* have to take this call," I pull up my roster on the computer, and begin verifying information. When I see that Melanie still hasn't left yet, I take my free hand and motion for her to move away. Melanie looks at me with sunken eyes, and I bulge my eyes out, giving her the "why-are–you-still-standing-here?" expression. Then, I focus back to the call at hand.

Melanie finally makes her exit, as another call beeps into my line. We don't bother to say goodbye, and frankly, I'm glad that the whole visit is over. The check I wrote should carry Melanie for the next month, therefore, I can look on the bright side, and *hope* that I *won't* have too see her; until her rent is due again!

Once I have a moment to take a breath from fielding calls, I search my desk for my date book, so that I can review my appointments for the afternoon. That's when I notice the check I wrote for Melanie.

She tore into pieces and scattered it across my desk!

MEKKA
Chapter 16

I walk into the hair salon to get my weave re-done, and the usual whispers and stares immediately greet me.

"That's the *bitch* right there," one patron whispers to another woman. She then points at me as I walk by wit' a bag of *Dunkin' Donuts* and two cups of coffee. "That's the *bitch* that *fucked* my girlfriend's husband and wrecked their whole marriage. She strips at that club downtown."

"*Dutch Gardens?*" the other woman asks.

"Yeah, that's the place. You know she got two kids by *two* different baby daddies?"

"Well, I heard the *bitch* turns tricks."

"I wouldn't doubt it."

"Hmmmph. She thinks she cute, with them too-tight *Apple Bottom* jeans on. And that weave, everybody knows that ain't her hair."

"Everything about the *bitch* is fake. Fake hair, fake nails, and fake contacts. Fake, fake, fake. Seems to me that if she gonna be strippin', she *need* to get them titties lifted. Then, she'll have fake titties, too!" they both laugh and slap each other hands.

As they burst into laughter, I turn to face them. I recognize one of the women from a photo that her husband carries in his wallet. Yeah, I *fuck* him on the regular, *strictly* for the cash, of course! My trick told me that his wife's name is Debra, and all she does is lay around and collect disability checks.

His wife never cooks or cleans. She just sits on her *fat...lazy...ass* all day, while my trick works his ass off at the *Budweiser* factory, twelve hours a day.

He said that when they first met in high school, his wife was the bomb. She was petite, light-skinned, and had long hair and dressed real fly, but since they've been married, his wife gained one-hundred and twenty pounds, chopped all of her hair off, and the only clothes she can fit into, are those pullover housedresses and house shoes.

No wonder my trick pays for sex!

Patrice, my stylist and the salon owner, waves me over to her empty chair: "Get over here, girl!" she says wit' a broad smile. "I know some of those donuts and coffee is for me."

"I can't have you *doin'* my head, first thing in the mornin' on an empty stomach. L-o-r-d *knows* what I'd walk outta here lookin' like if I did," I tease.

Patrice playfully snaps a hair cape at me. I sit down in her chair, and she pumps the pedal wit' her foot until I'm at the right height. Then, Patrice drapes the cape around me. I hand her a cup of coffee, and she picks out a chocolate éclair from the bag, leavin' me wit' the glazed.

"*Bitch,* that's the one I wanted," I say, referring to the donut.

"Too late!" Patrice teases and takes a bite. "So, what's been up, girlfriend?" she then asks with her mouth full.

"You know me, just tryna get that paper."

"You and me both, girl," Patrice now pours Kemi oil onto my bonded weave tracks, and massages the oil into my scalp. She uses this technique to loosen up my hair from the glue. "How's the kids?"

"They cool. Gettin' big," I say with a tinge of regret.

"Yeah, they grow so fast, don't they?"

"You ain't *never* lied. And Man-Man—thinks he's grown. Don't wanna listen to a *word* I say. He got suspended from school for fightin' again, and now they talkin' 'bout puttin' him in an alternative school for kids wit' disciplinary problems."

"What?"

"Yeah, girl. I had to see a social worker and everything behind that shit. She had the *n-e-r-v-e* to ask me where his father was."

"Oh, no she *didn't* go there!"

"Oh-yes-she-did, I told her, *'when you find his sorry ass, let me know'.*"

Wit' finesse, Patrice pulls my tracks out one at a time, until all that remains is my own shoulder-length hair. I continue wit' my story, "Then, the social worker had the *n-e-r-v-e* to ask me how long I planned to strip, in order to *support* myself; and if I thought that I was *settin'* a bad example for my daughter."

"Well, Mekka, people do talk around here."

"Fuck people! Ain't *nobody* payin' my muthafuckin' bills!"

"That's not what I'm sayin', girl. The last time you were here, even you said that you were ready to quit."

"I know, Patrice; but it ain't as easy as it seems. What the *fuck* am I gonna do when I give it up? I dunno how to do shit!"

"Mekka, you're not dumb...you just *think* you are. And with that attitude, you're never gonna get anywhere in life. What about college? You could go to school and get an Associates degree—"

"You know me and school don't get along."

"That's *just* an excuse," Patrice says, full of compassion.

I have always secretly admired Patrice. She's the same age as me, owns her own salon, makes good money, raises her children, and is engaged to one of the Philadelphia *Eagles* football players.

Patrice's life is a far stretch from the life of strippin' and prostitution that I lead. She didn't sell her soul to get the things she wants. Patrice has got it all. When it comes to advice, she is about the *only* woman I listen to.

"I'm gonna quit one day. I *just* gotta get myself a plan. Right now I don't have one."

"Well, you need to get one soon. With all that money you make, you could've owned your *own* business by now. Have you ever thought about investing?"

"I dunno the first thing about how to invest."

"It's not as hard as you think," Patrice replies, as she wraps a towel around my neck, and walks me over to the shampoo station.

"Mekka, if you *really* want to get out of the game, then I can help you. You *gotta* stop making excuses for yourself, and create a better life for you and your children."

Patrice then leans me back into the sink. I close my eyes, and enjoy the feelin' of the warm water rushin' through my hair. As she now lathers shampoo into my hair, I let Patrice's words sink in. I think about the possibility of maybe startin' my own business. If I continue on my current path, things will only get worse.

My children deserve better!

*   *   *   *   *

Two hours later, Patrice has me lookin' like a million bucks! My long weave is bone-straight, and the jet-black,

Hawaiian silky hair flows down my back. I walk to the counter to pay her, and as Patrice hands me my new appointment card, she holds my hand and gives it a gentle squeeze.

"Remember what we talked about, girl. If you want help, I'm here for you. I know someone that you can talk to about investing and handling your finances. Just think about it."

SHAWN
Chapter 17

As I look at each of the thirty-one faces that make up my fourth-grade class, I wonder if they can tell that I am struggling through the last fifteen minutes before the end-of-the-day school bell rings.

My body is running on fumes.

Yesterday's fiasco with Mike left me feeling used and abused. I was emotionally and physically drained by the time that I kicked him out. I ended up drowning my sorrows in a bottle of white wine, and a cloud of weed smoke.

Now, I live to regret it.

When I woke up this morning I had a hangover, my period came on, my last pair of pantyhose had a huge run in them, I couldn't find my car keys, and to top it off, I left the house wearing two, mixed-matched earrings; which one of my students politely pointed out during roll call.

What else could go wrong?

All I have to do is make it through these last, fifteen minutes, and I'll be home free.

I look at the clock...

The hands haven't moved...

I *still* have fifteen minutes to go before freedom.

"It seems that we have time for one more presentation," It pains me to announce to the class.

Today is the day that the children are scheduled to present their oral reports on the person that they admire most. So far, I've heard reports on *Serena Williams, Allen Iverson, Alicia Keys,* and, believe it or not, Jesus.

Mekhi, a round-faced boy with milk chocolate complexion, raises his hand.

"Yes, Mekhi."

"Miss Shawn, can I go next?" he asks eagerly.

"Why not. Come on up and let us hear your report."

Mekhi walks up to the front of the class holding his report in one hand, and a rolled up poster in the other. When he reaches the chalkboard, Mekhi turns to face the class and smiles broadly.

"Mekhi, who is your report on?"

Mekhi's face radiates with pride as he begins to speak: "The person I admire most is the rapper, 'Mike B.'."

When Mekhi unrolls the poster and exhibits it to the class, I nearly lose my balance. Immortalized on glossy, poster paper is a picture of "Mike B."...*my Mike*.

Several of the kids began to clap and sing lyrics from Mike's new single *Street Life*. They are obviously big fans of the *very* same man that I despise, and *never* want to see again! In front of thirty adoring fourth-graders, Mekhi is forcing me to confront the biggest mistake of my life.

"Class, settle down. Let Mekhi finish. The sooner he's finished, the sooner we can all leave for the day."

I want Mekhi's report to be over as soon as possible!

"Mekhi, go on," I urge.

Mekhi continues, "The person I admire most is the rapper "Mike B.". "Mike B." is cool. He raps about his life in Philadelphia, and that's where we all live! I like "Mike B.'s" video, because he drives the hottest cars and *always* has a lot of pretty women dancing around him. My favorite part of the video is when "Mike B." has the sexy women around the swimming pool.

"'Mike B.' has women doing *whatever* he wants...like cook and clean for him. I like "Mike B.'s" platinum chains and his big, fancy house. "Mike B." keeps it real in his music, and *that's* why I admire him the most! The end."

The class claps, and I give Mekhi the obligatory "job well done" response. Just as I am about to dismiss the class a little early, one of my more enthusiastic female students, Felicia, raises her hand.

"Yes, Felicia."

"Ms. Shawn, why is it cool for rappers to have a bunch of women hanging all over them dancing freaky and stuff?"

I am startled by her question, but at the same time, I *appreciate* the fact that she is aware that these images are derogatory and disrespectful to women.

"'Cause, "Mike B." is cool," Mekhi belts out, and the rest of the boys slap hands in agreement.

"Hold on, Mekhi, Felicia has a valid question. 'Mike B.', does he *really* need a lot of women to be cool?"

"Heck yeah! Having lots of women like 'Mike B.' does makes you cool."

"And why?" I ask Mekhi. Little did they know, this issue is *very* personal to me.

"Just because. All the coolest rappers have a lot of women in their video. Felicia needs to get a grip!"

"That language will not be tolerated," I chastise him. "Mekhi, let me ask you this. Your mom and dad are married, right?"

"Right?"

"So how would you feel if your father had tons of women around? Would that make him cool, too?"

Mekhi was stumped, but another male student called out: "Well, those women wouldn't be dancing for him if they didn't think he was cool. Why would *a-l-l* those women do that if he *wasn't* cool?"

"Because they're stupid and they don't respect themselves," Felicia blurted out. "My uncle told me that a man won't respect you if you don't respect yourself. That's why guys like "Mike B." get away with it, because the women he deals with are stupid, and they don't know any better—right, Ms. Shawn?"

Felicia's question hits me like a bullet!

As I contemplate the question, I reflect on my turbulent relationship with Mike, a.k.a. "Mike B.".

I recall how he never returned my calls. How Mike would *only* visit if he wanted sex. I then ponder how Mike never took me anywhere, or did anything special for me. I think about how Mike avoided me, and *never* once, invited me to his place, or asked me to meet his friends. Most of all, I consider the fact that Mike two-timed me, and left me for a White woman!

"Ms. Shawn, you didn't answer the question," Felicia says. "Would you be with a man that uses and abuses women?"

Just then the bell rings, and I am saved.

"Class dismissed."

MELANIE
Chapter 18

An eviction notice taped to the outside of the door, greets me when I arrive at my apartment. The *Housing Authority* gives each tenant a five-day grace period, in order to pay their past due rent. I had planned on making that payment this morning after I saw Tristan, but I let my pride rip up her check. Now, if I can't find another way to come up with the cash, I have to face the reality of being kicked out.

I pull the notice from the door, toss it on the coffee table and *slam* the door shut behind me.

All day while I was customer reppin' at the *Water Department,* I kept replaying my argument with Tristan inside of my head. I felt bad 'bout accusing her of being like our mother, even though I knew it was true.

I could have been a little bit more humble.

After all, I was the one *begging* for money at 7 AM on a Monday morning. Why should I expect any courtesy from Tristan, when all I do is continually hold my hand out for charity, month after month? I'm a *grown* woman, and I should be able to handle my own responsibilities.

I have *never* been responsible, because I know that I can *always* count on Tristan to bail me out.

It's time for me to stand up on my own two feet!

I look around at the *disgusting* condition my apartment is in. There are *Heineken* beer cans and empty pizza boxes scattered around. There's also a layer of dust at least an inch thick all over my furniture, and my kitchen *reeks* of dirty dishes soaking in the sink.

Dirty clothes are strewn along the hallway, my bed is unmade, and the bathroom sink and tub are both full of grime; and my venetian blinds are hanging crooked in the windows.

I think 'bout cleaning up the apartment, but I don't know where to begin…I sit on the coffee table and look around the room, until I'm tired of lookin' at the filth. But, I just *can't* seem to motivate myself and get my *ass* up off of this coffee table!

Maybe I need some theme music to motivate me.

I walk over to stereo and sift through a stack of CDs piled on the console. *The Miseducation of Lauryn Hill*. If anybody can get me going right now, it's *Lauryn*.

Lauryn sings my frustrations away, as I move from one task to the next. First, I conquer the dishes in the sink, clean out the fridge and scrub the counter tops. Next, I pick up the pizza boxes and beer bottles. Collect all of the clothes from off the floor, and give the *entire* apartment a good vacuuming.

I follow that up with a good dusting job. In the bathroom, I wipe down the sink, scrub out the tub and *Windex* the mirrors. In the bedroom, I change my bedding and put a clean comforter set on the bed. To top everything off, I open all the windows to let some fresh air in, burn incense all around, and light a few candles.

For the first time in a long time, it looks and smells *hell-a-good* in here! The only problem is that, after the heavy duty cleaning I just did, I'm sweaty and funky. I run a bath, and since I'm out of bubble bath, I pour in some *Herbal Essence* shampoo for effect.

Just as I'm 'bout to climb inside, I hear someone knocking at my door. I let out a sigh of frustration before yelling, "WHO IS IT?"

"It's me."

I recognize my homeboy, E's voice. E has been my best friend since I moved into Section 8 housing two years ago. He comes over just 'bout everyday after I get off from work.

E doesn't have a "real job".

He makes his livings hustling, which means E can pretty much hang out anytime he feels like it.

E knocks on the door again.

"Hold up!" I reached for my towel, walk to the door and let him in. Before greeting me, E's eyes travel over the entire apartment. *Lauryn Hill* has just finished preaching, followed by *The Roots* philosophizing, and *Jill Scott's* crooning, *Music Soulchild's* romancing and *Bilal's* begging from the speakers. The burning lavender-scented candles cast a warm glow over the living room.

"Damn, Mel, whachu do...hire a maid?"

"Naw, nigga, I got tired of lookin' at this triflin' place. And it's just like you to show up *after* the hard work is all done!"

"Considering that I helped create the mess," E acknowledges. He then takes off his denim *Marc Echo* jacket and

93

tosses it onto my second-hand ottoman. E cops a squat on the sofa, and looks up at me with those hazel-green colored eyes, ones that remind me of pretty glass marbles. His skin is the color of cappuccino, and E's thick cornrows are freshly done in neat little rows. "I just came by to see what's up," E says.

"Not much, I was just 'bout to take a bath and chill. Why, what's up with you?"

"Not a *damn* thing! The streets is hot, so I figured I'd lay low for a while," E replies as he looks me up-and-down.

The towel wrapped around my body barely covers me. E studies my bare shoulders, my cleavage, my thighs and legs. It's the first time he has ever looked at me this way. I adjust the towel so that it covers me a little more.

"Well, you can stay and hang out while I take a bath. I don't have nothing in here to eat, so if you're hungry, you're gonna have to order something."

"What else is new?" E says sarcastically. "I got a taste for a cheese steak. Can I call *Lehigh Family Pizza* and have some delivered," E asks, all the while, still staring at my half-naked body.

"Yeah, cheese steaks sounds good. It's gotta be your treat, 'cause I'm *dead* broke."

"Duh, what else is new? Girl, I know you ain't *never* got no dough."

I give him the middle finger before quickly retreating to the bathroom. The way E was lookin' at me, kinda freaked me out. I always thought he saw at me as just "one of the guys".

*   *   *   *   *

While I soak in the tub, I hear E dialing the phone and ordering our food. Then the sound of the TV coming on fills the room. E flips through the channels before settling on a classic episode of *Star Trek*. I can now hear his footsteps, as E makes his way into my kitchen.

The fridge door opens, and E pulls out a bottle of *Heineken* beer, removing the bottle top. His footsteps move back into the living room, and I hear the sofa cushions squeak, as E makes himself comfortable.

The food arrives as I finish my bath. I walk back out wearing my robe. My hair is wet and curly, giving me a more feminine appearance. I couldn't afford to keep my last two barber appointments, and my hair has grown freely.

E takes notice of my curly locks. His eyes tell me that he likes the feminine thang he sees going on.

"Just in time for the food," E announces, and the smell of cheese steaks with fried onions fills my nostrils.

"Good, 'cause I'm starving," I reply, as I sit down on the couch next to him. "Um, E, I'm *not* 'bout to watch this *same* old episode of *Star Trek.*"

E tosses me the remote control, and I flip through the channels. I notice that he hasn't opened up the food yet; E's just sitting there, *staring* at me—like the cat that swallowed the canary.

"Why are you sitting there lookin' stupid?" I jokingly ask. E picks up the eviction notice from the coffee table.

"Were you gonna tell me about this?" he asks, catching me off-guard.

"What's there to tell? I can't make the rent payment. Either I come up with the money soon, or I'm outta here."

"What about your sister?"

"I can't go there," I state, before explaining the argument that Tristan and I had earlier this morning.

"Why don't you call the *Housing Authority* and make some payment arrangements."

"I've already done that too many times before. They *won't* give me an extension," I answer before throwing down the remote control, no longer caring 'bout watching TV. "Look, can we just drop it."

"H-e-l-l no we *can't* just drop it! Do you wanna be homeless?" E asks rhetorically. "Or do you want my help?"

My stubborn nature doesn't allow me to answer. I attempt to unwrap my food, and E places his hands over mine.

"No eating until we settle this thing," E demands. "I've got plenty of money stashed away. I could break you off a coupla dollars and cover your rent."

"No! I can't let you to do that!"

"Mel, would you *let* me finish?" E exclaims. I fold my arms across my chest and relinquish. "Good, now, hear me out. You can *have* the money. Don't consider it a loan, consider it a gift. If I had my back against the wall, I *hope* you'd be willing to help a brother out."

"...I can't ask you to do this," I respond while lookin' E in the eyes. His hazel-green eyes are full of concern and sincerity. "E, I'll just suck up my pride and ask Tristan for the money again."

"Thought you couldn't do that again," E says, as his eyes search mine.

"I *really* don't wanna go crawling back to her."

"Then don't! Show your sister that you can make it without her. Let me help."

I don't say a word...

I let E's proposition sink in...

I know that I would rather take money from E, than to let Tristan win this battle.

"If you'd stop *throwing* away your hard-earned money on those *strippers*, you *might* not be in this situation! Don't you know that you don't mean *shit* to them? All they see is green."

E is beginning to sound just like Tristan! "Do I *tell* you how to live your life?" I scoff.

"No, but I'm not the one who's on the verge of not having a place to stay," E responds before pausing. "...Mel, I'm *only* telling you this for your own good. You *need* to stay out of those clubs. Those girls are just *using* you! Do you think they care about your situation? H-E-L-L NO! They're probably off somewhere getting their hair and nails done, while you can't even afford to keep a barber appointment!" E replies, as he rubs his fingers through my hair playfully.

"Okay, okay!" I throw my hands up and surrender.

"So I'll give you the money, and first thing in the morning, you take your *ass* down to the rent office."

"Okay, okay!"

"DON'T OKAY ME!"

"Okay," I answer for good measure, and E playfully punches me in my bicep. I punch him back before changing the tone of the conversation. "Yo, E, I promise, I'll find a way to pay you back.

"Don't worry about me, I got bricks that I can sell...Aye, if you wanna make a couple of extra dollars, I could use a mule."

"A what?"

"A mule. All you'd have to do is take a package and deliver it for me, pick up another package and bring it back to me. If you do that, I'll break you off a hundred dollars each time."

96

"And all I'd have to do is drop something off and pick something up?"

"That's it," E assures me. His phone then chirps. "Looks like one of my regulars is tryna reach me. Mind if I use your phone to call her back?"

"Naw, go ahead. Use the phone in the bedroom."

E then walks away, and I roll his proposition around in my head. I take a bite out of my cheese steak and think it over.

Somehow, it sounds *too* good to be true.

MEKKA
Chapter 19

After Patrice tightened up my weave, I went over to the ritziest spa in the city for the elite, *Adolf Biecker Spa,* for a full day of beauty treatments and relaxation. I figure if it's good enough for all those rich White folks, then it's *definitely* good enough for the M-to-the-E-to-the-K-K-A!

I treat myself to a LaStone therapy body massage, an elemental nature facial for radiance, a Carribean body therapy wrap, and a hand and foot paraffin treatment. Afterwards, I have lunch by the Olympic-size pool, and catch up on my magazine readin'. When I finished pamperin' myself, I switch my focus to Sheka and Man-Man.

I stop by the *Gallery Mall* and pick up some *Rocawear* gear for Man-Man, and some really cute outfits for Sheka from *Baby Phat.* Then, I visit *Toys-R-Us* and rack up all the latest *Xbox* video games for Man-Man, and pick out *Barbie* dolls for Sheka.

Finally, I head home totally refreshed, and wit' a new attitude. As I cruise down *Broad Street* in my convertible, I call my neighbor, Maria, and tell her that I'm on my way to pick up my kids from her house.

Maria watches Sheka for me durin' the day, and Man-Man sometimes goes to her house after school to do his homework. I ask her what the kids want me to pick up for dinner, and they request "Mickey D's", as usual.

I breeze through the *McDonald's* drive through, and I'm a block away from Maria's townhouse when my cell phone rings. The caller ID tells me that it's someone callin' from *Dutch Gardens.* They probably want to know if I'll be on the roster for Thursday. I press the talk button and Trish's voice floods into my ear piece.

"What's up, hoe?" Trish asks.

"What up?"

"Got something for you."

"What is it? Don't be *callin'* me wit' no b-u-l-l-s-h-i-t."

"Whatever. You ain't gonna believe this."

98

"Will you just spill it?" I already know it's about money. Trish only gets excited about money, and she's never afraid to share the wealth. "What the *fuck* has got you all giddy?"

"'Mike B.', bitch!"

"'Mike B.', the rapper?" Trish now has my *full* attention, but I have to play it off like I'm not pressed. "What about him?"

"He booked a party for Friday night at *Dutch Gardens*. His manager just called, looking for girls to keep his entourage happy, and be eye-candy for the press. If you're down, you'll need to be available Friday from midnight until, dressed to impress, and you know the rest."

"How much *money* we talkin'?

"Three Gs a piece. Plus, whatever extra you can negotiate on the side," Trish whispers. Trish always whispers when she quotes figures.

"How many *niggas* are in his entourage?"

"'Bout twenty-five."

"Me and you *can't* handle that many niggas! Not even in my prime could I pull off a stunt like that!" I then pull up in Maria's driveway and sit in the car, while I finish my conversation.

"Hoe, it won't be just you and me. But I do want to keep our numbers low. The more hoes we take with us, the more ways we have to split up the cash. Nothing funky is gonna happen. We'll have big Smitty with us, just in case some *shit* pops off."

I'm thinking...Trish senses my hesitation.

"Mekka, this could really put us on! It'll be like old times! Can you imagine? They might even ask us to be in a video, and before you know it, we'll be movin' out to L.A., where the *real* ballers are!"

I wanted to tell Trish to get her head out of the clouds! There is *no* way that those dudes are gonna take two tricks like us anywhere! And being in a video? Who is she fooling? They only hire "professional models" for one thing: they hire us to *fuck!*

Plain and simple.

No need to get it twisted.

"Okay, I'm down," I concede. "But I want my *money* up front!"

"Cool. Meet me at the club around midnight on Friday."

I knock on Maria's screen door. Sheka runs towards me on her tip-toes. Man-Man looks up at me from where he's seated on the floor, doing his homework on the coffee table. Man-Man doesn't smile at me. He turns back and finishes reading his textbook.

"It's open," Maria calls from the kitchen. "I dunno know why chu insist on knocking."

The aroma of arroz con polla wafts past me, as I enter her living room.

"Smells good in here," I say politely, but now I feel guilty about buyin' *McDonalds*, instead of cookin' my children a home-cooked meal. *I'll have to make it up to 'em later.*

Sheka has her arm wrapped around my legs, hugging me tight; smiling up at me.

"Guess what, mama?" she says excitedly. I look over at her brother who is still ignoring me.

"What, baby?" I ask, refocusing my attention on her.

"I colored you a picture, and I want you to hang it on the fridge when we get home."

"Where is it? Let me see."

Sheka runs to get the picture from the coffee table, and Maria comes out of the kitchen, wiping her hands on her apron.

"Hey, Miss Mekka. Don't you look like a million bucks?" she says, checking out my new hair style.

"I wanna thank you for watchin' the kids for me," I reach into my *Coach* "Soho" bag, and pull out an envelope filled wit' cash. "This is for this week and next week." Maria takes the envelope and stuffs it into her front apron pocket.

Sheka runs back towards me, holdin' a picture of stick figures that she'd drawn. She holds it up for me to see. I bend over to take a closer look.

"Mama, this is me," Sheka says, pointin' to the shortest stick figure in the middle. "This is Man-Man and Miss Maria, holding my hands," she indicates, pointin' at the two stick figures on both sides of her. In the background, there is a small stick figure alone in the distance.

"Who is that way back there?" I ask.

"Oh, that's you, Mama!"

I can't believe my eyes...*What am I doin' way in the background?* I feel completely left out.

"Guess what we're doing in the picture?" Sheka quizzes me.

"...Um, I dunno."

"This is all of us going to *Chuck E. Cheese* on Friday, like you promised."

SHIT! I had forgotten all about that. Now I committed myself to doin' that thing for "Mike B." wit' Trish, and I'd have to cancel wit' the kids.

"Look, Sheka, mama forgot she had to work that night."

Man-Man looks up at me, shakes his head disappointedly and rolls his eyes. Maria catches an eyeful of all of this. *Time for me to get my kids and handle this in the privacy of my own home.*

"Man-Man, grab your jacket, and you and Sheka meet me at the house."

Man-Man gets up, hugs Maria, and walks pass me without saying a word. Once they're both outside, Maria feels comfortable enough to speak.

"Don't worry about it, Mekka, he's too young to understand that you're a single mother, and chu have to work to provide for them."

"Yeah, but Man-Man's behavior is *gettin'* ridiculous."

"...This may not be any of my business, but Man-Man told me why he's been getting into fights at school."

"And why is that?" I ask, wit' an attitude brewin' beneath the surface of my words. I am *outraged* that Man-Man confides in her! I'm *pissed* that Maria knows more about my family than I do!

But it's not her fault.

Maria spends more time wit' 'em than I do. She cooks for 'em, and studies wit' 'em. Plays wit' 'em and reads to 'em.

How can *I* compare to that?

I'm not easily threatened by anyone, but Maria's relationship wit' my children was beginnin' to make me look real bad.

"...Some of the boys in Man-Man's class have been teasing him about chu being a stripper."

"WHAT! How in the *hell* do they know about that?"

"Apparently, a father of one of the boys in his class talks about chu, and the little boy went back to school and told everybody. Man-Man is only fighting to defend you."

I'm now speechless.

"Chu think that Man-Man didn't already know? Mekka, he's not stupid. Man-Man has eyes, and he sees things. He's very perceptive. You need to sit down and have a talk with Man-Man before this gets worse."

TRISTAN
Chapter 20

Monday night is Cornelius' night off, so after he drives me to *Rittenhouse Square*, I am left in the condo, alone. I slip off my shoes, walk into the kitchen, and heat up the Chicken Marsala and roasted potatoes that Cornelius has prepared for me. I take a seat on one of the kitchen stools, and watch the dish as it spins slow circles in the microwave.

It is completely quiet, except for the humming sound coming from the microwave, and the low crackling of the fireplace in the living room. I pour myself a glass of *Merlot*, pick up the remote control, and flick on my *Sony*, 55-inch flat screen, plasma TV, hanging on the wall.

CNN comes on, and I instantaneously switch over to the *Pay Per View* channel. It's my Monday night routine: enjoy a good meal, rent a romantic comedy, and vicariously live through the characters, as they live happily ever freaking after!

The evening ends as usual; my plate of Chicken Marsala is empty, and the male lead of the movie is racing to the alter— stopping the woman he's in love with from marrying another man. The movie is a complete cliché, and ends with the obligatory kiss.

It's such *bullshit* how everything wraps up nice and neat at the end of these movies. I wonder why I subject myself to such asinine crap, which only serves to keep a woman's ideas of love and marriage in the stone ages.

Disgusted at the crap Hollywood markets to women, I hit the off button on the remote control and toss it onto the ottoman. The TV goes blank. The room goes dark.

Having given up on TV romance, I decide to sort through the mail, then take a shower and retire early. I walk into the study to retrieve the mail, and flip through countless credit card bills, credit card offers and clothing catalogues, before reaching a crisp, white envelope with the words *"You Are Invited"* scripted on the front. I lift the seal, and it reveals a wedding invitation from one of my old college girlfriends.

Over the years, it seems as though I am the *only* one left who hasn't announced a wedding or a new baby. Aside from

Shawn, who is hopeless, I am the only one from my college clique who isn't married. I'm not even attached, and I don't have *any* prospects on the horizon.

At least crazy-ass Shawn gets laid from time-to-time! Me, I've been on a drought, and I am *ashamed* to say how long it's been. My mind takes me on a mental journey of the handful of men that I've dated over the years—more like speed-dated!

The trip down memory lane is brief. All of my relationships ended bitterly because of my lack of willingness to commit. Or, their interest dwindled, due to my lack of availability. Either way, *none* of my relationships have withstood the test of time.

That's fine with me.

Men are *only* a distraction.

I take a quick shower, moisturize, throw on my favorite, perfectly-broken in, Pima cotton nightshirt, and I hit the sheets.

I lay there, wide awake.

My mind is tired, but my body isn't. In fact, I'm horny; which is unusual, because masturbation was certainly not on my list of things to do today—I'm not scheduled to masturbate until Wednesday.

I tuck the bed spread between my legs, and the contrast of the cool, soft fabric against my warm thighs, gives me the briefest fleeting sensation. It creates an urge that I *wish* would go away.

To avoid succumbing to the desire, I change my sleeping position.

I re-arrange pillows.

I toss and turn.

No matter what I do, the yearning does not leave. My body longs for release. So I guess I have no choice. The sooner I get this over with, the sooner I can fall asleep.

I pull a standard fantasy from my mind, and go through the motions of pleasuring myself. I know *exactly* what buttons to push to get me where I need to go. My technique is quick, mechanical and methodical. There's no need for all the fuss, trying to make the moment seem real.

Because it's not real.

It's just me in the dark, doing what needs to be done for the desired end result…sleep.

Nothing more.

Nothing less.

SHAWN
Chapter 21

I wake up in a haze. I must have dozed off as soon as I got home from school. Tiny jackhammers are pounding inside my head, and there is a puddle of drool by my mouth. I lift my head, which feels like it weighs a ton, and realize that I have fallen off the couch, and was crashed out on the floor.

I am face-to-face with two empty bottles of *Alizé*.

I muster up enough strength and push myself up onto my knees. I reach for my cell phone, which is lodged in between two sofa cushions, and try to read what time it is: "8:30 PM". *Fuck!*

I must have been tired as hell. All I remember is driving home from school, stopping at the liquor store, coming home, making a phone call, grading papers, sipping *Alizé* and smoking half a blunt.

I am way too tired and foggy to try to stand up.

So I lay back on the floor and stare long and hard at the ceiling. My cell phone rings and scares the *shit* out of me! I forgot that I was still holding the *damn* thing in my hand.

"Yo, it's E. You chirped me a little while ago?"

"Did I?" I ask, trying to remember, but it's pointless.

"Yeah. You hit me up like six times."

"E? Oh, yeah. Now I remember. Can you make a delivery?"

That's E, my weed supplier, with his light-skinned, green-eyed, fine ass. He must have been the person I called before I passed out. I probably would've given up smoking weed a long time ago, if E didn't make house calls. Now that Mike was out of the picture, maybe I could give E a test ride.

"I can get some to you in about a half. Cool?" he says in his usual breezy tone.

"Yeah, that's cool."

"Same address?"

"Yeah."

"Later."

In the time span that elapsed, I managed to get myself together by taking a quick, ice-cold shower, using the freezing

104

cold water to shock life back into my system. I brushed my teeth and gargled before changing into my hot pink *Betsey Johnson Lycra* tank top, and my pink, mini gym shorts with hot pink trimming.

I pinned up my dreadlocks, put on my reading glasses and finished grading papers while I waited on E to arrive.

The doorbell finally rings.

I look at myself in the mirror that's hanging over my sofa. I adjust my boobs for maximum cleavage, and touch up my lips with some pink *MAC* "Viva Glam" lipstick. Tonight will be the night to make Mike history, and create a future with E. I don't actually think that E was the best substitute, nor is he an upgrade, but E will definitely keep me occupied in the meantime.

The poor boy won't know what hit him!

I pull the door open without checking the peephole first. When I see that it's not E standing in the doorway, my jaw drops down to the floor.

"You're not E," I say disappointedly. I look at the young woman standing before me, and suddenly, wish that I had more clothes on. "Who are you?"

"E couldn't make it," she says.

The woman looks like a man, but I can tell she isn't. She checks me out hard from head-to-toe. *Damn, she's worse than a man!* At least most men try to play it off like they're not really checking you out, when then actually are. This woman is making it completely obvious that, if I was an ice cream cone, she'd take a lick!

"E asked me to make the delivery for him. I hope that's not a problem."

"Well, it *is* a problem! E is the *only* person I deal with!"

"Yeah, I can tell," the manly-looking woman says sarcastically, as she takes inventory of my skimpy clothing. "Look, I'm not 5-O. I'm just here to hook you up, and I'll be on my way."

"E could've at *least* told me he was sending somebody else."

"I'm sure he didn't think it would be a problem. Look, I got your stuff right here," she says while holding up a *Ziploc* sandwich bag full of weed. "If you don't want it, then I'll be on my way. You can take up your grievance with E later."

The sight of weed is more tempting than I care to admit.

"Okay, let's get this over with. Stay here and I'll grab my wallet," I command, as I walk away and search the living room for my purse. By this time, she is looking pass me and into my apartment.

"Nice crib," I hear her say. I completely *ignore* her compliment and continue to search. I look in all the usual places. Before I know it, ten minutes have gone by and she's still standing in the doorway waiting.

"WHERE THE *FUCK* IS MY PURSE?" I yell out in aggravation. I then look over my shoulder, and the young woman seems to be amused at me making a spectacle of myself. She's now wearing a smirk on her face.

"Maybe I can help you out and make this easier on both of us. What does your purse look like?"

I look at her suspiciously, but for some reason I answer: "It's a brown *Dooney & Burke.* You know the kind with the little D and Bs printed all over it?"

"Where is the last place you remember having it?"

"If I knew that I wouldn't be *running* around here like a chicken with my head cut off!"

"What I meant was…try to retrace your steps. You came home, walked through the door, then what?"

I stop moving for a moment and I try to remember...

"Just try to remember what you did, one step at a time. Trust me, I been where you are now," the manly-looking woman says and smiles. She knows I'm buzzed.

"…I came home, sat my keys down on the island in the kitchen."

"Then what?"

"…Sat my briefcase on the desk over there to the left."

"Then what?"

"…Carried my bottles of *Alizé* over to the couch and made a phone call. Chirped E."

"And then?"

"…I walked over to the cabinet to get a glass. Reached in the freezer for some ice cubes. Sat down…Poured myself a drink…I can't remember much after that."

The young woman now holds up her hand to tell me to pause: "Do you mind?" she asks before stepping inside. "I think I know where your purse is."

I plop down on the couch and watch her walk into the kitchen. She then opens the freezer and pulls out my purse. I must have put it in there by mistake when I reached for the ice cubes.

"Okay, *David Copperfield,* what other tricks can you do?"

We both laugh! The manly-looking woman then tosses the bag to me, and I reach inside for my wallet.

"You having a party or something?" she asks.

"No, why?"

"You bought two bottles of *Alizé,* and now you're buying all this weed. Figured you must be planning a party."

"A party for one."

"Damn. You know they say that's the first sign of trouble."

"What's the first sign of trouble?"

"Drinking and getting high by yourself. That's a no-no. Sure sign of depression."

"And who are *you* supposed to be, Dr. Phil?"

"Like I said before, I been where you are now. It's not healthy to get high alone. At least not to the extreme that you are."

"So, what do you suggest I do about it?"

"Thought you'd never ask."

MELANIE
Chapter 22

She ain't as sexy as Mekka, but *definitely* a good runner-up! I can tell honey's a *freak* by the way she answered the door half-naked. E must get more *pussy* thrown at him than he can shake a stick at!

At first, this woman with henna-colored dreads looked disappointed to see me standing there instead of E, but after I helped honey find her purse, I knew I was in like Flynn! I made the comment 'bout not getting high alone, and she took the bait.

Just like I knew honey would!

I suggested that we spark up the "purple haze" weed, smoke together and chill out. So, here I am, sitting on her couch, waiting for honey to come back. I expected her to have thrown some clothes on, but when she comes back in the room a few minutes later, this chick still hasn't covered up. As a matter of fact, honey has let her hair down, and even ditched the glasses.

That's a good sign for me!

As she slowly leans over to pour me a glass of *Alizé,* her ass sticks up in the air, and I get a close up view of honey's cleavage.

I know right off the bat that she's game!

Now honey puts some music on. A cool jazz CD: *Verve: The Remixes,* and an updated cut by *Nina Simone* tells me that this chick is feeling fine.

We pass the blunt back-and-forth.

Vibe to the music.

Sip on the *Alizé.*

Let the weed soak in.

I then look around at all the test papers on the table: "You must be a teacher."

"Yep."

"What grade?"

"Fourth."

"Wish I had a teacher like you. I would've *never* cut class, might have even made something of myself."

We smoke some more. Chit-chat a little.

Honey's light-brown eyes are now heavy. The "purple haze" must be hitting her hard. I pour this chick another glass of *Alizé* to top her high off.

Honey sips.

Closes her eyes.

Now I can stare at this chick's body without worrying 'bout making her nervous.

O-O-H!

Honey's nipples are now hard and standing at attention, pushing at the fabric of her slinky tank top. I want to lean over and kiss them!

We drink, smoke and flirt. This goes on for 'bout an hour.

"So what's your name?" I finally ask.

"No names."

Her eyes are still shut, and honey hasn't moved in a couple of minutes. She's gone!

"If you're tired, I can leave," I suggest. This way the ball is in her court.

"No, I want you to stay," she says, with her eyes halfway closed; they look like slits. Now honey motions with her finger, "C'mere."

She slowly spreads her curvaceous legs. Only a thin layer of pink cotton fabric separates my lips from the feminine "V" between honey's thighs. I lean over until my face is deep in this chick's crotch, and I smell her.

I love the way honey smells!

I then push her mini gym shorts to the side, and stare at the bald, puffy, pink lips between her thick thighs...

I lightly graze my mouth across her "sweet lips".

Honey moans.

This chick now grabs the back of my head, pulls me closer, and I dive my wet, curious tongue deep inside, slowly.

Her back arches.

She then pulls her tank top down, and honey's perky titties point straight out. I tweak her left nipple while I lick the "kitty cat".

I tickle this chick's fat pussy faster-and-faster!

Honey's sweet juices begin to flow!

I don't want this to end so quickly, so I *s-l-o-w* it down.

I slide up and take her right, full breast into my mouth. She reaches for me and kisses me, full-blown on the mouth. Our tongues dance in each other's mouths, and I can tell honey is hungry for me.

I squeeze her nipples as we continue to kiss.

She tugs at the back of my shirt, trying to pull it over my head.

Her hands now search my back.

Outta all the times I messed around with a girl, I've *never* had one come on to me like this! Most women are usually content with me getting them off. They never worry 'bout me.

But honey's different.

Her hands are everywhere!

She now squeezes my ass.

Then honey slides her hand inside my *Cardhart* jeans, reaches between my thighs and touches my clit. She then tries to slip her finger inside my pussy. I jump up and startle her!

Her eyes pop open: "What's up? I thought you were down," she says, sounding slightly ticked off.

I don't speak.

I can't speak.

"When I saw you at the door, I *knew* you weren't a guy. I was just playing along, sweetie. You're gay, right?" Honey asks, like it's no big deal.

I nod my head yes.

"I knew that. You don't have to be embarrassed because I touched you down there. I know you don't have a dick."

"That's not the problem," I reply, as I contemplate explaining to her why I freaked out; but decide it's too embarrassing. "Look, I gotta get outta here."

Honey sits up and pulls her shirt back down. I can tell she's *pissed* off by how fast I put on the brakes.

"Why are you leaving? Did I do something wrong?"

"No…it's not you…look I just gotta go…um…I'm sorry," I answer as I adjust my clothing.

"Oh, I get it…you don't like being touched there. It makes you feel like a girl. Okay, well, I'll play along," Honey says as she pats her lap. "Now, why don't you come back over here."

I can't even look at her. I just want to get outta here as soon as possible! I turn away from honey, and tuck my white "wife beater" T-shirt back inside my jeans. "Look, I'm sorry, but—"

This chick now stands in front of me.

Tries to coax me.
Rubs her hands up-and-down my back.
She's trying to warm me back up.
But I freeze at her touch.
"Look, I said that I won't touch you there. What's the big deal?"
"'Cause, that's not it. Let's just drop it."
"You gotta be *kidding* me! You come up in here, get me all hot and horny, then you start acting like a virgin?" she retorts, as her eyes pop open.
"Just leave it alone!"
"That's it, isn't it?"
I make a beeline for the door.
"You're a virgin?"
I don't answer.
"So you like to make out with women, but you're *actually* a virgin?"
I can't answer.
I'm too embarrassed.
In the background, I hear her laugh.
Honey's laughter mocks me.
I have my hand on the doorknob and I'm twisting it open.
"Sweetie, I don't mind if you go. That's cool, no hard feelings but first, I got one question for you…If you're a virgin, and you've *never* had a man inside you, then how do you know you're gay?"
I turn back to look at honey, and her question *hits* me like a ton of bricks!
It's the same question that haunts me when I am alone.

THANK GOD IT'S FRIDAY!

Most people think Wednesday is "hump" day, but for me, wrapping up business at the end of the week is a bigger hump for me to get over.

I quickly hustle into the office first thing in the morning, anticipating the closure of the Morgan Baxter deal. I expect to see his signature on the dotted line of the Letter Of Intent before close of business today. With this deal sealed, I can move forward feeling that I had jumped one major hurdle this week; and finally accomplished something significant.

I want more than *anything,* to close Mr. Baxter's contract! This deal will bring in approximately a quarter of a million dollars in revenue for my firm, and Philadelphia will finally have its first independently, black-owned and operated, financial institution.

The best part about the whole deal is that my firm will get all the credit! I imagine myself being interviewed by the press, and having my office *swamped* with so many offers, that I'll have to turn most of them down! Maybe I'll even hire a COO, so that I can manage the firm from a distance, and take time to travel like I always planned. But for now, I have to make it through the morning first.

I reach for my *Rolodex,* which Anissa finally returned to me, and phone the *Cigar Shop,* to place an order for a box of Cuban cigars. Although they're illegal in the states, I have my connections. I'll have the Cubans delivered over to Mr. Baxter and Drew's office this morning. It may be a premature celebratory gesture, but I *know* I have this deal locked, so what the hell!

I phone the *Cigar Shop,* and Frederique, the proprietor, answers on the first ring.

"Frederique, this is Tristan from *Capital Appreciation,* how are you?"

"*Mademoiselle Vincent, always* a pleasure to hear your voice. What can I do for you?

"I'd like to order a box of Cubans and have them delivered."

"Wow, *another* box? Someone must have been *v-e-r-y* good this week."

I'm taken aback by his comment: "…What do you mean *another* box?"

"Yesterday, a box was ordered on your corporate account, and sent over to a 'Morgan Baxter'."

I think for a second, and quickly tap my *Mont Blanc* fountain pen against the desk.

"Anissa phoned the order in," Frederique offered.

"Oh, very well then. She beat me to the punch. You know what they say, great minds think alike."

"Is there anything *else* I can do for you this morning? *Anything* at all?"

I blush: "No, thank you, Frederique; that will be all."

My next move is to phone *Zanzibar Blue,* an upscale restaurant in the heart of the city; which offers live jazz and elegant ambiance. It is my hope to convince Mr. Baxter to dine with me in celebration. I'd have Anissa phone his secretary to confirm.

"Reservation for two, please, under the name Vincent."

"What time?" the hostess asks.

"Six-thirty, please."

"Vincent at six-thirty… for two. We'll see you then."

We hang up, and I lean back in my chair. I reflect on the past week, and revel at how amazing Anissa has been through this whole deal. She has done *everything* in her power to rectify the *Fed Ex* fiasco.

All week long, Anissa's taken extra work home, she's been borrowing books from my library, Anissa's also taken initiatives to personally deal with clients, and she has even maintained her new, professional attire. Anissa has been one step ahead of me the entire time.

In the past, I've been very harsh when dealing with her, but, I can *never* forget that *no* one made it easy for me on my way up. It seems as though my approach with Anissa has *finally* paid off.

By mid morning, Mr. Baxter still hasn't phoned. I try to keep myself preoccupied by attending to other clients. Yet, they aren't as challenging or time consuming, and I find myself twiddling my fingers, waiting for the phone to ring.

Anissa buzzes my intercom: "Drew Cunningham is on the line." I say a prayer before answering, and hope that this is the phone call I've been waiting for.

"Drew, Tristan speaking," I say, being overly anxious.

"Tristan, I apologize for not phoning you sooner. It's not like Baxter to take so long."

"I completely understand. A deal of this magnitude takes time. I hope that he's satisfied with all of our efforts to expedite this transaction as smoothly as possible."

"As a matter of fact, Baxter is highly impressed."

I smile.

"However," Drew continues, "there was another offer that came in right under the wire. The other proposition is just a little more thorough with its strategy, and the bid was lower than yours."

"That can't be. There's *no* way this deal can be pushed through at a cheaper bid. I *cut* every corner possible, but I have expenses to cover, and there is *no* way I can make this deal happen for any less than what I quoted. Is Baxter trying to play hard ball?"

"No, it's not like that at all. The other firm that bid against you is a small independent firm, so it was able to under bid you. It seems as though they're a lot hungrier than you are, and they were relentless at pursuing Baxter. Quite frankly, their offer is outstanding, and they are using many of the same resources as you."

"Well, what can I say to that?" I say in a somber tone. "Someone beat me to the punch."

"Nothing personal, Tristan; it's just business. We do look forward to utilizing your firm in the future, if possible."

"Yes, of course."

I CAN'T *BELIEVE* WHAT I JUST HEARD!

I worked my fingers to the *bone* on this deal! What *more* could I have done? Should I have devoted more time?

IMPOSSIBLE!

Could I have worked harder?

UNFATHOMABLE!

No one works as *hard* as I do! I'm practically *married* to my job, so much so, that I have neglected *everything* and *everyone* else in my life!

I'll just have to regroup.

Restructure. Refocus. Reprioritize.

115

And *who* is this firm that underbid me? Probably one of Mr. Baxter's "good old boys". I know better than *anyone*, how hard it is to break into the "men's club", when it comes to business. I'll just have to go to more golf games, attend more business functions.

Make myself more visible!

It is time for me to *show* these men that Tristan Vincent is still a force to be reckoned with!

I buzz Anissa: "Anissa, please see to it that the files for all of our unclosed deals are placed on my desk immediately. I want to attend to any accounts that still have loose ends."

Anissa instantly breezes into my office. She's exquisitely dressed in an iridescent gray, chalk-stripe suit, and a white shirt with French cuffs, all by *Armani;* with powder-pink, high-heeled *Dior* mules. Anissa's also wearing five-carat, diamond-studded earrings, and a matching diamond-studded broach.

She's a little *too* sharp this morning, if I do say so myself.

"That was quick. I thought that it would take you more time to get that all together," I say.

"Actually, I was already working on them. All files with red tabs have the highest priority, then yellow, and green. There are task lists attached to each file, outlining measures that still need to be taken to finalize each individual deal. I've also placed follow-up calls with each client, informing them of our progress, instilling into them that they're our number one priority."

I am flabbergasted!

How's that for a girl with only an Associate's degree? Anissa now thinks to herself.

Wit' Man-Man *actin'* out all week and *gettin'* suspended again, I haven't had a moment of peace! I've decided that I won't talk to him until after I figure out my next move. There's *no* point in havin' this conversation if I can't find another means of bringin' a steady income into this house.

Until I come up wit' a plan, I'll just have to keep a low profile, and let Man-Man get away wit' *actin'* like an asshole! I'll sit him down, and explain all, when the time is right.

I sent Man-Man to school this mornin' wit' his overnight bag. That way, Man-Man can go straight to Maria's house afterwards, and I can get ready for my rendezvous tonight wit' "Mike B." and his crew. Three-thousand extra dollars in my pocket is my *sole* motivation!

But, oh no, the *buck* doesn't stop there!

If I play my cards right, I might be able to finesse even more cash than Trish has already negotiated. In order to do that, I'd need a killer outfit, and the only place to find an ensemble sexy and exotic enough for tonight is on *South Street.*

There's a little boutique on Sixth Street where I can find all the hottest outfits straight outta New York and LA. I can buy the latest trends that these other *hoes* don't know nothin' about! It may cost me a little extra, but *scared* money don't *make* money!

I get dressed in a comfortable, pink, *Juicy Couture* velour sweat suit. It's my favorite outfit to shop in because, it's easy to get in-and-out of, and it's still hip enough for me to be seen in; when I feel like takin' it down a notch. I pull on my pink, rhinestone-studded *Dior* glasses and head out the door.

I leave the boutique wit' an outfit and shoes so hot, that *I* can't even stand myself! Tonight, I'm definitely gonna shut these *hoes* down!

Shopping has made me hungry. Just as I'm 'bout to cross the street and head over to *Haagen Dazs,* my cell phone rings. I answer before the first ring ends.

"Mekka...Mekka...Mekka, you're a hard woman to catch up to," Eugene says, wit' excitement in his voice. Eugene is obviously thrilled that I have finally taken a call from him. He's been one of my most faithful tricks. Eugene's been hangin' around for 'bout two years now. He's the type that likes to be dominated. The more you ignore and mistreat him, the stronger he comes after you.

"You know me, Eugene, I keep myself busy. It's hard to stay idle when you're in high demand," I brag.

"Well, I hope you're not too busy to stop by my office for a little afternoon delight."

I play hard to get: "I don't know. I've got plans tonight, and I just want to chill and relax all afternoon."

"I won't keep you long; I promise. An hour, tops."

"And *how* much is it worth to you?"

"How about a shopping spree on me?"

"I can afford my *own* clothes."

"I'm not talking clothes, I'm talking *Tiffany's*. You know, little turquoise boxes with white silk ribbons?" Eugene teases.

Music to my ears!

"It just so happens that I'm in town," I say, having a sudden change of heart.

"How about you swing past my office in about an hour for a quickie? I'll call ahead to *Tiffany's,* leave them my credit card info, and let them know to expect you."

"You know the way to my heart, don't you? See you in an hour."

I hang up, and nearly float the rest of the way to the ice cream parlor. Today was turnin' about better than I expected.

Why would a woman *ever* want to quit this life?

I make my own schedule. I earn more money in a week than most people earn in a month.

There's *no* way I'm givin' up a good hustle like this!

Everybody will just have to deal. So what if my son is havin' a little trouble adjustin'. He'll just have to get *over* it!

SHAWN

Chapter 25

I can tell it's been a bad week because it's only 11 AM, and I've already finished off a four pack of *Smirnoff* "Twisted Apple" wine coolers. While I'm at school, I've resorted to pouring liquor into my lunch thermos and pretending that it's coffee. The worst part is that, lately, if I don't have any alcohol in my system, I get a pounding headache.

"Shawn, may I have a word with you?"

I look up and notice that Principal Palmer has entered the room, wearing her trademark color red. I was in such deep thought—I didn't even hear her come in. I sit the thermos on my desk and twist the cap back on. I grab a stick of spearmint gum from my desk drawer, unwrap it and pop it in my mouth.

"Ms. Palmer, how can I help you?" I ask with a fake smile plastered to my face. She sits on the corner of my desk and looks me squarely in the eyes.

"Shawn, I've received complaints from some of the parents, and I wanted to take a minute to talk it over with you, before I take action."

"Take action? What could possibly be the problem?"

"I'll get straight to the point, if you don't mind?"

"No, please do," I say, trying to sound indifferent when I'm actually nervous as hell.

"Timothy Geyer's mother called me, informing me that he hasn't brought any homework home in a week, and she thought that was odd. I thought it was unusual as well, but I told her I would check with you. Have you been assigning homework?"

"Um…actually, I haven't," I answer. It hadn't dawned on me until now that I have been slacking off.

"And why haven't you?"

I try to think fast, and as a result, I come off sounding stupid: "I thought that the children needed a break."

"A break? That's what summers and holidays are for," Ms. Palmer replies, before standing up and examining the papers on my desk.

"I assure you that it won't happen again," I say in my defense.

"Well, you see the problem is that, I *may* have been able to let that one slide, but that's *not* the only complaint that I've gotten," Principal Palmer states, as she picks up my lesson plan book, and discovers that I have nothing filled in for the entire week. A look of suspicion fills her face.

"What else have you heard?" I ask. A drunken haze has clouded me for the past week, and I can't remember a *fucking* thing. A part of me wants to know *exactly* what has been said about me; the other part of me *really* doesn't care. I just want to get this conversation over with as soon as possible, so that I can finish my *drink* before my class gets back from recess!

"I find it inconceivable that James Carter told his mother that you fell asleep while they were having silent reading time."

I feel my Adams Apple sink into the pit of my stomach.

"Yet, Shawn, I find it even *more* inconceivable when the parents tell me that you've been coming in late every morning, and dismissing the class early, every afternoon. All of these accusations can't *possibly* be true, can they?" she asks with her left eyebrow raised. Principal Palmer then stands and turns away from me. I watch as she walks around the room, taking inventory of the entire classroom setting.

"Ms. Palmer, let me explain. I haven't been feeling well. I think I'm coming down with a virus or something. I—"

"Let me stop you before you *dig* yourself deeper in the *lie* you're about to tell. Whatever *it* is you're *coming down with,* I *trust* that you'll have *it* taken cared of over the weekend, because *it* is *obviously* interfering with the way you interact with these children. I *cannot* and *will not* allow you to *neglect* your class any longer!

"From *this* day forward, you will turn in a lesson plan to me, every week. You will also contact the parents who filed complaints against you, and apologize for your behavior, a.s.a.p. Furthermore, I am going to document what we discussed here on a formal reprimand, which will be placed in your personnel file. *This* will affect your raise eligibility at the end of the quarter!"

With every word that falls out of Principal Palmer's mouth, I feel the pounding in my head getting worse. Mentally, I turn down the volume of her berating voice, and occasionally nod my head, as if I'm actually listening. Eventually, I completely drown her voice out.

Her lips are moving, but I don't hear a thing. My thoughts wander to the thermos sitting on my desk.

The thermos calls my name.

Principal Palmer walks towards the door. Each step she takes away from me, draws me closer to the moment when I can be alone with my thermos. She then stops dead in her tracks and turns back around to face me.

"I will *not* tolerate this type of behavior. Shawn, I suggest that you straighten up and fly right. You're a young kid, you don't want to screw up your career by making *stupid* mistakes. Any more mistakes on your part, and I'll be *forced* to terminate you!"

Principal Palmer finally exits the room and leaves me feeling like a scolded child.

I reach for my thermos.

I twist the cap off and hold it to my mouth.

I take a long, hard swallow.

Then another, and another and another.

Until I've drained it dry.

MELANIE
Chapter 26

All week I've been doing double duties. I've been customer reppin' at the *Water Department* during the day, and hustling orders for E at night. Only four days have gone by, and I've already made an extra four-hundred dollars! Under normal circumstances, I would've taken that extra money and blew it all away at *Dutch Gardens,* but after the debacle with the pot head teacher on Monday—I'm *not* in the mood for tits and ass.

Instead, I do something completely outta the norm. I call Tristan and tell her that I've got a couple of dollars, and that I want to pay back the last loan.

Tristan sounds happy for me.

She tells me this is the *best* news she's heard all day. Tristan doesn't even bother to ask where I got the dough from. Turns out that some dinner plans she'd made for a client fell through, so she now invites me to some fancy-shmancy restaurant called *Zanzibar Blue Blue.*

"Do you have something appropriate to wear?" Tristan asks in a motherly tone.

"Uh, probably not."

"Then you'll just have to borrow something of mine. I'll have Cornelius pick you up at five o'clock. That'll give us time to rummage through my closet. There's got to be *something* in my closet that would look good on you. You're about a size six, right?"

"I guess," I really don't have a clue. I've been buying men's clothes for so long—I have no idea what my size translates to in women's clothing.

"Don't worry about it. We'll find you something. But what about that *nappy* head of yours."

"Nappy? You mean afro?"

"Whatever you call it. When's the last time you had that puff ball cut?"

"A whole minute."

"Well, don't touch it! I'll call over to *Quincy's* and have him give you a relaxer."

"I don't want no perm! That's *too* much maintenance. I like to get up and go!"

"I'll have him press it. Afterwards, you can wash it and go back to being happy and nappy if you want."

Tristan then puts me on hold to call Quincy's salon and make a reservation for me. A minute later, she comes back on the line and tells me to hustle over to *Quincy's* on 20th and Walnut Street.

"I'll have Cornelius pick you up from there."

A press-and-curl later, I'm staring at myself in Quincy's mirror, and I don't recognize the reflection staring back at me. He has my hair styled in that *Halle Berry* inspired Pixie cut. Then he has his make-up artist hook my face up with some foundation, a little eye shadow and lips gloss; all by *Nars*.

Quincy seems pleased with his latest creation: "Miss Thing, you are f-i-e-r-c-e!" he exclaims with a finger snap for emphasis. "Who knew Tristan had such a beautiful sister hiding under all of those *h-o-r-r-i-d* clothes! I can't *wait* to get Tristan in my chair, I need to hook her up with a new look. It's long overdue to get Tristan out of that uptight, neat little bun."

"Quincy, you know that Tristan is too stuck-on-stupid and scared to try a new look."

Quincy clears his throat and points at me: "D-a-r-l-i-n-g, look who's talking. I practically had to *drag* you in here and *force* you into my chair!"

By the time Cornelius arrives to take me to Tristan's, Quincy has closed up shop, and has invited himself to our "girl's night out". On the ride over, Quincy fills me in on all the latest gossip in Tristan's life. Apparently my sister hasn't gotten laid in over a year, she doesn't have a man, doesn't even have any prospects, and Tristan's thinking about buying a kitten.

"Oh, Lord! Quincy, I hope Tristan doesn't turn into the crazy cat lady," I say, shaking my head.

"My dear, it's *candles* now. The new thing for lonely women is to buy candles all the time. It's pathetic!"

When we get to Tristan's condo, we make a beeline for her unbelievably enormous walk-in-closet. Tristan's closet is as big as my living room and bedroom combined! Quincy gracefully sits on the edge of the bed, sipping on a glass of *Riesling,* and vetoes half of the outfits I model for him.

It's not until I try on a skimpy, silk, turquoise, vintage camisole tank top by *Anna Sui,* with a skin-tight pair of *Seven* blue jeans and strappy, turquoise *Via Spiga* pumps, that he jumps up and does the holy ghost dance.

"W-O-R-K! That's the one, Miss Thing! Yes, chile! This is the outfit you need to step out in tonight, honey!"

Tristan comes running into the closet, still dressed in her work attire, trying to figure out what's all the commotion 'bout. When she sees me, Tristan's eyes pop. It is the first time she's seen me with my new, sassy haircut, and dressed in form-fitting, feminine clothes.

Tristan then witnesses how hard it is for me to maneuver in these high-heeled shoes. I stumble, trying to get acquainted with the way they feel. Tristan slowly circles around me to see if I am up to par. She intensely performs her inspection, then nods with approval.

"About time," Tristan blurts out.

I shake my head.

I can't *believe* the spectacle Quincy's making over my new hairdo and clothes, until I catch a glimpse of myself in a full body mirror. I look like I stepped outta *Essence* magazine! Okay, maybe not *Essence,* more like *Vibe,* but I still look *damn* good for my first time outta the starting blocks.

Quincy then stops praising me long enough to eye Tristan's business suit: "Now, *what* are we gonna do about *you?*"

"What do you mean?" Tristan asks.

"Miss Crab Tree, You *need* to get out of those *t-i-r-e-d* work clothes, and get on the same page as your sister, or else *girlfriend* is gonna steal the show tonight. O-K-A-Y! And puh-lease let your hair down. That *tight,* little neat bun is *not* the *Jordache!*"

"The *Jordache?*"

"The look, Tristan! Oh, by the way, you have *got* to let me borrow your new *Gucci* belt," Quincy says while immediately trying it on. His waist is tiny enough, and it fits Quincy perfectly. "Cute! This belt is *exactly* what I need to set my outfit off!"

Tristan then changes into a Quincy-approved-outfit: A black and white satin *Diane Von Furstenberg* wrap halter top, with black wide-legged parachute pants by *Epperson;* black stiletto heels by *Giuseppe*. Tristan then loosens up her bun, and lets her hair fall to her shoulders.

"It's *Destiny's Child* in person! Looks like we're ready to turn it out!" Quincy shouts, as he puts his arms around Tristan and I, as we now head towards the front door. "The three of us stepping out: the diva, the queen and the lesbo! Who would've thunk it?"

* * * * *

After consuming dinner, desserts and way too many martinis, Tristan, Quincy and I say our good-byes, and I hail a cab. During the ride home, I sit with the back windows wide open, and the cool night air kisses my face and breezes through my hair. I am completely drunk, and I'm hoping that the fresh air will revive me.

I reflect on the exciting evening I've just had.

Hanging out with Tristan was more fun than I thought. Quincy was a *riot*…"queen" of the one-liners. For the first time in a long time, I looked good, and felt good.

Inside and out.

I now tip the cab driver and watch him drive off. It's close to midnight, but most of the neighborhood guys are still hanging out on the corner, sitting on the stoop of an abandoned house.

Although it's dark outside, I recognize E's silhouette amongst the crew. I wave to him before heading to my walkway.

E doesn't wave.

He doesn't recognize me with the new hairdo and sexy clothes.

E squints his eyes and tries to make out who I am. It's not until I slide my key in the door that E figures out that it's me; he then jumps off the stoop, and jogs toward me. His crew encourages him; they make catcalls.

They still haven't figured out that it's *only* me.

I walk inside and flick on the light. E is ten steps behind me. When the light hits my face, he stops dead in his tracks. As I walk inside, E notices my outfit. His eyes take their time making their way along my body, slowly, starting with my hair, and not finishing until the journey has reached the tips of my toes.

"Mel?"

"Yeah, fool. Who do you *think* it is?"

E just stands there with a star-struck expression.

"You coming in? Or are you going to stand there lookin' stupid?"

"My bad. It ain't everyday that I see you this way."

"What way? A little hair, a little make-up, new clothes. You'd *think* you never saw a woman before."

"Well, you don't usually look like a woman," E replies, still standing in the doorway.

"Come in and shut my door. You got everybody in our business."

E then looks over his shoulder, and all the guys' faces are staring in our direction. He then slams the door shut, as if he doesn't want to let a good thing out.

"So, where are you *coming* from?" E asks, sounding slightly jealous. He checks his watch. "Kinda late, ain't it?"

I don't answer…I can't believe E just had the *nerve* to act like he owns me or something!

"Did I ask you where you *been* all night?"

"No, but I ain't walking around this muthafucka looking like I just had an extreme makeover."

"Well, maybe if you ask *nicely*, I just might tell you," I tease, and take of my shoes. I now walk to the hall closet, pull out my fuzzy slippers and slide them on. The whole time, I can feel E's eyes glued to my tight- ass jeans.

"So where were you?"

"If you gotta know, I went out to dinner."

"WITH WHO?" he responds, sounding even more jealous than before.

"My sister."

"Bullshit! Ya'll don't even get along."

"Well, believe what you want to believe."

E gives up the interrogation for a minute. I grab a *Corona* beer bottle from the fridge and toss it to him. E sits on the sofa and changes the subject, but I can feel him *burning* to ask me more questions 'bout my new look!

I'm flattered.

E then changes the subject: "So you made out pretty good this week making runs for me?"

"Yeah, I did aiiight."

"Must feel good to have a little extra cash for a change."

"Yep, I appreciate it, E. Good lookin' out."

"Might need you to take over some more of my customers for me. More cash, of course."

"Cool," I say while popping the top of my beer; I take a sip.

"You could take that extra money and buy some more of those nice clothes; get your hair done again."

"Maybe."

"Maybe I could take you out; help you spend all that money you're gonna be making."

"Take-me-out?"

"I mean, hang out; kick it, you know."

"Oh, yeah, kick it, like boys, right? Like we always do."

"Yeah, you know how we do," E tries to play it off.

"Lemme make the money first. Then we can *talk* 'bout spending it," I say before I yawn. Fatigue now comes crashing down on me, and I can feel my eyes lids getting heavy. I lay across the sofa and snuggle against a throw pillow.

"E, it's been a long day for me. Think I'm 'bout to crash."

E looks disappointed. Doesn't want to leave.

"I'll catch up witchu tomorrow," I say through another yawn.

"I guess going to dinner with your *sister* wore you out, huh?" E says sarcastically.

He still doesn't believe that I went out to dinner with Tristan.

E then stands up to leave. Gives me a long look. A look that expresses more than he can verbally say to me right now.

"See ya tomorrow?" I ask.

E nods. Tries to be nonchalant. Lets himself out and closes the door behind him.

I close my eyes, and hope "Sandman" visits me soon. All I want to do is sleep off these martinis, but as soon as I shut my lids, E's face keeps *popping* up. Memories of his facial expressions, ones that I wasn't even aware were stored in my brain, present themselves to me.

And that's when I hear honey's voice, *"If you're a virgin, and you've never had a man inside you, then how do you know you're gay?"*

The sound of her voice is bangs inside of my head.

And I can't will it away.

AFTER MIDNIGHT

MEKKA

Chapter 27

Klymaxx says it best: *"The men all pause, when I walk into the room."*

It's not just song lyrics for me, tonight it's a reality. I step into *Dutch Gardens* just as cool as you please, wearin' a white, loosely crochet, body-huggin' *Nicole Miller* mini-dress, wit' vintage, rope-tied jute, platform espadrilles by *Viktor and Rolf.*

I'm carryin' the latest leather and crochet, monogram bag by *Louis Vuitton*, and my face is framed by gold, oversized, retro *Stella McCartney* sunglasses. Thanks to my "afternoon delight" wit' Eugene, and my shoppin' spree at *Tiffany's,* my neck, ears and wrists are drippin' wit' "Mother of Pearl" on gold-filled necklaces and bracelets.

My skin has that "new bronze look", since I used a secret make-up technique that was taught to me by an old school dancer—apply a foundation color slightly darker than your natural color, then boost your base with gold-highlighted *Chanel* "Sheer Brilliance" in "Sunkissed".

I look like I just got back from the beaches of San Tropez.

These *hoes* ain't ready for me tonight!

A bourbon flavored, vanilla breeze of "Pink" by *Nanadebary* perfume, follows me as I walk pass the roped off entrance. It's slightly past midnight, and there's a line of tricks and groupies a mile long, waitin' to get inside to catch a glimpse of "Mike B." Amazin' what a person will subject themselves to, *just* to be able to say that they were in the same room as a celebrity.

"Hateration" is *thick* in the house tonight! The other dancers, dressed in cheap outfits, who *thought* they looked good until I popped on the scene, have *nothin'* but disdain for me! I been in this game too long not to be able to spot the fake ones. Their faces wear a smile, but I know deep down inside, they wanna *knock* a bitch off her throne!

Two of the dancers, Diamond and China Doll, have been plottin' on me since the day I got here. Every time I come to work, I gotta hear those *Payless* shoes-wearin' *hoes* talkin' *shit* about

129

me. I guess I should take it as a compliment. If I wasn't doing so well, they wouldn't talkin' about me.

Smitty is the first person that opens his mouth to speak to me. He's standin' by the "VIP" area dressed in a tux. In Smitty's right hand, he's carryin' a taser wit' a high voltage count, yet, it's illegal to carry one, unless you're law enforcement. I can tell by the way that Smitty's tuxedo jacket doesn't drape quite right that he's wearin' a double holster.

"Hey, Miss Mekka."

"What's up, Smitty? What's it lookin' like tonight? Are these *niggas* really tryna drop some cash, or are they just here to window shop?" As Smitty gently shakes my hand, I slide two C-notes into his palm. "I *trust* that you will direct me to the real ballers."

"Sho' nuff," he says. Smitty takes the money, but not before eyein' the diamond ring on my index finger from *Doris Panos* "Dazzling Diamond Diva Collection".

"Is Trish around?"

"In her office. She's been waiting on you. You know Trish don't like to wait."

I then walk pass the main bar, and up the spiral staircase leadin' to Trish's office. As I wind up the stairs, I look down on all the patrons mixin' and minglin'. I inconspicuously take inventory of the entire room, and spot a few *NBA* stars, a couple of actors, musicians, and some 'round-the-way ghetto superstars.

From the distance, I check out their watches, belts and shoes. I can tell who's *really* got it goin' on by payin' attention to fine details.

I don't bother to knock before enterin' Trish's office. Her office is stark-white, brightly lit and freezin' cold. I'm guessin' that's how Trish keeps alert in this business full of night crawlers. I walk in, and catch her snortin' a line of coke from her glass top desk. Trish isn't startled by the intrusion, just a little pissed.

"Shut the damn door," Trish commands. She looks up at me, wipes the dust from her nose, dips her pinky finger into the pile of powder, and wipes it along her gums. "Gotta get my head right. Want some?"

"Naw, I'm cool. I just stopped by to see what's what."

Trish now stands up. She's wearin' a tailored, silver metallic, trench coat dress wit' clear *Casadei* heels, studded wit' *Swarovski* crystals. Trish's ash-blonde hair is swept into a carefree updo, givin' her that freshly fucked look; diamond chandelier earrings dangle from her ears.

Trish is the *only* bitch in this club that I can halfway tolerate, because she never lets anything get personal. Trish is strictly business, all about the Benjamins, and has impeccable taste.

I watch Trish walk over to the *Gustav Klimt* paintin' hangin' on the wall. She tucks her French-manicured fingertips behind the frame of the paintin', and pulls it away from the wall' revealin' a hidden safe. Trish then punches in the combination and it slowly opens. She pulls three small stacks of cash, and tosses it on the desk in front of me.

"Three thousand, as we discussed," Trish says. I pick up the money and quickly fan my fingers along the edges. "It's all there," Trish states. She then walks over to her mini bar, and begins to open a bottle of *Cristal* that's been chillin' on ice. "Want a drink?" Trish asks.

"No thanks, I'm gonna have Josh fix me a *Ketel One* martini when I go back down." Although I'm not particularly thirsty, I know her drink offer is a cue for me to sit down and chill for a moment, so I cop a squat in Trish's acrylic bubble hangin' chair.

"C'mon, don't make me drink alone."

Trish now pours me a glass of *Cristal,* despite my reservations. She hands me the drink and takes a seat on her white leather sofa, before crossing her legs and lighting up a *Newport* cigarette.

"Mekka, here's the deal. 'Mike B.' and his crew will be here any minute. I just got a call from his manager; they're on the *Ben Franklin Bridge.* When they get here, the two will go straight to the private lounge. I'll have a few girls down there to keep them occupied.

"Of course those girls won't have *nothin'* on you and me, so around about one-thirty, after they've done all their lap dances and hard work, we'll waltz in and take it from there. You and me are responsible for taking care of 'Mike B.' and his manager exclusively. No one else is allowed to touch us. It's all been arranged."

At that moment, I remembered readin' somethin' 'bout 'Mike B.' in the *Philly Weekly.* Rumors 'bout him bein' engaged to get married. I guess he considers himself a "free agent" until the weddin' ring is on his finger. *Niggas ain't shit, but hoes and tricks!* I focus back to the matter at hand. "Who's handlin' security for this little soiree?"

"Smitty and Cool Hand Luke."

"Refreshments?"

"Weed, coke, liquor...nothing heavy."

It sounds like a smooth operation. Trish ain't no slouch, she's got all the bases covered.

"How's about a toast to start the evening off right, Mekka?" Trish asks, holdin' up her champagne flute. I close my eyes and try to think of somethin' appropriate to say for the occasion. I raise my glass and recite a famous P-Diddy lyric.

"I got, no time for fake ones. Just sippin' *Cristal* wit' these real ones."

"No doubt!"

We touch glasses and sip down our drinks.

Butterflies flurry in my stomach.

I *never* get butterflies.

Precaution. Prediction. Premonition.

SHAWN
Chapter 28

I go to *Lou and Choos,* the neighborhood bar, right after school let out, and the bartender greets me like I'm "Norm" from TV show *Cheers.* His name is Frank. Before I even get a chance to take my favorite seat at the bar, he already has my scotch on the rocks waiting for me.

Frank is one of those old heads that still keeps himself in good shape. His head is always freshly shaven bald, and he sports a salt-and-pepper sprinkled mustache and beard. I *think* Frank has a crush on me, but that's something that we've never spoke on.

Since I've been here at the bar today, I haven't gotten up from my stool, except to take a piss. Eventually, Frank fills my glass and threatens to cut me off, if I order another drink. I tell him that, "I'm a *grown* woman and I know when I've had enough!"

"Sure about that?" Frank asks.

"Sure as I'll *ever* be. Now, quit acting like my father and *do* your job."

Frank now wipes the counter where another patron had been sitting, then throws the towel back over his shoulder.

"Tough week teaching the brats?"

"The week from Hell! Just when I thought I made it through the workweek without a hitch, the dragon lady, Principal Palmer, jumped on my case. Seems like I've been *fucking* up lately. But what else is new?"

"Can't be that bad."

"Bad is the *understatement*-of-the-year."

I don't bother to tell him about my encounter with Mike or the disaster with the "so-called dyke".

That would be *too* embarrassing!

There are just some things that you have to keep to yourself. Not even tell your hairstylist, therapist or friendly neighborhood bartender.

I now try to wash away the memory of my week with the scotch. I stare at the bottom of yet another empty glass, and jiggle the ice cubes around; listening to the clinking sound.

"Let me get another!"

133

Against his better judgment, Frank pours me another drink: "Last one, Shawn," he threatens. I wave him away with my hand. Frank pours my drink, then walks away to greet another customer.

Thirty minutes goes by and I am *still* holding my position at the bar, but barely. I'm beginning to teeter off the stool. Frank has busied himself with a pretty group of older women at the opposite end of the bar.

Someone drops four quarters into the jukebox—*Distant Lover* by *Marvin Gaye* plays. That same someone then joins me by the bar. I listen to *Marvin,* and drift to the memories that he brings back.

"Can you remember the first time you heard that song?"

I turn and find a *beautiful* Puerto Rican man seated next to me at the bar. He's got dark wavy hair, dark, deep-set eyes and a butter pecan complexion. Papi is casually dressed in a black V-neck T-shirt and carpenter style jeans. I'm so taken aback by his good looks, that I *can't* even open up my mouth to respond!

The guy then answers his own question, "I remember the first time I heard *Distant Lover*. It was back in my high school days. I was at one of those "red light" basement parties in The Bronx. I was grinding up against this girl named Tasha. She was hot! It was getting pretty good, 'til her pops came home early from work, and shut the party down."

I still don't respond.

Papi then grins, exposing a sexy gap between his two front teeth. "My name is Manuel, but my friends call me 'Manny'."

"Good for you," I answer. I guess that any attempt at co-existing at this bar without having a conversation is futile.

Manny then asks: "Can I buy you a drink?"

That gets my attention!

Manny now orders me another scotch. Frank is too preoccupied to care anymore. He pours us both a drink, and gets back to his female company without missing a beat.

"I see that you like scotch," Manny says.

"Not hard to miss," I reply.

"It's not often that I find a woman who drinks single malt scotch. You should try *Glenlivet* if you're looking for a good Highland malt."

134

"I see you know your Scotch."

"My mother used to drink scotch."

For the first time since he sat down, I turn to him: "So did mine, but only when she was depressed...or lonely."

"Looks like we picked up our mother's bad habits," Manny answers, before taking a moment to ponder. "...Here we are talking about our mothers, and you still haven't told me your name."

"It's Shawn," I try to brighten up a little bit. "Sorry for my rudeness, but I've had a rough week, and one too many of these," I say, holding up my glass.

"Been there before. Care to talk about it? Might make you feel better."

"I seriously doubt that. Besides, I'm *not* in the habit of exposing all my deep, dark secrets to total strangers," I say before chasing my scotch down with *7-Up*.

"Everyone's got secrets. But that's no reason for a *beautiful* lady such as yourself to be drinking all alone."

I push my dreadlocks away from my face. I look at Manny and begin to wonder, *what is a handsome, charming, seemingly educated man doing in a place like this.*

So I ask him.

Manny tells me that he's was visiting a female friend who lives in the neighborhood. It was his first time in her home. Manny then explains that her crib is a pigsty. He was so disgusted by how she lived, that he ended the date early; left skid marks on her carpet on his way out the door. Manny later found this bar on his way home; decided to stop and have a drink.

"You would have *never* thought that a woman that fine, would be living so trife!" Manny states.

I give him points for being honest.

"And why are you here?" Manny asks.

"Let's just say that I'm a woman scorned."

Manny clinches up his face and says, "Oh, you're one of them."

"Hate to admit it, but, that's the skin I'm in right now."

"A brother do you wrong?"

"I just put faith in the wrong person...people in general. Just call me "Little Red Riding Hood". Are you another wolf that I have to watch out for?"

"Maybe in my former life, but nowadays, I like to think of myself as one of the good guys. The last of a dying breed."

Manny finishes his drink.

Pays the tab.

"I've got a long ride home. I hate to have to cut this short, but I really gotta go. Maybe I could get your digits," Manny now suggests.

"I can do you one better. I live not too far from here. I've got *plenty* of scotch in the liquor cabinet. Who knows what *trouble* we could get into together?" I place my hand on Manny's shoulder. He gently slides it away.

"As tempting as that sounds, I *really* gotta go."

"So soon?" I answer, as I reach for a napkin, accidentally knock over my glass, and spill the rest of my drink on the bar. There's nothing more unattractive than a sloppily drunk woman!

"Look, Shawn, don't take this the wrong way. I came in here for a quick drink. I saw you sitting at the bar and you looked like you needed some company. I really didn't have anything else in mind.

"Well, maybe I could *change* your mind," I plead. "Look, there's a room in the back. We could go back there, have another drink in private...play things by ear," I whisper.

I now stand up.

Stumble drunkenly.

We then close the tab.

Manny and I end up in the old poolroom in the back of the bar. My slacks and panties are now down around my ankles.

Manny didn't even bother to undo his jeans.

He just pulled his big, pretty penis through his zipper hole, and began pounding his rock-hard dick inside of me doggy style.

Got me bent over an old, dusty pool table.

The side of my face is pressed against the green felt. My dreadlocks flail along the dusty table top, like a mop washing over a dirty floor. Every time Manny pounces inside of me, I bang my head.

He now pounds me harder!

I cry out, "Isaiah!"

Manny then stops in mid stroke.

Looks at me like I'm a mad woman!

Backs away from me.

"My name is Manny...Manny. Don't you remember?"

136

I stare at his face, but all I can see is the image of Isaiah.

Manny then zips up his pants.

"Crazy drunk bitch," he murmurs, as Manny leaves me there in the room.

Alone.

BREAK OF DAWN

TRISTAN
Chapter 29

The dream has me back in that...*old familiar apartment. I find myself in the kitchen. It's a galley kitchen. There is a window right above the kitchen sink. I'm washing dishes and looking out over* One Western Avenue and Peabody Terrace. *I marvel at its classic red-brick buildings, tree-lined walkways and grassy courtyards.*

I live in Soldiers Field Park, *located on* Harvard Business School Campus. *I'm not eligible to live in residence halls because of my father's income, so he pulls some strings, and finds this apartment for me through* Harvard Real Estate Services Affiliated Housing.

This weekend, my sister, Melanie is coming to visit. She's three years my junior, sixteen at this time, and rebelliously full of fire. My father phones me earlier this week, telling me that he's sending Melanie up to Cambridge Massachusetts, *by train. She's to stay with me for the weekend, and I'm suppose to take time and "talk some sense into Melanie".*

Melanie recently was caught having a sexual relationship with a girl on the basketball team of her high school. She and the girl had ditched school one afternoon, and was caught making out in the living room, when my father came home early from his private practice.

After my mother left us, my father took it very hard...to say the least. He became a recluse, and very seldom did anything but work. I'm left to take care of our family affairs, manage the estate, balance the bank accounts, and pay the employees.

I also mail off the holiday cards, do the grocery shopping, prepare the meals, have the cars serviced, oversee the landscaping, pay the property taxes, attend chamber of commerce meetings in my father's stead, and most importantly, I look after my sister.

I am the one who keeps up the facade that my family isn't devastated by my mother's betrayal. I pick up the pieces, maintain

139

the status quo, and conduct myself as if life in the Vincent home is picture perfect.

My sister and I absorbed the pain in contrasting ways. Determined to earn a scholarship and a one-way ticket out of Hell, I buried myself in my studies. I retreated inside of the fantasy world of books. I read voraciously: Whitman, Shakespeare, Dubois, Morrison, Angelou, Walker, Achebe, Wright, Nabakov— *anything I could get my hands on. I'm active in school, joining the honor society, the chorus, and every social club available.*

I keep myself busy.

Action is the enemy of thought.

As long as I preoccupy myself with trivialities, I don't have to face my life.

Melanie is the complete opposite.

She wears her pain on her sleeve, and doesn't care who sees it. Melanie is on a path of self-destruction. She disappears for days at a time. Melanie ditches school, sasses teachers, and is expelled. She is now a petty thief. Also steals cars, and takes joyrides. Recently, Melanie made it all the way to Florida before the cops found her.

Melanie is my nightmare, and I, hers.

We hate each other!

Because it's easier than loving.

Melanie and I know we can't save each other. We coexist, but really don't exist at all.

We rarely speak.

And when Melanie shows up at the train station in Cambridge, *I barely recognize her. She arrives in baggy* Girbaud *jeans, a* Woolrich *plaid shirt and* Timberland *boots. Melanie walks off the train, and steps onto the platform with her headphones blasting so loud, that the whole concourse could hear the lyrics to* Dr. Dre and Snoop Doggy Dog's "Deep Cover".

As soon as I see Melanie, my eyes well up with tears. I fight them back and paint a smile across my face. I want to hug her, but instead, I tightly cross my arms.

"'Sup, big sis," is all she says, as Melanie throws her luggage, a trash bag filled with clothes, into the trunk of my yellow Volkswagen Beetle.

When we reach my apartment at Soldiers Park, *Melanie steps inside of my sunlit living room, drops her bag on the floor, and takes a look around the place. She opens my closet doors, looks through my kitchen cabinets, and my refrigerator.*

Melanie also opens all of my shoeboxes, digs through my school bag, listens to my answering machine messages, thumbs through my albums, and eats peanut butter and jelly sandwiches.

Later on, Melanie sits on my futon in the living room, smokes cigarettes and drinks cheap Olde English *beer, until she crashes and falls asleep.*

Melanie sleeps for nineteen hours before she finally awakens. Melanie groggily steps into the kitchen like she has walked The Green Mile. *She finds me washing dishes, and staring out at the courtyard through the window above the sink.*

"I bet that you've never *even stepped foot on the courtyard, but you stare at it every day," Melanie says.*

And she is right.

My sister, Melanie, the person who I haven't spoken to since I left for college, is still the only person who truly knows me.

"Mom says you're a dyke *now?" I say blatantly. Melanie lights a cigarette: "You say that like it's an occupation."*

"She's worried about you, Mel."

"What 'bout you? You worried, too? Looks to me like you got it made at good ol' Harvard; probably got yourself a preppy, White *boyfriend."*

She's right, again.

"This is not *about me!"*

"When is it ever *'bout Tristan? Tristan is too busy living her* Andy Warhol *existence—she doesn't even know what's* real *anymore."*

"And how you behave is real? *Tell me, what's so* real *about your life?"*

"I'm not the one pointing fingers here. I know I'm fucked *up! I can deal with my* own *shit! I don't need dad forcing me to come up here so that I can listen to* you *preach to me 'bout what's right and what's wrong."*

"Since when was dad able to force you to do anything?"

Melanie knows that I know, that deep down inside, she was here because she wanted to be.

"Dad told me that mom took away the Trust fund she set aside for you," I say knowingly. "What are you going to do without money?"

"Whatever I want to do! I'll get by without mom! I've been getting along all this time. I'm tired of her dangling money in front of us like bait, just because she's finally ready to acknowledge us. You're *the one with your eyes still* glued *to the prize!"* Melanie challenged, as she sits at my second hand kitchen table, using a paper cup as an ashtray.

"I can put my share of the Trust to good use. Make a life for us."

"That's mom's guilt money! That money don't mean shit to me. Not after what she did to us and dad!"

"It's his own fault! Dad let a woman destroy him! He was weak! If I never see him again, it'll be too soon!"

Before I see it coming, Melanie jumps up from her seat, raises her hand, and slaps me hard against the side of my face.

I drop the dish that I was washing.

It crashes on the floor and shatters into pieces.

"How can you say that 'bout our father? How could you take her side?"

But I'm not taking sides. Melanie doesn't understand that.

She turns away from me.

Leaves the kitchen.

Leaves the apartment.

Leaves my life.

And my heart feels like the dish.

Shattered on the floor.

"MELANIE...MELANIE! DON'T GO! MELANIE, I'M SORRY!" I scream, "MELANIE, PLEASE COME BACK!"

I scream out into the night. I feel like I'm sailing away on a ship that's rocking on the turbulent waves of my mistake. And the ship is carrying me away on the dark desolate sea.

The sea is rocking...

...And rocking...

...Back-and-forth...

...Slowly rocking...

...And rocking...

...I wake to find Cornelius sitting on the edge of my bed, gently rubbing my back.

Soothing me.

The motion rocks me awake.

Pulls me away from the turbulent waves of my nightmare.

Back to reality.

Cornelius is whispering softly, "S-s-s-s-s-s-s-h, it's going to be alright. It was just another nightmare. I can hear you in my quarters, screaming all the way down the hall. It's going to be alright, Tristan. Try and get some rest."

But I can't....

MELANIE

Chapter 30

I am dreaming that...*I just scratched off a winning lottery ticket,* when I'm awakened by a knock on the door.

FUCK!

I *hate* it when I'm in the middle of a good dream and something wakes me up! You can never fall back to sleep and pick up where the dream left off.

Once it's lost, it's lost.

It's pathetic when you prefer a dream over your real life.

KNOCK-KNOCK-KNOCK!

I'm still on the couch.

I toss the pillow that has been covering my head onto the floor and yell out: "WHO THE FUCK IS IT?"

"Damn girl, you kiss your mother with that mouth?" a voice says from behind the door.

It's E.

I shoulda known.

"E, Do you *know* what time it is?"

"It's not that late. Quit acting like you got a curfew and open up."

"Didn't I *just* kick you out a few hours ago?"

"Open the *damn* door before I kick it down."

I get up from the couch.

Blow breath into my cupped hand.

Take a whiff...

I'm still cool.

When I open the door, E is standing there smiling, wearing casual, blue velour *Enyce* sweat suit, and a fresh pair of "S. Carter" *Reebok* sneakers. He's got a diamond stud in his right ear, and a diamond-studded cross medallion hangs from a platinum gold chain around his neck

He looks like a breath of fresh air.

I stand in the doorway: "Whachu want, *boy?*"

E grabs his crotch: "I got your *boy* right here."

"Whatever," I roll my eyes. "I hope you don't need me to make a run, 'cause I don't feel like it right now. I'm off the clock."

"Good. Get dressed," E commands, as he bombards his way pass me and enters the apartment.

"Damn, nigga, *can't* you say excuse me?"

"There is *no* excuse for you!" E jokes.

"Ha, ha, not funny," I reply and shut the door.

"C'mon, Mel, hurry up and get dressed. And *don't* put on *no* baggy sweats. I want you to throw on that outfit you had on earlier; you know, the sexy jeans and tank top."

"For what?"

"I gotta drop off something at this nightclub, and I want you to come with me."

"Whachu *need* me for?"

"I want you to meet an associate of mine. I'm trying to put you on. Now, get dressed!" E says before he snaps his fingers. "Hurry up!"

"Nigga, you better *fall* back!"

E gives me a shove.

I return the shove.

I then saunter inside the bedroom to get dressed.

Quiet as it's kept, I'm happy to see him.

Fifteen minutes later, I'm dressed. E and I hop into his snow-white "Escalade" *Cadillac* and head over to *Gotham,* the hottest urban nightspot in the city. The butter-soft, camel-colored leather seat swallows me up. Aside from Tristan's cars, I never been in a whip like this fancy.

E's got the speakers on full blast.

Usher tells us his *Confessions.*

We take a shortcut down *Ridge Avenue.* We bang a left onto *Broad Street,* and take *Broad* to *Spring Garden.* The statue of *William Penn* atop *City Hall* comes into view. We follow *Spring Garden* to Delaware Avenue.

Delaware Avenue is a metropolis filled with hip-hop spots, reggae joints, three-story techno warehouses, jazz lounges, and classic rock venues. The sidewalks are filled with party people. The streets are lined with pimped-out *Porsches, Benzs, Hummers, Jags, Land Rovers* and *Ducati* motorcycle squads.

The scene looks like the "ghetto Grammys".

E and I valet park. When we get to the door, the bouncer recognizes E and tells the hostess to escort us inside.

"Damn, E. I didn't know you had it *goin'* on like this."

"There are a lot of things that you don't know about me," E says with a wink and a sly smile. He then tells the hostess that we're here to meet his friend, Will, and she shows us to the "VIP" area.

Bass thumps from the speakers.

The dance floor is jam-packed.

Crowds of dancers gyrate and grind against each other.

People parlay by the bar.

Along the way, several people come up to E and engage him in "ghetto handshakes"—slapping fives of the hands while giving half hugs simultaneously. E then exchanges a few words before we continue our path to the private room in the back.

We come to a hallway lined with red carpet. At the end of the hall, E and I are met by a steel door with a built-in window slot.

E knocks once.

The slot opens.

A pair of eyes greets us.

The eyes study E's face and register recognition.

The slot slams shut and the door opens.

The room is small, and decorated like a gambling parlor straight out of the Harlem Renaissance era. A group of well-dressed, stone-faced gangsters are seated at a round table playing "Spades".

Cigar smoke fills the room.

As soon as E steps into the room, one of the men sitting at the table acknowledges him with a head nod. He then lays his cards on the table and stands up to greet E.

"My nigga, Eazy E!"

"What's up, Tone."

They shake hands. Tone's eyes then leave E's face and travel towards me.

"Where you been hiding this one?" Tone asks, as he looks over the entire frame of my body. Like a man marking his territory, E subtly slides his arm around my waist.

"Never *mind* where I been hiding her."

It's obvious that Tone is flirting with me, and even *more* obvious that E doesn't like it.

E then clears his throat.

Tone catches the hint.

"My bad, E," Tone states.

"Yeah, don't let it happen again."

Tone then lets the tension roll off of his back. "You here to see Will?"

"Yeah, is he around? Will told me to meet him here 'bout two o' clock," E says and looks at his *Tag Heuer;* checking the time.

"Will's here. He went to handle something right-quick. Why don't y'all sit down and chill; he'll be back in a sec."

E and I walk over to a sitting area in the corner of the room.

"What's up with dude?" I ask, referring to Tone.

"Niggas see a pretty lady and start acting like vultures."

Pretty lady? ...Me?

We take a seat on the burgundy velvet couch and a waitress comes over to take our drink order. E gets a *Corona* with lime and a shot of tequila, and I order a rum and coke. The waitress smiles a syrupy sweet smile at E, and switches her hips as she walks away.

I feel a little out of my element.

E senses my nervousness.

He grabs my hand.

Gives it a gentle squeeze.

Rubs my hand tenderly.

"It's cool. Just act like we're back at the crib hanging out."

"But that's the problem, E. We're not at the crib. We're at this fancy club, I'm dressed in this *sexified* outfit with this new hairstyle, and I'm not used to it all."

E then pauses as if he's considering what he's going to say very carefully: "...Well, you look *very* nice...and I'm happy that you came out with me tonight. But if you feel uncomfortable, we can go back home as soon as I get done. Cool?"

The waitress now comes back over. She flirts with her eyes as she serves E his drink. The next time she looks at him that way, I feel like I might *knock* her teeth out! I now stare her down. *I don't even know why I'm trippin'.* I drain my drink in one long gulp, and order another before the waitress has a chance to walk off.

"You like rum and coke?" E asks sarcastically.

"Love it."

"Do you?"

At that moment, a brother who looks like he could be *Shemar Moore's* twin, walks up to us and approaches E. He's dressed in a starched, white *Sean John* button-down shirt with French cuffs, black slacks, black crocodile *Stacy Adams,* and a *Movado* watch adorns the man's left wrist.

E now stands up. They greet each other with a fraternal hug that tells me that they've known each other for a long time.

"This is my friend, Will. The man I told you about earlier. Will, this is my friend, Melanie Vincent."

I don't think that I've *ever* been introduced to anyone that way. I'm so used to being called "Mel" that, for a moment, it doesn't even sound like E's talking 'bout me.

"It's nice to finally meet you, Ms. Vincent," Will says. His smile is full of boyish charm. "E talks about you all the time."

"Is that so?" I ask, turning to face E.

E tries to play it off by nonchalantly sipping his beer as he sits, but I can tell by E's silence that Will just let the cat outta the bag.

E now looks nervous.

I place my right hand over his and comfort him.

"Just like were hangin' at home, right?" I say

E grins and gathers his composure.

Will then studies E's face: "Did I say something wrong?"

"You always did *talk* too much."

I sit and watch as the two of them catch up on old times. I begin to enjoy listening to the stories of how E and Will grew up together. Will talks about how E used to have a *Gumby*-style hair cut back in the day. E says that Will used to have a high-top fade like *Kid* from *Kid and Play.*

We all laugh and share a few more rounds of drinks. The tension of tonight feeling like a date has subsided. We're back to just being good ol' E and Mel again.

Nature calls.

I excuse myself to the ladies room.

E watches as I walk away.

I can *feel* his eyes following me down the hall. E's checking to make sure that none of the other brothers are trying to step to me.

The line outside of the ladies room is a mile long. It takes forever to get to the stall. When I finally make it inside, there's a gang of women jam-packed in front of the mirror, trying to make sure there faces are still holding up. I push through and find an empty stall.

When I get back from the bathroom, it looks as though E and Will are wrapping up business. Will hands E a folded manila envelope. E stuffs the envelope into his back pocket. I approach, and the two men stand up and begin to say their good-byes.

"Hit me up when you finish flippin' it, and we'll take it from there," Will says.

"It shouldn't take me more than a week."

The two shake on it.

"I'd love to stay, but I got this party to go to. So, I'll let you get back to *your date,*" Will states playfully.

E gives him an icy stare.

"Oops!" Will blurts, but I can tell that his disclosure was no accident. Will turns to me: "Ms. Vincent, it was a *pleasure* meeting you."

"You, too."

"E, I'll catch you later." Before Will walks away, he turns back and tells E, "Good luck tonight."

Will makes his exit.

And once again, E and I are alone.

Just when it seems like the vibe is 'bout to return back to normal, the *last* person I want to see on the planet walks into the room.

Theresa!

Her boney, little frame is dressed in the skimpiest outfit she could find; it looks like it came from the *children's* department.

Theresa walks pass where E and I are seated.

Leans against the bar.

Orders a drink.

She now looks at me, without any recognition, sees E, and then looks back at me, and puts two-and-two together.

Theresa now has the "oh, shit" look on her face.

I'm *not* in the mood for another run in with Theresa!

I grab E's hand: "Lets get out of here," I suggest.

"Ready to go home?" E asks with disappointment.

"Not exactly. It's just getting a little crowded in here. I need a change of scenery."

I then stand up and E follows my lead. We leave the confines of the "VIP". The steel door slams shut behind us, and we are immediately bombarded by reggae music coming from the main dance floor. It is so crowded, that we have to push our way through the crowd.

People are coming and going in every direction. E grabs my hand so that we won't get separated, and we swim through the crowd; heading in the direction of the stairs leading up to the balcony, overlooking the dance floor.

We find two stools and sit by the rail.

E now searches for a waitress.

MEKKA
Chapter 31

The "VIP" lounge is constructed in the same manner as a skybox in a sports arena. It has a tinted window that overlooks the entire club. It's equipped wit' its own sound system, gourmet buffet and a fully stocked private bar. There are custom-made chenille lounge chairs, sofas, high-top bar tables, pool tables, a heated Jacuzzi, and a floor-to-ceilin' projection screen.

The vibe is crazy bananas!

Champagne poppin'. Lap dancin'. Weed smokin'. Booties clappin'. Coke snortin'. Lesbo shows. Dick suckin'. Ménage-a-trois. Butt-naked bitches jumpin' in-and-out of the Jacuzzi.

Temptation. Fornication. Degradation.

You have to walk through the "VIP" lounge, in order to get to the secret adjacent room where the rapper, "Mike B." is. When I enter, he's sittin' in a leather chair, lookin' through a two-way mirror, which gives him full view of the "VIP" lounge.

"Mike B." looks like a king on a throne, keepin' an eye on his lowly subjects. The only other people that's in the room wit' "Mike B." is his manager and Trish, who's sittin' in the chair next to him—Trish now givin' the manager a lap dance. *Damn! She beat me here. Trish sure didn't waste any time!*

The rapper is dressed in a navy washed velvet blazer, a *Roberto Cavalli* tattoo print T-shirt and a pair of *True Religion* distressed jeans. "Mike B." is also wearin' a navy blue velvet driving cap by *Paul Smith,* a white and canary diamond-embezzled *Marc Jacobs* watch, and a pair of black *Prada* dress shoes. I do a quick calculation on his outfit and jewels: *fifty Gs.*

Impressive.

"Mike B." now looks me over like a lion stalkin' his prey: "Mekka. Your reputation precedes you."

"As does yours," I answer.

"Why don't you have a seat?" he motions me to the empty chair beside him. "Can I get you something to drink? *Moet? Cristal? Alize'? Remy?* Some *Hennessy?*"

"White wine will be fine."

"Classy lady," "Mike B." states. He then snaps his fingers, and the rapper's manager looks over at him. "Go to the bar and get Mekka some white wine."

"They ain't got no waitress up in here?" his manager asks, while in the midst of gettin' a seriously seductive lap dance from Trish—he doesn't want to get up and ruin the moment.

"Mike B." then gives him a stern "what-did-I-tell-you?" facial expression. His now manager hops up, and walks over to the private bar.

"Now where were we?" "Mike B." asks, refocusin' his attention on me.

"We were talkin' about reputations," I reply, lookin' at the rapper's ring finger, tryna find out if the rumors are true or not. It's still unadorned. "Mike B." now catches me lookin'.

"Reputations or rumors?" "Mike B." curiously asks. "Well, why did you agree to meet me?"

"I'm searchin' for some *intelligent* conversation."

"Mike B." laughs. "Your conversation comes with an expensive price tag."

I laugh. "I guess when you consider it, *all* conversations come wit' a price tag in some form or another."

"How so?"

"For example, you see a beautiful woman—you want to get to know her better. You ask her out on a date. Show up to her door with flowers—take her out to dinner. Have cocktails and desert; see a movie. During the course of the evenin', you engage her in conversation. Ask her favorite color, what her middle name is—her zodiac sign. When it's all said and done, at the end of the evenin', you know *all* these new things about her...through conversation, but look at how much *money* you had to spend to accomplish that."

"So you're saying that every women has a price tag."

"All women may not be as up front about as I am, but, *yes,* all women come wit' a price."

"Mike B." now contemplates my theory. Acquiesces. The rapper takes the wine glass from his manager and hands it to me.

"Do you require anything *else*, Miss Mekka?"

I take a sip of my wine. "What I require, you are *not* equipped to provide me wit', but thanks for askin'."

"Mike B." grins. He's enjoyin' the mental sparrin' thang we've got goin' on. When it comes to *shit* like this, I am the master! And I'm playin' wit' my A-game tonight.

"Mike B." then drinks his cognac and rubs his goatee. "What is it that you require that I *can't* provide?"

"As you can see, I'm an *independent* woman. I can *afford* the finer things in life. I can pay my *own* bills, my car note. I can afford fancy restaurants, designer clothes, bling—"

"But would you be able to afford those things without the generosity of men like me?"

"I wasn't *finished.* I haven't gotten to the best part yet."

"Go on."

"Like I was *sayin',* I can afford *all* those materialistic things. What I *require,* is considered the epitome of all things."

"And what might that be?"

"What I *require,* is money...power and respect. Can you provide that?"

"Mike B." doesn't answer.

"I didn't think so."

"Touché," he responds while raisin' his glass to me simultaneously. "Mike B." then glances over at Trish and his manager—they're practically fuckin' right next to us.

"What's that perfume you're wearing? I don't think that I've ever smelled anything so intoxicating."

"It's 'Pink' by *Nanadebary.*"

"What? By who?"

I laugh. "It's *Madonna's* signature scent."

"And that makes it good?"

"Good enough for me."

"I see. So, tell me, what else does Miss Mekka require?"

"Are you *serious?*" I ask cynically.

"I'm absolutely, positively serious. I like the way your mind works; I wanna hear more."

"What else do I require?" I repeat the question, rolling it around in my head. "Peace of mind. What I would give for a day...just *one* day without drama."

"Self-imposed drama?"

"Drama is drama! No matter who imposes it. But, yeah, I guess it's self-imposed. If I wasn't livin' this lifestyle, then I guess that I wouldn't feel like *Mary J. Blige,* 'tired of a-l-l the drama'."

"Yeah, I know what you mean. Sometimes being a celebrity ain't all what it's cracked up to be. People start buying into all the hype, and forget that deep down inside, you're a real person."

"Doesn't sound like you have *much* to complain about," I throw out.

"I guess you're right. I wouldn't trade this for the world. It's what I've *always* wanted. What about you? Would you trade it all?"

"...No, I wouldn't trade. Wit' the exception of one thing."

"Mike B." asks with sincerity: "What's that one thing?"

"Well, I have two kids. I wish I could give 'em more of me, but the longer I stay in the game, the more it chips away at me; a little at a time. Soon, I won't have nothin' left to give 'em."

"Don't be so hard on yourself. When I was comin' up, my mama didn't have two nickels to rub together. She couldn't afford to give me *shit!* You might not have quality time with your kids, but at least you can afford to take care of them, and that's more than *most* single moms can do."

"I guess you're right, but, what about the fact that I haven't had a *date* in five years?" I say to lighten the mood.

"Bullshit."

"I'm not *talkin'* 'bout any ol' kind of date. I mean a real, ol' fashion, pick-you-up-at-the-door, and candlelight dinner type date."

"It would be intimidating for the average brother to step to a woman like you. You're the self-proclaimed 'independent woman'. As you said earlier, you can pay your *own* bills and buy your *own* bling, so don't whine about being lonely. You can't have it both ways."

"Don't get it *twisted.* I'm not whinin'. I'm simply statin' the facts. I'd settle for a *big* bank account over a *big* dick to keep me company, any day."

"Well, Mekka, for the sake of argument, you *wouldn't* have to settle with me—I have a big bank account, *and* a big dick...Both!"

I raise my glass to "Mike B.". "Touché!"

Seconds turn to minutes.
Minutes turn to hours.

Night turns to day.

The party has died down.

Most of the people are beginnin' to leave.

The "VIP" lounge is empty.

And "Mike B." and I are *still* talkin'!

When "Mike B." finally escorts me out to the door of the VIP, not even so much as a kiss has taken place. Wit' the exception of a few flirtations, he's been a complete gentlemen the entire evenin'. I can't remember the last time a *trick* paid me that kind of cash wit'out expectin' to, at least, get his *dick* sucked! I had such an easy, breezy time tonight, that it almost didn't feel like work.

"It's been a pleasure, Miss Mekka."

"The pleasure was all mine."

"Maybe we can do this again sometime." "Mike B." hints. "Can I have my manager get your number from Trish? Continue this conversation behind closed doors? Where there aren't so many spectators."

I look down at his empty ring finger: "Reputations or rumors?"

"Mike B." smiles. "It's true."

"And *just* when I was beginnin' to *think* you were a good boy. Have you're manager holla at Trish. She knows how to reach me."

I wave good-bye and wish "Mike B." a goodnight.

SHAWN
Chapter 32

The dream has me back...*in the House of the Lord. I find myself in the choir's dressing room. It's spacious, with plenty of mirrors, dressing tables and vanities.*

I am standing in front of the mahogany chival beveled mirror. I'm a twenty-one-year-old, beautiful, young caterpillar of a woman, who is about to blossom into a butterfly.

At this time, my dreadlocks are only tiny twists. I'm wearing a Moshood *cream-colored, African-inspired, strapless wedding gown, beaded with carie shells. Instead of a contemporary veil, I'm wearing a traditional African head wrap.*

I'm nervously trying to wrap the five yards of silk fabric around my head while my mother stands behind me. I can see the reflection of her flawless, chocolate-brown face appear over my shoulder. My mother's a beautiful statuesque woman, with short silver-gray hair, a graceful neck and thin-framed body. She's wearing a mother-of-the-bride white pantsuit—one with wide-legged, flowing palazzo pants.

My mother looks like a guardian angle.

She possesses the distinguished beauty of Diahann Carroll.

Without saying a word, my mother grabs the delicate fabric from my hand, and helps me fashion the wrap around my head. When she has the silk fabric draped perfectly, my mother slides the stem of an African violet over my ear. She tucks the stem inside the lining of the head wrap, so that only the blossom shows. Then she turns me away from the mirror to face her.

"Perfect," she says.

My mother, Elizabeth, is the matriarch of my family. She held it together when my father died of a stroke. It's been hard for her, but my mother is always strong.

She and my father got it right. They embodied the true essence of a take no prisoners, soulful, God-fearing, deeply-rooted love. They had honesty and integrity. Their marriage was a true testament that love endures all things.

It was real love.

I remember how they danced in the living room to their old school jams. My mom loved Patti Labelle, *and my father loved* Carlos Santana. *They used to "step in the name of love" before R. Kelly made it popular.*

When pop had his first stroke and had to quit working on account of his disability, my mother worked two jobs; schoolteacher by day, and she cleaned a local beauty salon on weekends. I would go there after school, do my homework, and listen to my mother and the women in the neighborhood gossip about who was doing who. Sometimes, she would take me to the salon to get a press and curl.

My mother was on the usher board of our church and the lead singer in the choir. I would sit with her on Wednesday nights and listen to them rehearse. I would rub her legs down with liniment oil on Sunday nights, and rod set her hair in puffy pink rollers.

She was a Nubian queen.

And I was her princess.

We were mother and daughter, and best of friends....

My mother straightens out the taffeta lining of my dress, then picks up the bouquet of lilies from the dressing table and hands them to me.

"Thank you, mom. I'm a nervous wreck."

"Come here, child," My mother says softly. She takes my hand and walks me over to the sofa, and we sit together. "I'm going to ask you something. And I want you to know that, no matter what your response is, I will stand by you. Understood?"

"Yes," I say, as I nervously rub my hands along the length of my train, and straighten it out alongside of me.

"Stop fidgeting!" my mother says sternly and looks me directly in the eyes. "Now, I know that I worked hard to make this day beautiful and perfect for you. I taught summer school every year after your father passed, so that I could put extra money aside for your college tuition and your wedding day. And here we are, nineteen years later..." she pauses.

Tears well up in her eyes. My mother smiles through the tears and continues to speak: "...I attended to every detail. Made all the arrangements, and fussed *over every little thing because, I have been dreaming of this day for a very long time. You are my child, and I am your mother; and this is what mothers do. Now, I must ask you something, and I want you to search the depths of your soul and answer me with honesty."*

"Yes, ma'am."

"I don't want you to feel that you have to do this because of all the trouble I've gone through. It's never too late to turn back. Are you sure *that you want to go through with this?"*

"What? Mom, how could you ask me something like that? I love Isaiah. We've been living together for over a year and, I know that you never approved of us living together, but I had to make sure that this was right for me; before I took this giant step."

"Shawn, I don't doubt that. But, I look at you, and you seem so nervous. If you are sure about this, then there should be nothing *to be nervous about."*

"Mother, why would I go through all *this trouble? The gown...the caterer...the florist.... We've flown family in from* all *over the country, and you're* asking *me if I'm sure?"*

"You still *haven't answered the question," my mother says dead on. "Shawny, you know that ever since you were a little girl you were always good at avoiding questions? I had always thought that you would make a good lawyer, but you decided to follow in my footsteps and become a teacher," she says, as my mother smiles a proud smile. "Now answer the question that I asked. Are you sure?"*

"Mother. I'm absolutely, positively, one-hundred percent sure."

My mother takes my hands in hers, and I stare at the tree-like veins that extend up the backside of her hands when she clutches my palm.

"Good. I am pleased to hear that. Now I am going to tell you what your grandmother told me, the day I married your father; God rest his soul." My mother closes her eyes and leans her head toward the Heavens, as if she's seeking divine inspiration to guide her words. "The key to a successful marriage lies in emotions and how you deal with them. You must remember that all painful emotions...anger, fear, jealousy, anxiety, rage, etc, are all reflections of loss of power. You must teach yourself to confront each emotion and ask yourself, 'how do I feel that I am losing power?'

"But first, you must determine the spiritual definition of power. My spiritual definition of power is, a sense of liberation, inward peace and strength, insight into truth, and joy. Power is

possessing a true understanding, true purpose, true speech, true conduct, and true effort. Shawn, if you understand these truths, and live by them, then you will never feel powerless.

"What most people fail to realize is that, you can tap into your greatest power by looking within. Integrate all of these truths into your daily life. It takes patience and practice, and you have to remind yourself that you are human, and your are prone to making mistakes. However, you have to understand that, you will constantly suffer from pain, until you accept these truths.

And remember that you cannot seek gratification from any source outside of yourself. As long as you do so, you will continue to be unhappy. The only place you can draw happiness from is within. Never let anyone steal your power. Without it, you will be lost."

My mother's words sends shivers up-and-down my back. The fine hairs on the back of my neck are standing at attention.

I sit there speechless.

In utter awe of this woman's divine intellect.

My mother never fails to amaze me!

"Shawn, I wish you and Isaiah love, peace and happiness. People throw the word "love" around like it's a trivial thing or a toy to be played with; but love is the most abundant resource. Love is God and God is love. Love is not jealous. Love is not vain. Love is not easily provoked. Love is not evil. Love rejoices in the truth. Love bears all things. Love never fails."

At this time, tears are falling from my eyes.

"Hold your head back and cry upwards. Don't mess your mascara," my mother says softly, as she slides a tissue from the cuff of her jacket and dabs my eyes dry.

"I love you, mom," I whisper, choking back my tears.

"I...love you, too."

For a moment, it seems as if my mother is straining to get her words out. Her breath appears labored. My mother now clutches her chest, inhales and exhales, slowly and rhythmically. Then as quickly as the pain set in, it disappears.

"Are you okay, mom?" I take my hand and rub her back, until my mother regains her composure.

"I'm fine. Just had a little chest pain is all. Don't worry about me. This old body has had so many aches and pains for so long, that I can't even remember life without it," she states and rises slowly.

"Are you sure?"

"Shawn, I'm fine," my mother assures, as she takes her hand and runs it through her freshly coiffed hair. *"Today is your day, and we aren't going to let anything steal your joy. Now, if you'll excuse me for a moment, I'm going to check to make sure that the guests are all being seated, and that we're still on schedule. I'll tell Isaiah that you'll be out in a moment, and the wedding procession will begin shortly. I'll be right back. Just think happy thoughts. This is supposed to be one of the happiest days of your life."*

My mother disappears through the doorway, and I sit there in my wedding gown, contemplating the words of wisdom that she just shared with me. Wisdom passed—passed down from her mother to her, and now, from my mother to me.

I feel honored!

Minutes later, I hear the pianist begin to play soft music, music that the guests are being seated to.

My heart flutters...

The gravity of the magnitude of what is about to happen finally sinks in: I am about to become Mrs. Isaiah Brooks!

I begin to feel anxious...

Nervous...

Hot!

My conscious is trying to manifest itself.

The ugly lie that I have been keeping is trying to expel itself from my body. Like a fever breaking, beads of sweat form over my brow.

Just then, my mother reappears. She whisks inside the room and quickly shuts the door behind her.

"You should see your Aunt Ellen," my mother whispers, as if somebody else could possibly hear her, *"she's wearing that same, old, tired dress that she wears at every family function."*

"That tired, yellow, too-small-dress? The one that Aunt Ellen should've retired, after she wore it to my eighth-grade graduation?" I disguise my guilt with humor.

"That's the one."

"She ought to be ashamed of herself! That's your sister," I poke.

"You know what they say: 'you can't pick your relatives'."

"Aint that *the truth! ...Is cousin Cassandra out there with her seven kids by seven different men?"*

"Seven-and-a-half."

"Shut up! Is she pregnant again?*"*

"Big-as-a-house!"

We gossip about every relative hanging from every branch of our dysfunctional family tree, like two old ladies sitting on their front stoop, talking about the people in the neighborhood. The humor eases away the anxiety that was brimming inside of me. As my mother and I gossip and giggle, she puts the finishing touches on my make-up. Then she stands behind me and adorns my neck with a b-e-a-u-t-i-f-u-l string of pearls.

"Are these the pearls *that you've been keeping in your jewelry box all these years? The ones I was warned against touching or I would draw back a nub?"*

My mother chuckles, "Yes, they are." She now closes the clasp and adjusts the strand of pearls, so that they drape against my décolletage just right. "I have been saving these pearls for you for this special *day, and I* hope *that some day, you will pass these pearls to your daughter on her wedding day."*

I run my fingers along the precious pearls, admiring my reflection in the mirror.

"Mom, there is something that I have to tell you," I say seriously. "I've been so *afraid of how you would react to the news, that I have been avoiding telling you. But now, for some reason, the moment seems perfect."*

"Shawny, you're talking like someone died."

"No mom, it's just the opposite."

My mother looks puzzled for a moment, before finally putting the pieces together: "Are you...pregnant?"

Silence...

Unsure of how to take the news, she asks, "Am I to be happy or sad about this?"

"I'm happy," I lie. "I hope you are happy, too."

"Does Isaiah know?"

"Of course. I told him as soon as I found out."

"And when was that?"

"Three months ago."

My mother's eyes bug out in surprise. "I can't believe *that you would keep something like this from me."*

"Well, I didn't intend to, but I knew that you would be upset if I told you I was pregnant out of wedlock."

"Foolish child! When did you start caring about what I thought, let alone be afraid to tell me something?"

"I don't know. It just seemed like everything was happening so fast."

She hugs me and sings: "My-baby-is-having-a-b-a-b-y!"

I feel safe inside my mother's warm, reassuring hug.

"I may not always approve of everything you do, but I promise you, I could never be disappointed. I am so very happy! Now let's get you married!" my mother exclaims.

KNOCK-KNOCK-KNOCK!

Someone knocks on the door. My mother opens the door and finds my Aunt Ellen standing there in her tired yellow dress, having a flushed expression on her heavily Fashion Fair make-up painted face. She looks at Aunt Ellen like she is the grim reaper.

"What is it Ellen?" my mother asks with reservations.

Aunt Ellen pouts her frosted-pink lips and says, "I hate to be the bearer of bad news, but the organist can't start the wedding song—the groom is M. I. A."

"WHAT?" I lift my dress train and race to the door.

My mother grabs Aunt Ellen's arm, pulls her inside and slams the door shut behind her. We both stand in front of her, waiting for an explanation.

"What do you mean, M. I. A.?" I ask frantically.

"Missing in action!" Aunt Ellen answers curtly.

"I KNOW WHAT THE HELL IT MEANS!" I snap. "WHERE THE HELL DID ISAIAH GO?"

"If I knew that, would I be in here bothering you?" Aunt Ellen asks with her hand on her hip. Not knowing what else to do, I turn to my mother, and she immediately springs into action.

"Ellen, get the best man in here a. s. a. fucking p." my mother demands. It's the first time I heard her swear since my father passed. "And don't say a word to anyone! Do you understand?"

When Aunt Ellen leaves, my mother instinctively closes her eyes and says a quick, silent prayer. Her eyes then pop open, and she musters up a display of calmness.

"Now, Shawny, don't panic. I'm sure he probably just went to the bathroom or something. There's no need to get all

162

riled up, since we don't even know what's going on. You know how dramatic *your Aunt Ellen is. She loves to stir things up. I...I," my mother says before struggling to get the words out. They seem to get caught in her throat.*

Next thing I know, my mother is hunched over clutching her chest. I reach for her, helping her over to the sofa.

"Grab my purse. Hand me my pain pills," my mother utters through the pain. Without question, or wasting a single solitary second, I quickly do as I was told.

I withdraw a bottle marked Valsatran *and a bottle marked* Captopril *from her purse, and pour her a glass of water from the pitcher on the coffee table. My mother swallows the large pills and chases it down with the water. When she's done and has regained her composure, I drill her with many questions.*

"What are these medicines? Valsatran *and* Captopril?*"*

My mother flags away my questions.

"Mother, I'm not going to ask you again, so you better be straight with me!" I say firmly.

"It's nothing."

"Mom!"

"Okay," she looks at me with faint embarrassment, "it fights heart disease...for heart attack survivors."

"Oh my God!" I blurt out before plopping down on the sofa beside her.

"Don't worry. The risk of me having another cardiovascular event is slim."

"Cardiovascular event? Do you mean heart attack?" I ask sarcastically. Aunt Ellen now storms back through the door with the best man, Rasheed, in tow.

"Rasheed, do you have something to tell us?" my mother strains through each word. Once again, she's back in action; always there when I need her—no matter how painful it is.

Rasheed now can't look me in the eye. His conscience causes him to hang his head before speaking: "No one knows where Isaiah is. He left without saying a word to anyone."

"And how long has he been gone?" I interject.

"An hour, tops."

I stand and march towards him: "And did you not think that this little piece of information was relevant to me?"

Rasheed now looks like a deer caught in headlights.

"I didn't start to get concerned until most of the guests had been seated. When Isaiah still hadn't shown up, I wasn't sure if I should come to you and get you all upset; without being sure that he wasn't coming back. But then I got this text message, and I knew something definitely was wrong. Your Aunt Ellen came and got me, and here I am."

"And what did the text message say?" I ask hesitantly. Rasheed hands me his two-way pager and I hit the "read" button. My mother and Aunt Ellen crowd around me, and we all read the message simultaneously. It reads: "I know everything. I tried, but I can't live a lie!"

I throw the two-way pager down, and watch it crack against the floor. I look up at Rasheed and demand, "YOU BETTER *GO OUT THERE AND LOOK FOR THAT MAN AS IF YOUR* LIFE *DEPENDED ON IT! AND* DON'T *YOU EVEN* THINK *ABOUT COMING BACK WITHOUT HIM, OR I SWEAR I WILL GO* POSTAL *UP IN HERE! THIS IS MY* FUCKING *WEDDING DAY! HOW IN THE* HELL *CAN THAT* BASTARD *LEAVE ME HANGING?"*

As Rasheed exits, several members of my wedding party storms into the room, including my best friend from college, Tristan. Tristan is at the head of the pack of people who want to know what in the hell was going on, and I don't know what to tell them.

"Do you want me to go outside and make an announcement?" Aunt Ellen asks.

"Nobody's making any damn announcements! There will be a wedding today, whether Isaiah likes it...or not!"

But I was wrong.

And the worse thing of all is that, in all the commotion, no one notices that my mother has fallen against the sofa, and is no longer breathing.

In the course of one day, I lose my fiancé, and my mother.

A week later, I have an abortion...

I would've had a girl...

I couldn't live the lie.

"Ma'am...Ma'am."

TAP-TAP-TAP.

164

"Ma'am!"

TAP-TAP-TAP-TAP-TAP.

I feel warm light on my face.
The inside of my eyelids register the brightness.
My eyes pop open, and the white light hits me.
Startles me back to consciousness.
Behind the beam of light, I see a hand holding a flashlight.
Behind the hand, I make out the image of a black shirt.
A silver badge.

TAP-TAP-TAP.

The image becomes clearer, and I begin to realize that I am sitting in my car. I roll down the driver's side window.
"Ma'am, do you know you've crashed into a stop sign?" The cop informs me.
I'm hunched over the steering wheel.
My neck is stiff.
My head aches.
My chest feels like somebody dropped a ton of bricks on me. Every time I take a breath, I feel like a knife is being jammed into my chest. I adjust my posture, and slowly attempt to sit up in the seat.
"E-x-c-u-s-e me?" I say.
My words slur.
My breath is foul.
I taste remnants of scotch.
I feel slobber in the corner of my mouth, and I wipe it away with the back of my hand.
"Are you aware that you've been in an accident? Are you hurt? Can you move at all?"
I rub my eyes, trying to see things through my blurred vision.
I slowly look around...
I am two blocks away from *Lou and Choos* bar. The right side, front fender of my brand-new *Nissan* "Maxima" is smashed around a stop sign. Half of my car is on the sidewalk; the other half is leaning into the street.
I now beat up the steering wheel, hysterically.
Then I begin to laugh.

Laughter masks the awful pain that is beginning to unearth from inside of me.

The pain of the accident.

The pain of my memories.

The pain left from Manny.

My laughter echoes defeat.

"I give up," I whisper, a whisper so low, that only I can hear the words.

My head bobs and falls back onto the headrest.

My eyes roll to the back of my head.

My eyelids flutter shut.

The police officer now looks at me with full of concern. He places his fingers against my carotid artery, the major artery of the neck that supplies blood to the head.

"Ma'am, I'm going to call an ambulance," the cop indicates, as he presses the "talk" button on the mini radio transmitter that's clipped to his shirt: "I got a 901-T."

A few seconds passes by before dispatch responds to the call: "What's your location?" the dispatcher asks.

"17th and Greene."

"901-K." The ambulance has been dispatched.

The police officer looks back at me.

My breath is shallow. I whisper, "I'm so tired. I just want to close my eyes and sleep."

He carefully grabs my hand gently, but firmly says, "Ma'am, hang in there. The ambulance is on the way."

My eyelids grow heavy.

The darkness begins to swallows me.

In my state of delirium I whisper, "I need to speak to Isaiah."

"Let's get you to a hospital, get you taken cared of, and then you can contact anybody you want."

"I *need* to speak to *Isaiah!*" I say; full of venom.

"Ma'am, do you know what you're saying?" the cop asks, puzzled.

"I need Isaiah. He's at *Oakview Estates. Oakview* on *33rd* and *Lehigh.*"

The police officer brow furrows: "What did you say?"

"Isaiah...he's...at Oakview."

"Ma'am, I think you're delirious. Do you know what you're saying? Oakview is a cemetery."

"Don't you think I know that? I'm the one who *put* him there..."

My breathing is shallow.

"...I killed Isaiah."

…I still can't sleep.

It's long past midnight, and ever since Cornelius woke me up from my nightmare, I've been in the den practicing my golf swing.

It clears my head.

I swing the putter with gentle precision, and it taps the white *Dior* golf ball. The ball slowly rolls down the 12-foot stretch of *Sharper Image's* fake, green grass, and sinks into the hole. The mechanism pops the ball back out of the hole, and it rolls back towards me.

I swing the iron, and tap the ball again.

It rolls away from me and plops into the hole; pops back out and comes back to me.

I position the ball and hit it once again.

I do this over-and-over-and-over again.

An hour passes by, the clock chimes once, and I am *still* abusing the ball. It comes back time-and-time again, awaiting more punishment.

When I first returned home from having dinner with Melanie and Quincy last night, I headed straight for the shower, then crawled into bed, and made a futile attempt at sleep.

But, after the nightmare, sleep didn't come.

I kept thinking of Melanie, and then the Morgan Baxter fiasco kept *popping* inside my head.

The Baxter failure has me worrying about *Capital Appreciation's* bottom line. Because I was so confident that the Morgan Baxter deal was sealed, I prematurely invested the company's additional assets. My plan was to replace the funds when the deal was finalized. Now that the deal isn't happening, I have to find a way to replace all of that money.

I tried a little yoga.

I stood in the middle of my bedroom, in mountain posture for ten minutes, trying to banish the negative energy; I hummed, chanted and *"Nam myoho renge kyo'd"*, but that didn't help either. So I escaped to my den, and have been hitting at this ball ever since.

For the first time in my life, I am uncertain.

This is *not* a good feeling!

It was only a year ago that I was ranked one of the fifty most-powerful, up-and-coming women executives in the U.S., by *Fortune* magazine. Before then, my firm, *Capital Appreciation,* had a quasi-obscurity. It wasn't until an editor at *Fortune* had met me at a *Harvard Alumni* function that my name got any recognition.

I was vaulted to the *highest* levels of the corporate hierarchy! After the article in *Fortune,* I became one of the few Venture Capitalists in the Tri-state area who was recognized by my first name only.

I became a pseudo-celebrity.

It was even rumored that one day I would move on to politics.

The question on everybody's lips was whether my world-wind success would last. After word of the failed Morgan Baxter deal, and news of my controversial investments hits the wire, the answer to the question of my longevity is doubtful. It won't be long before these vaguely-based opinions will be reflected in the press.

Just as my earnings made headlines, so will my decline...

I drop the golf club onto the soft turf. My bare feet slap against the marble floor as I walk to my desk. I boot up my accounting software, and hack away at the figures. I examine my skewed business portfolio, revenues, operating earnings, corporate investments, company reports, etc.

I made a huge error in asserting the Morgan Baxter deal. I knew that the prodigious strength of a partnership with Baxter would keep my firm looking respectable. But as I sum up the damaging mathematics on my accounting software, and hedge the figure against the potential earnings of my investments, the outcome is condemning.

If my investments don't pay off soon—I'll be in jeopardy.

What can I do to make my firm au courant again? It's a question of whether I can trade-off the bottom line for buzz. *How can I create a higher profile with lower-profit margin? Can I translate my hard work and innovative ideas into profits and market shares? Will I be in any shape to thrive in this brutally competitive world?*

If *Capital Appreciation* can't survive this financial setback, then I suspect that there must have been something wrong with the strategy that I created in the beginning.

Or a weakness in execution.

This is suspicion that I will never confirm. It will only serve to further damage the company, hurt the employees' confidence, sales efforts and stock price.

So I must keep quiet.

Forty-five minutes later, the railing in front of us is filled with empty beer bottles and shot glasses. By this time, E and I are seriously drunk, and we don't give a *fuck!* A hip-hop classic from *Slick Rick* and *Doug E. Fresh* blasts from the speakers, and E and I sing together: *"LA-DI-DA-DI, WE CAME TO PARTY. WE DON'T CAUSE TROUBLE. WE DON'T BOTHER NOBODY."*

We sing along to every song, and talk until our voices are hoarse from yelling over the music. E then turns to me.

"Mel, you know what?"

"What?"

"You're my best friend."

"Nigga, I know that," I say as I bop my head to the hip-hop beat. I am floating.

"I got a question for you," E says. The beat of the conversation changes. It slows down. Gets serious. He hesitates and asks, "…What do you want?"

I look at E with a puzzled expression: "What do you mean?"

"Out of life. What do you want?"

"I never really thought about it. I just take things, one day at a time."

"Well, do you want to work for the *Water Department,* reading meters all your life?"

"Hell no!"

"What do you want then?"

I shrug my shoulders.

Take a sip of my rum and coke.

"What about the women?" E now asks.

"What women?"

"The women you *mess* around with."

"What about them? E, I don't like the direction this conversation is going in," I say, getting defensive. This conversation is starting to turn into an interrogation.

"Do you plan on being with women for the rest of your life?"

"E, I don't know. *Why?* What *difference* does it make?"

"I wanna know."

"Well, I *don't* want to talk about it!" I feel an argument brewing.

"Well, I *wanna* know!"

"E, you're acting stupid," I reply and turn around on my stool; facing the opposite direction.

"No, you're *acting* stupid."

I spin back around and face E: "Why are we *even* having this conversation? We were just chillin' a second ago. Now you're going *Oprah Winfrey* on me."

"Because, all we ever do *is* chill. I'm *tired* of spinning my wheels with you. I need to move forward."

"Well, move forward then," I say stubbornly.

"Let me explain something to you, Melanie. Tonight, my man, Will offered me an opportunity of a lifetime. If I can pull this thing off, I stand to make a lot of money, and I can finally go legit; like I always planned. Do you think I want to be a *hustler* all my life? Is *that* what you think? That we can go on playing *Xbox* in your living room until the end of time. Mel, you *gotta* have a plan."

"Sounds like you got yourself a pretty good plan—why are you worried 'bout me?"

"Because, I...I...um...because my plan includes *you,* stupid!" E blurts out.

I *slam* my glass down.

Rum and coke splatters everywhere.

"Dammit, E, don't do this."

"Why not?" his hazel-green eyes now search mine.

"Because."

"Because what?"

"Because if we go there, then that means that *everything* in my life until this point has been one big lie! You can't *expect* me to be *gay* one day and *straight* the next, just because you want us to ride off in the sunset together.

"What about *all* the women I've been with? What about that? Do you think this is all just a *fucking* illusion? This is who...I...am!"

172

"Bullshit! I *refuse* to believe that! I see the way you look at me."

"You see what you *want* to see," I snap.

"I see the truth."

And just like that, E's managed to rip my fucking world apart. It was as if this whole time...my whole life, I had been living in a dream, and tonight would be the night that E would force me to take ownership of my feelings.

But that would be utterly impossible without dredging up all the pain, and hurt. Pain that has existed on the inside for so long.

Pain that I buried.

Until now.

E opened his mouth, and like a shovel, dug up all my layers and layers of bullshit!

Nobody says a another word.

We are at a standoff

The hip-hop song ends.

A slow groove begins to play.

Diffuses the tension.

The bass line is slow and sexy. Violins and synthesized melodies dance together and form perfect harmonies.

E confesses, "Do you know that I had to get *drunk* tonight? Because otherwise, I wouldn't have the courage to tell you something."

"Tell me what?"

"I can't tell you...I have to show you. Come with me," E commands. He now grabs my arm and leads me down the stairs to the dance floor.

I stand there as *stiff* as a board.

I am ashamed to admit that I've never slow danced before.

"It's okay," E says patiently, leading me to the center of the floor. "Close your eyes."

I close my eyes.

"Really listen to the music."

I listen closely.

The bass *pounds* inside my chest.

Like a heartbeat.

It feels like the melodies are flowing through me.

"Now, wrap your arms around my shoulders."

I slowly place my arms around E's shoulders.

"Don't think about anything else."

He now pulls me close.

The warmth of E's body surrounds me like a blanket.

I lay my head against his chest.

I can feel E's heartbeat racing a mile a minute.

He wraps his arms around me.

It's the first time I have *ever* been in the arms of a man. E feels strong. Solid. His chest is firm. E's scent is warm. Heat escapes from his body and penetrates me. E's hands then travel up-and-down my back, and just when I feel like we can't get any closer, he holds me tighter.

We sway to the rhythm of the *intoxicating* groove.

As soon as our heartbeats synchronize, *Prince's* soulful falsetto voice pours *The One* from the speakers; into the atmosphere surrounding us.

Prince sings, and it's like he's singing through E, to me: *"If you're looking for the man that will walk away from responsibility...I aint the one."*

E now holds me as if he never wants to let go.

"If you're looking for the brother that will treat you like anything but a queen...I ain't the one."

E's hand searches for mine.

Prince continues to sing to me.

Then E stops dancing. He locks eyes with mine and says, "I can't go on just being your friend. Every time I come over to your house, it *kills* me not to be able to touch you, and to hold and kiss you. Mel, I want to be the man in your life." He then leans over and whispers softly in my ear, "If you feel the same way that I do, I need you to tell me right now."

The club is barren, except for a few men at the bar, who look like they're engaged in a heavy business discussion. One of the men at the bar looks up at me.

He's a cutie pie.

The man smiles at me.

Diamond and China Doll are *still* hangin' around, standin' by the door of the dressin' room. They must be waitin' for the men at the bar, tryna score a last minute trick.

I walk past the bar on my way to the employee exit.

The house lights are low.

The cleanin' crew is sweepin' up.

Trish has gone home.

I look at the clock over the bar. It reads "5 AM". *No wonder nobody else is around.* I've been *fuckin'* around wit' "Mike B.", and lost track of the time.

Smitty's massive *Shrek*-like frame bounds its way over to me. He looks like he has good news for me. I guess the tip I gave him earlier has paid off.

"Mekka, I have a gentleman waiting for you in the champagne room. He's been hanging around all night."

"What's the 411."

"I had one of the dancers check the guy out real thorough. Dude dropped about five-hundred dollars on her earlier. He's a big oilman from Houston. Old money. Only in town for one evening, and he's been requesting to see a lady of the darker persuasion, if you know what I mean."

"This cat is White?"

"White and big-as-a-house. Dude must weigh over four-hundred pounds. Makes me look small."

"Damn, he *must* be huge."

Smitty looks slightly offended at my comment. He's one of those big, fat men who classify themselves as "husky", but Smitty is fat! He's just in denial

Smitty adds, "He's been drinking whiskey all night, so he's pretty full. Even scored coke a couple of times."

If there's one thing that I've learned along the way, it's that a man that's been drinkin' and doin' coke all night, *can't* get it up. This should be a pretty easy.

"I'll meet him. Sure he's not 5-O? Has he discussed cash wit' you?"

"He's straight. Even dropped his drawers for one girl earlier tonight, just to prove he wasn't law enforcement."

"Cool. I'll take it from here."

Like eggs, I *scramble* to the champagne room. The cutie pie at the bar studies me from head-to-toe. He examines the way I walk. The way I flip my hair over my shoulder. Looks at me obscurely. Almost wit' scrutiny. Then nonchalantly turns away, and rejoins his discussion.

Usually men look at me like a sexual object, but cutie pie's eyes looked like he was searching for something other than sex.

Can't quite put my finger on it.

I feel weird for a second, and then I brush it off. If I tried to try to figure out every man that looked at me a certain way, then I wouldn't have time to do shit else.

Inside the champagne room sits the biggest man I've ever met in real life. Not only is he fat, but he has the stature of that wrestler, *Andre the Giant.* A big, grizzly bear of a man wit' long brown hair and a long beard like *ZZ Top.* The trick looks like he's born and bred to ride a *Harley Davidson.*

Jammed in the pocket of his lower gum is a big wad of chewing tobacco. He now stares at me like a hunter observin' a fawn.

"You got a hairy bush?" the fat man asks. "I like a hairy bush."

"No. Bare as a baby's bottom"

"You got one of them shaved pussies?"

I nod my head.

"Well, come here, let me get a closer look at you."

I approach him.

I then stand there and let the obese trick examine me wit' his eyes. I now rub my fingers together slowly while lookin' in his eyes, in a gesture that lets him know that he's got to pay-to-play. The fat man then digs in his pocket, and tosses a money clip wit' the outline of the state of Texas engraved on it.

The clip is *stuffed* to its capacity!

"Take what you need, sugar."

I pull two Gs from the clip. Shit, I should've taken more, but I didn't want to *fuck* myself by bein' greedy. My mama always said, *"Don't get greedy, 'cause that's when you fuck up. Always play it safe. Be smart. Trickin' is an art form, just like any other."*

"Now get over here, sugar and lift up that dress," the trick commands.

I tuck the money into the linin' of my *Louis Vuitton* handbag, next to the three Gs that Trish gave me earlier. I walk over to the big, grizzly bear, sittin' on the sofa. He spreads his tree stump legs, and motions me with his fingers to step a little closer.

I stand between his legs.

The trick slides his hand between my thighs, and slowly crawls his fingers up towards my crotch.

"Turn round."

I turn around.

He then lifts my dress up around my waist, and rubs my backside.

"L-o-r-d hammercy, sugar! You got an *ass* that a man could sit his drink on! Turn back around and let me see that pretty face of yours."

I turn back around to face him.

"Here's what I want you to do. I want you to cock that leg up right onto my shoulder. Can you do that for me, sugar?"

I cock my leg up and place it on his shoulder, so that my thick thigh is right up against the trick's cheek.

"Now, here's what I need you to do next. I'm gonna hand you a bullet of coke. Open the bullet and sprinkle some dust onto your thigh."

I do as he says.

The fat man turns so that he's facin' my thigh. Takes a long, loud snort of the line, then follows it up by lickin' the residue.

"Now, unbuckle my pants, pull out my *cock*, and show daddy what you can do with that thing."

I reach under the big, grizzly bear's jellyroll, tug open his gaudy, gold belt buckle, and unzip his *Wranglers*. I dig under the huge man's gut, and search for his dick between the creases.

I am met by a rank, musty odor.

When I finally find his sweaty, shriveled up dick, it's about the size of my pinky finger. I make tweezers out of my thumb and pointer finger, and hold the man's tiny, smelly dick between my fingertips like a straw.

"Don't be shy. Put that *cock* in your mouth."

I lean in closer, and the *funk* hits me full force!

I have to keep myself from gaggin'.

When I touch the tip of his dick wit' my tongue, I taste remnants of old piss. I feel the acid in my stomach bubble up.

My gag reflex contracts, releases, contracts, then releases.

I feel like I'm 'bout to upchuck in dude's lap. He then places his hand on the back of my head and shoves it in his lap. The big, grizzly bear's sweaty belly is pressed against my forehead.

"Suck it. Wrap those *chocolate* lips around my *cock,* sugar."

I take the tip of my tongue and flicker it against the side of his pencil-sized dick, barely touchin' it wit' my tongue.

He grunts and groans.

The trick is tryin' his damndest to get it up, but the fool's so full of coke and whiskey, that he can't get a hard on.

"Fuck, girl, *can't* you do no better 'n that? I heard you was a r-e-a-l pro-fessional," he says, as the man continues to pump his limp dick against my lips, with no results.

This goes on for about twenty minutes.

Then, the big, grizzly man finally blows his load, and soaks my face wit' his funky spunk.

It smells like trash-truck juice!

"L-o-r-d hammercy, girl! You are a gift on God's green earth."

Dude now tosses a white handkerchief in my face. I rush to the locker room and wash the sticky, smelly spooge off of my face, but some smells leave an indelible mark in your brain. I can't wash my face enough times to *rid* myself of the stench!

When I get done cleanin' up, I make tracks to the nearest exit. I don't even bother to look around for Smitty, who usually waits around for me, and walks me to my car.

I push open the emergency exit door, and step out to the dimly lit parking lot.

Dusk is turnin' to dawn.

I dig in my purse, searchin' for my car remote. My hand wades through the contents: tubes of lipstick, breath mints, wads of cash, sunglasses, spare change—and eventually, reaches the bottom linin' where my car remote is.

I yank it from the purse, lose my grip on the remote, and it falls to the ground. When I bend over to pick it up, I hear footsteps behind me.

I turn to see who it is.

But it's too late.

A heavy object comes *crashin'* down on the back of my head wit' blunt force.

I fall back onto the concrete.

Drop my purse.

The contents spill onto the pavement.

I am hit again.

And again.

And again.

I scream!

A sharp pain *shoots* through my skull. A river of blood runs down my forehead—spills into my left eye. I hold my arms up, tryna block my head from another attack, and I am kicked in the face. The sole of a high-heeled shoe comes *crashin'* down against my lips and nose. Then another shoe slams into my stomach.

I hear voices.

Whispers.

I am beginnin' to lose consciousness.

Everything becomes shadows.

A blur.

I see the silhouette of a hand reachin' towards my neck. My new necklace from *Tiffany's* is violently ripped from my throat.

"BITCH!" I hear Diamond's voice say. She jams her stiletto heel into my shoulder. "Get the bracelet," Diamond then says.

China Doll snatches my bracelet from around my wrist, steps on it, applies all of her weight and cracks my wrist bone.

I scream out in agony!

My pink diamond ring is now pulled off of my finger.

"FUCK YOU!" I hear China Doll yell. Then she spits in my face.

My pocketbook disappears.

I hear the door of the club burst open.

179

Heavy footsteps run towards me.
I hear Diamond and China Doll run off.
"Ma'am, are you okay?" I hear a man's voice say.
I then feel a strong hand holdin' my head up.
The other hand cups my face.
He wipes the blood drippin' from my eyes wit' his shirt.
I see the shadow of the man's face.
The cutie pie that had been watchin' me from the bar.
He immediately pulls out his cell phone.
Pushes three buttons: 911.
Devastation. Brutilization. Elimination.
I fade to black....

GLOSSARY

5-O - Police
Aiiight - Alright
A & R - Artists and Repetoire
A half - Thirty minutes
Arroz con pollo - Rice with chicken
Au courant - Fully familiar
Ballers, Shot-callers - Power players
Bling - Diamonds, jewelry
Booty call - A phone call for sex
Break you off - To give someone money
Bricks - Cocaine
Benjamins, C-note - One-hundred dollars
Catch it - About to get hurt
Chit-chat - Talking
Chu - You
COO - Chief Operating Officer
Cooch, Coochie - Vagina
Coupla - Couple of
Crib - Apartment
Dat - That
Dis - Disrespect
Do-the-damn-thang - To proceed with enthusiasm
Dunno - Don't know
Du-rag - Stocking cap
Dyke, Lesbo - Lesbian
Errythang - Everything
'Em, Nem - Them/And them
Freak on - Sex
Flippin' - Selling drugs
Funky spunk, spooge - Semen
Gassed up - Overly convince
Gs - Thousands
Gumby - Sloped haircut
Hateration - Hatred
Herre - Here
High post - Conceited
Hood rat - a female who's a lowlife

Kicked it - Hung out
Kinda - Kind of
Layin' the pipe - Penetrating
Lemme - Let me
Mademoiselle - Miss
Minute - Short period of time
Mo' - More
Mos' def - Most definitely
Mule - A drug transporter
My bad - Mistake
New growth - Hair growth
Nip-and-tuck - Plastic surgery
Notha - Another
O' - Of
Outta - Out of
Pimped-out - Flamboyant
Po' - Poor
Poo-putt - Faggot
Press - Move forward
Press-and-curl - Hair styling techniques
Pushin' - Driving
Que sera sera - Such as life
Right-quick - Fast
'Round - Around
'Round-the-way girl - Local neighborhood urban girl
Sexified - Very appealing
Sho' nuff - Sure enough
Slapping fives - Handshakes
Stuck-on-stupid - To be idiotic
That's what's up - The real dea
Trife - Trifling
Trippin' - Acting crazy
Trickin' - Prostituting
Tryna - Trying to
VIP - Very important person
Weed - Marijuana
Whachu - What you
Whoop - To beat up/Inflict pain
Wild-out - To start a fight
Wife beater - Tank top
Yo' - Your

Excerpts from *AND GOD CREATED WOMAN* by
MIKA MILLER
A GHETTOHEAT® PRODUCTION

MELANIE

All I'm trying to do is *bust* a nut this morning, and shit keeps fuckin' with me. Just as I'm 'bout to get my *shit* off to my favorite DVD *Rumpshakers and Shake Dancin'*, part 3, (yeah, I got parts 1 and 2) the damn thing freezes in my DVD player, right at my favorite part. Damn, can't I *masturbate* in peace?

I pull my fingers out of my crotch, and I get up with sticky-icky-icky juice still on my fingertips. I go over to my entertainment center to eject the DVD, so that I can clean it off with the oversized wife beater I'm wearing. I clean the smudges off with my shirt, insert the DVD back into the player, and hop back onto the bed.

The DVD begins to play. I hit scene selection, so that I can pick up right where I left off. Once again, loose booties start *clappin'* on the screen! Pussies start *poppin'* in my face! I prop my head up against a pillow. Spread my legs. Lick my fingers. Slide my hand back down to my crotch. Get to rubbin'…

My phone rings. Ain't this a *bitch!*

SHAWN

The last thing I solidly remember is fucking…Pablo? …Carlos? …Manny, or *whatever* his name is…then I left *Lou and Choos*…am I remembering correctly? …Did I crash my car? …Did I wake up in the emergency room? And now…I'm in a prison holding area.

The question is, how in the *hell* did I end up here? I stare at the ceiling of the cold, musty jail, and try to remember the events of this past weekend. I sift through the alcohol-induced haze, and start to recall bits and pieces of what happened. I metaphysically trace my steps back to the car accident.

The first thing I remember is, the police officer that found me. I remember the sounds of the siren, as I was taken to the hospital's emergency room for observation.

This morning, when the doctor finally cleared me for discharge, I was immediately taken into police custody. I was charged with "driving under the influence", and learned that my license would be revoked. But that wasn't the worst part.

The worst part was when the officer read me my rights, told me to turn around, for me to place my hands behind my back, and was restrained by the cold, steel handcuffs; closing shut around my wrists.

Talk about shame? I was so ashamed to be seen as I was escorted down the halls of the hospital, taken onto the elevator and walked out of the lobby. When we exited the building, the police squad car was parked right out front.

I remember a little boy and his mother walking towards me holding hands. When the boy saw me in handcuffs, he pointed at me, and I heard him ask his mother, "Mommy, is she *going* to jail?" The little boy's mother quickly shushed him, averted making eye contact with me, and pulled her son inside the hospital.

I was humiliated. And had no one to blame but myself.

TRISTAN

5:00 A.M. My bedroom television is tuned to *CNN*. The stock market opens like a bull. *CNN's* "Market Watch" informs me that U.S. stock futures are indicating a modest rebound, *Dow* futures edged up 22 points to 10,913, *NASDAQ* 100 futures rose 8.5 points to 1,736, while *S & P* 500 futures rose 3.30 points to 1,287.

Though the market lacks a true catalyst, my forecast is that it will rally to new highs, due to a better-than-I-expected performance on Friday, before market closing at 4 PM. This gives me a sliver of hope that my lackluster investments will, at least, remain calm, if not thrive in the face of my adversity. The thought of no longer being in financial jeopardy is an inspiration to me.

However, no sooner than I'm lifted up into the clouds of prospective profitability, market analyst, Maria Baritoromo, hits the screen like the financial cougar she is, and informs me that the *Dow Jones Industrial Average* fell 41 points to 10,854. The *NASDAQ Composite Index* tumbled to a two-week low, sliding 23 points to 2,279, while the *S & P 500 Index* dropped 4.99 points to 1,277. My bubble is busted. And I fall back to earth.

MEKKA

I been *yellin'* at nurses *a-l-l* morning long. How many times do I have to tell these *stupid-ass* nurses to leave me the *fuck* alone, and let me *be,* goddammit? I keep thinkin' of the scene from that movie, *The Color Purple,* when "Shug Avery" shows up on "Celie's" doorstep, sick as hell, and "Albert" is tryna do the best he can to make her feel better. And "Shug" screams at Albert: "Turn loose my goddamn arm."

I feel like "Shug". That's exactly how I feel. Just as soon as I get ready to drift back to sleep, another nurse enters my hospital room. This one looks like she *just* graduated from high school. The nurse is a pale-faced, white chick wit' short red hair and freckles. She enters the room like *Molly Ringwald,* and I just want to *punch* her in the face for bein' so *fuckin'* chipper this *fuckin'* early in the *fuckin'* morning!

"And how is my patient doing this morning?" the nurse asks wit' a broad smile.

"How the *fuck* does it look like I'm doin'?"

"O-o-o-h, I see somebody woke up on the wrong side of the bed. But that's understandable, Miss Mekka, considering the circumstances. I just wanted to check on you and see how you are feeling?"

I don't answer. I stare at her…. Like they used to say back in my day, "I grit on her" and don't blink. My eyes *dare* her to say anotha *fuckin'* word.

The nurse is now reluctant, but she forges ahead.

"O-k-a-y, why don't I check your bandages."

"Whateva!"

"Molly Ringwald" sits her clipboard down onto the bedside table, and prepares to strap that thing 'round my arm that checks your blood pressure. When she's done, the nurse pulls a pen from the chest pocket of her jacket, and jots something down on her clipboard.

Then she pulls out that thing wit' the light, and checks my left eye. My right eye is all bandaged up.

"Miss Mekka, if you'll follow my finger with your eye, I can check to see if your vision has been affected." She holds up the pointer finger of her right hand in the air, and takes the posture as if she is 'bout to conduct an orchestra.

Gimme a *fuckin'* break!

185

An excerpt from ***GHETTOHEAT*®** by
HICKSON
A GHETTOHEAT® PRODUCTION

GHETTOHEAT®

S-S-S-S-S-S-S!
Can you feel it? Scaldin' breath of frisky spirits
Surroundin' you in the streets
The intensity
S-S-S-S-S-S-S!
That's GHETTOHEAT®!
The energy – Electric sparks
Better watch ya back after dark!
Dogs bark – Cats hiss
Rank smells of trash and piss
Internalize – Realize
No surprise – Naughty spirits frolic in disguise
S-S-S-S-S-S-S!
INTENSITY: CLIMBIN'! CLIMBIN'! CLIMBIN'! CLIMBIN'!
GHETTOHEAT®: RISIN'! RISIN'! RISIN'! RISIN'!

Streets is watchin'
Hoes talkin' – Thugs stalkin'
POW! POW! POW!
Start speed-walkin'!
Heggies down – Rob that clown
Snatch his stash – Jet downtown
El Barrio – Spanish Harlem:

"MIRA, NO! WE DON'T WANNO PROBLEM!"

Bullets graze – I'm not amazed
GHETTOHEAT®!
Niggas start blazin'
Air's scathin' – Gangs blood-bathin'
Five-O's misbehavin' – Wifey's rantin'-n-ravin'!
My left: The Bloods – My right: The Crips
Niggas start prayin' – Murk-out in ya whip!

186

Internalize – Realize
No surprise – Naughty spirits frolic in disguise
S-S-S-S-S-S-S!
INTENSITY: CLIMBIN'! CLIMBIN'! CLIMBIN'! CLIMBIN'!
GHETTOHEAT®: RISIN'! RISIN'! RISIN'! RISIN'!

Mean hoodlums – Plottin' schemes
A swoop-down – 'Bout to rob me – Seems like a bad dream
Thugs around – It's goin' down
'BOUT TO BE SOME SHIT!
But I'm ghetto – Know how to spit
Gully mentality – Thinkin' of reality of planned-out casualty
I fake wit' the trickery:
"ASS-ALAMUALAIKUM"

"STICK 'EM UP!"

"YO, DON'T FUCK WIT' HIM – HE'S MUSLIM!"

Flipped script wit' quickness
Changed demeanor – The swiftness
Not dimwitted – Felt the flames of evil spirits!
Hid chain in shirt – I don't catch pain – Don't get hurt
No desire gettin' burnt by the fire
Thermometer soars, yo, higher-and-higher
In the PRO-JECTS – Fightin' to protect ya neck
Gotta earn respect – Defend ya rep
Or BEAT-DOWNS you'll collect
The furor – The fever – My gun – My cleaver
Bitches brewin' – Slits a-stewin'
Sheets roastin' – Champagne toastin' – Gangstas boastin':

"The ghetto – Nuthin's mellow
The ghetto – Cries in falsetto
The ghetto – A dream bordello
The ghetto – Hotter than Soweto"

Internalize – Realize
No surprise – Naughty spirits frolic in disguise
S-S-S-S-S-S-S!
INTENSITY: CLIMBIN'! CLIMBIN'! CLIMBIN'! CLIMBIN'!
GHETTOHEAT®: RISIN'! RISIN'! RISIN'! RISIN'!

Red-hot hustlers – Broilin' at the spot
Boilin' alcohol – The lucky crackpot
Streets a-scorchin' – Crackheads torchin'
Stems ignited – Junkies delighted
Money's flowin' – Pusherman's excited
The first and fifteenth: BLOCK-HUGGERS' JUNETEENTH!
Comin' ya way – Take ya benefits today
Intoxication – Self-medication – The air's dense
Ghetto-suffocation – Volcanic maniacs attackin'
Cash stackin' – Niggas packin' – Daddy Rock's mackin':

"The ghetto – Nuthin's mellow
The ghetto – Cries in falsetto
The ghetto – A dream bordello
The ghetto – Hotter than Soweto"

BedStuy – Do or die

BUCK! BUCK! BUCK! BUCK!

They don't give a FUCK!
In The Bronx – You'll fry – Tossin' lye – WATCH YA EYES!

Walk straight – Tunnel vision – False move – Bad decision
So hot – Starts to drizzle – Steamy sidewalks – Begin to sizzle
HOT-TO-DEF! Intense GHETTOHEAT®

"DO YOU FEEL IT? DO YOU FEEL IT?"
"THE HOTNESS IN THE STREETS!!!™"

So hot – Got ya mase?
Too hot – PEPPER SPRAYIN' IN A NIGGA'S FACE!
The Madness – Sadness
Don't you know the flare of street-glow?
OH!
Meltingly – Swelteringly
S-S-S-S-S-S-S!
HOOD IN-FER-NO!
Internalize – Realize
No surprise – Naughty spirits frolic in disguise
S-S-S-S-S-S-S!
INTENSITY: CLIMBIN'! CLIMBIN'! CLIMBIN'! CLIMBIN'!
GHETTOHEAT®: RISIN'! RISIN'! RISIN'! RISIN'!

INTENSITY: CLIMBIN'! CLIMBIN'! CLIMBIN'! CLIMBIN'!
GHETTOHEAT®: RISIN'! RISIN'! RISIN'! RISIN'!
S-S-S-S-S-S-S!

An excerpt from ***HARDER*** by
SHA
A GHETTOHEAT® PRODUCTION

When I finally arrived back home, Tony was heated. I didn't even realize I was out that long.

"Where the *fuck* you been, Kai?!" he yelled as I walked through the door.

"I went to the range and then shopping. I had a lot on my mind to clear and I just needed to get away. Damn, is there a law against that?"

"Nah, ain't no law, shorty! Just watch yaself, cuz if I finds out different, we gonna have major problems."

Tony was taking on a "Rico" tone with me that I did not like whatsoever.

"Who the *fuck* is you talking to, Tony? I *know* it ain't me. Ya better keep that *shit* in ya back pocket before you come at me with it."

I had never seen Tony like this before, and it made me very upset. I knew I had to calm down, before I said something that I would live to regret.

"Oh word? It's like that, Kai? Fuck you forget or something? This here is *my* house! *I'm* the star, baby girl! You *used* to be the co-star, but now you just another *fucking* spectator! Show over, get the *fuck* out!"

Just when I thought things couldn't get any worse!

"Get the fuck out? You get mad over some *bullshit* and now it's 'get the fuck out'? Tony, think about that shit for a minute." I started talking slowly and softly. "I'm ya 'co-star' alright, but do you *know* what that means? ...It means, everything you own, *I* own. All the work you put in, I put in, too.

"You forget who sees over the cooks and make sure ya deliveries are made on time? That's me, *motherfucker*. You *sure* you wanna have me running the street with all ya info, baby boy?"

That weird laugh echoed out of me again. This time, it set Tony off. He grabbed me by my throat, and *threw* me into the hard brick wall! When I hit the floor, Tony started to strangle me as he screamed, "BABY BOY?! BABY BOY? HUH? YOU FUCK THAT NIGGA?! HUH?! DON'T YOU *EVA* IN YA LIFE CALL ME 'BABY BOY' AGAIN, YOU FUCKING SLUT!"

Tony let go, and I hit the floor again. It took all the air I had in me, but I managed.

"Tony-I-ain't-fuckin'-nobody!"

"Oh word? You come in here acting brand-new, and you ain't *fucking* nobody? We'll see!"

Tony then picked me up by my waist and ripped my jeans off. He proceeded to remove my panties. I didn't know what Tony was up to, until he threw me onto the couch. Tony then spread my legs wide-open, as he stuck three fingers in me at the same time.

I screamed in pain...

Tony bowed his head in regret.

"I'm sorry, Kai," was all that he said, before Tony left the house for the night. I laid there until he came back early the next day. When Tony walked in the house, I'd pretended to be asleep, as he started to play with my hair.

"Kai, I hope you're listening to me. You know shit's been kinda hard since *Five Points*. You know it's hard knowing that I can't make love to you. I be seeing how dudes look at you and shit. I know your type, ma, you got the sex drive of a 18-year-old man."

I stifled a giggle.

"I just be thinking when you're gone, you out there getting the only thing I *can't* give you. I know you've been on my side since I came back home, but I still be bugging. You're a trooper, baby and that's why I love you. Please don't leave me—I need you. All this shit, is 'cause of you. I know that, ma-ma; I love you."

That became my driving force. The man that ran Queens *needed* me. It's true that behind every great man, was a great woman. I wanted to go down in history as being the greatest.

Tony would be my link to the city. I already had him in my back pocket, so that meant I had Queens in my back pocket! All I needed was the other four boroughs to fall in line.

Sure, I would step on some toes, but I would stand to be retired at twenty-five—with enough money to finance my life, for the rest of my life. AJ was right, but I had a point to prove, and money to make! After that was done, I would be game to anything else.

I started stashing away as much money as I could. I told Tony that I would no longer sleep at his house, since he put his hands on me.

Tony begged for me not to.

Instead, we came to the "agreement" that, I would *only* sleep over two or three nights out of the week, and I *had* to be on his payroll.

Tony agreed.

Every Friday morning, I got five-thousand in cash.

I *never* put it in the bank.

I used some of it as pocket money, and had my checks from work directly deposited in my bank account every Thursday. I used my work money to pay my bills and other expenses. I didn't want to give "Uncle Sam" a reason to start sniffing up my ass! Instead, I hid the money that Tony gave me in my bedroom closet at my father's house.

My game plan was clear: I would be the Queen-of-the-NYC drug empire.

I had Tony do all of the dirty work, and I stopped managing the cooks. I became his silent partner, so to speak. With a little coaching from me, and a lot of strong-arming, Tony could definitely have a heavy hand in the other boroughs.

In case the Feds were watching, I had a sound-proof alibi:

I was a student...

I worked full-time, and I lived at home with my pops.

Technically.

The only way I would be fucked was if they ever wanted to search my father's crib. Tony *never* came to my house, so I doubt that would ever happen.

An excerpt from ***SONZ OF DARKNESS*** by
DRU NOBLE
A GHETTOHEAT® PRODUCTION

"They *won't* wake up! What did you let that woman do to our children, Wilfred?" Marilyn nervously asked.

"GET IN THE CAR!" Wilfred shouted. The expression on her husband's face told Marilyn that he was somewhat scared. She hurried into the passenger's seat, halting her frustration for the moment. Wilfred didn't bother to glance at his wife, as he started the vehicle's ignition and drove off at rapid speed.

Marilyn stared silently at the right side of Wilfred's face for ten minutes. She wanted to strike her husband so badly, for putting not only her, but their two children through the eerie circumstances.

"I know you're upset, Marilyn, but to *my* people this is sacred; it's normal," Wilfred stated, while his eyes were locked on the little bit of road the headlights revealed. Marilyn instantly frowned at his remark.

"Andrew and Gary were *screaming* inside that hut, and now they're sound asleep. This is *not* normal, I don't care *what* you say, this is wrong, Wilfred. That *bitch* did something to our kids, it's like they're drugged! Why the *hell* did you bring us out here? WHAT DID SHE DO TO THEM?" Marilyn loudly screamed, budding tears then began to run down the young, ebony mother's face.

Wilfred then took a deep breath, trying his best to maintain his composure.

"Take us to the hospital!" Marilyn demanded.

"They don't need a doctor, they're perfectly healthy."

"How can you say that? Just look at them," Marilyn argued.

"Listen to me."

"I don't want to—"

"LISTEN TO ME!" Wilfred roared over his wife's voice. Marilyn paused, glaring fiercely toward her husband as he spoke. "The Vowdun has done something to them, she's given them gifts we don't yet know. Marilyn, the Vowdun has helped many people with her magic, she once healed my broken leg in a matter of seconds. The Vowdun has brought men and women fame, wealth, and cured those stricken with deadly diseases. It was even told that she made a man immortal, who now lives in the shadows."

"I'm a Christian, and what you're talking about is satanic. You *tricked* me into coming out here to get Andrew and Gary blessed—you're a liar!" Marilyn interjected.

"That is why we came to Haiti, and it has been done—the worst is now over."

As the couple argued, Gary Romulus eyes opened. He remained silent and unknown to his parents. The infant was in a trance, detached from his surroundings. Wilfred wasn't paying attention to the road ahead, his vision was locked on his wife as they feuded. Gary was however. The newborn saw what his mother and father didn't see, way ahead in the black night.

Two huge glowing crimson eyes stared back at the baby. They were serpentine, eyes Gary would never forget. They were the same eyes he and his brother, Andrew had seen in the hut; the Vowdun's eyes. Gary reached across and gently touched his older brother's shoulder, strangely Andrew awoke in the same catatonic state as his sibling.

"Everything is going to be okay, Marilyn. I tried to pay the Vowdun her price, but she refused," Wilfred said. Marilyn gasped.

"A price?" Marilyn replied annoyingly, refusing to hear her husband's explanation.

Andrew and Gary glared at the large red eyes, which were accompanied by an ever growing shadow that seemed to make the oncoming road darker. Lashing shadows awaited the vehicle.

"WHAT PRICE?" Marilyn then retorted, consumed with anger; she could easily detect the blankness of her husband's mind. Wilfred now was at a loss of words, even he had no knowledge of what the Vowdun expected from him, that was the very thought that frightened the man to the core.

The car was moving at seventy miles per hour. The saddened mother of two turned away from Wilfred's stare, at that moment, Marilyn couldn't even bare his presence. When her sight fell on the oncoming road, Marilyn franticly screamed out in terror. Wilfred instinctively turned forward to see what frightened his wife. His mouth fell ajar at the sight of the nightmarish form ahead of them. Filled with panic, Wilfred quickly tried to turn the steering wheel to avoid crashing.

It was too late.

The sudden impact of the collision caused the speeding car to explode into immense flames that roared to the night sky. The creature that had caused it suddenly disappeared, leaving behind its chaotic destruction and the reason for it.

Out of the flickering flames and screeching metal came young Andrew, who held his baby brother carefully in his fragile arms. An illuminating blue sphere then surrounded their forms, which kept Andrew and Gary unscathed from the fires and jagged metal of the wreckage; incredibly, the two brothers were physically unharmed.

Andrew walked away from the crash feeling melancholy. In the middle of his forehead was a newly formed third eye, which stared out bizarrely. Not until he and Gary were far enough away from the accident did Andrew sit down, and the blue orb vanished.

Gary then looked up at his older brother and cooed to get his attention. Andrew ignored him, he was staring at the flaming vehicle as their parents' flesh burned horridly, causing a horrible stench to pollute the air. Through glassy eyes, Andrew's vision didn't waver, the child was beyond mourning.

Finally, Andrew gazed down at his precious baby brother before he embraced Gary. Gary smiled assured, unfazed by the tragic event. With his tiny arms, Gary then tried to reach upwards, to touch the strange silver eye on his brother's forehead, playfully. Gary was as amused by the new organ as he would've been about a brand new toy.

"Mommy and daddy are gone now," Andrew then sobbed, as streams of tears rolled down his young face. He was trying his best to explain his sorrow. "I will *never* leave you, Gary—I promise," The young boy cried. Gary giggled, still trying to reach Andrew's third eye as best he could.

For the price of the Vowdun to bestow her gifts from her dark powers to the children, Wilfred Romulus had paid the ultimate price—he and his wife's lives. Their children were given gifts far beyond their father's imagination, and for this, they were also cursed with fates not of their choosing. The future held in store untold suffering.

Andrew and Gary were no longer innocent, no longer children of Wilfred and Marilyn Romulus—they were now *Sonz of Darkness.*

An excerpt from ***CONVICT'S CANDY*** by
DAMON "AMIN" MEADOWS & JASON POOLE
A GHETTOHEAT® PRODUCTION

"Sweets, you're in cell 1325; upper bunk," the Correctional Officer had indicated, as he instructed Candy on which cell to report to. When she heard 'upper bunk', Candy had wondered who would be occupying the cell with her. As Candy had grabbed her bedroll and headed towards the cell, located near the far end of the tier and away from the officer's desk and sight, butterflies had grown deep inside of Candy's stomach, as she'd become overwhelmed with nervousness; Candy tried hard to camouflage her fear.

This was Candy's first time in prison and she'd been frightened, forcefully trapped in terror against her will. Candy had become extremely horrified, especially when her eyes met directly with Trigger's, the young, hostile thug she'd accidentally bumped into as she'd been placed inside the holding cell. Trigger had rudely shoved Candy when she first arrived to the facility.

"THE *FUCK* YOU LOOKIN' AT, HOMO?" Trigger had spat; embarrassed that Candy had looked at him. Trigger immediately wondered if she was able to detect that something was different about him and his masculinity; Trigger had hoped that Candy hadn't gotten any ideas that he might've been attracted to her, since Candy had caught him staring hard at her.

She'd quickly turned her face in the opposite direction, Candy wanted desperately not to provoke Trigger, as the thought of getting beat down by him instantly had come to Candy's mind. She couldn't exactly figure out the young thug, although Candy thought she might've had a clue as to why he'd displayed so much anger and hatred towards her. Yet, this hadn't been the time to come to any conclusions, as Candy was more concerned with whom she'd be sharing the cell with.

When Candy had reached cell 1325, she glanced twice at the number printed above on the door, and had made sure that she was at the right cell before she'd entered. Candy then peeped inside the window to see if anyone had been there. Seeing that it was empty, she'd stepped inside of the cell that would serve as her new home for the next five-and-a-half years.

Candy was overwhelmed with joy when she found the cell had been perfectly neat and clean; and for a moment, Candy had sensed that it had a woman's touch. The room smelled like sweet perfume, instead of the strong musk oil that was sold on commissary.

Right away, Candy had dropped her bedroll and raced towards the picture board that had hung on the wall and analyzed every photo; she'd become curious to know who occupied the cell and how they'd lived. Candy believed that a photo was like a thousand words; she'd felt that people told a lot about themselves by the way they'd posed in photographs, including how they displayed their own pictures.

Candy then smiled as her eyes perused over photos of gorgeous models, both male and female, and had become happy when she'd found the huge portrait of her new cellmate. Judging by his long, jet-black wavy hair, facial features and large green eyes, Candy had assumed that he was Hispanic.

Now that she'd known the identity of her cellmate, Candy then decided that it would be best to go find him and introduce herself; she'd hoped that he would fully accept her into the room.

As Candy had turned around and headed out the door, she'd abruptly been stopped by a hard, powerful right-handed fist to her chiseled jaw, followed by the tight grip of a person's left hand hooking around her throat; her vocal cords were being crushed so she couldn't scream.

Candy had haphazardly fallen back into a corner and hit the back of her head against the wall, before she'd become unconscious momentarily. Within the first five seconds of gaining back her conscious, Candy had pondered who'd bashed her so hard in her face.

The first person that had come to mind was Trigger. Secondly, Candy also had thought it might've been her new cellmate who obviously hadn't wanted Candy in his cell, she'd assumed by the blow that Candy had taken to her flawless face.

Struggling her way back from darkness, Candy's eyes had widened wide, at that point, being terribly frightened, as she was face-to-face with two unknown convicts who'd worn white pillow cases over their heads; mean eyes had peeked from the two holes that was cut out from the cloth. The two attackers had resembled members of the Ku Klux Klan bandits as they'd hid their faces; both had been armed with sharp, ten-inch knives.

Overcome with panic, there was no doubt in Candy's mind that she was about to be brutally raped, as there was no way out. Candy then quickly prayed to herself and had hoped that they wouldn't take her life as well. Yet, being raped no longer was an important factor to Candy, as they could've had their way with her. All Candy had been concerned with at that moment was continuing to live.

An excerpt from **GHOST TOWN HUSTLERS** by
CARTEL: CASTILLO
A GHETTOHEAT® PRODUCTION

It was early in the morning when I heard someone knock on the door, calling my name. I sat up and reached for my watch that I'd placed on top of the nightstand.

It was seventy-thirty.

"WHO IS IT?"

"Senor! Lo estan esperando pa desallunar! (Sir! They're waiting for you to come have breakfast!) I hear the voice of Maria yell from behind the door.

"Dame unos cuanto minutos!" (Give me a couple of minutes!"

I hear footsteps going away. I get out of bed, walk over to a table on the far left corner of the room, where a vase full of fresh water has been set. Once downstairs, I see the boys sitting down at the table along with Emilio. I sit next to Pedrito.

"Where's Martha?" I ask.

"She didn't want to eat," Pedrito says while shrugging his shoulders.

Minutes later after we'd eaten, Pedrito and I got up and walked out onto the porch, sat down and lit up our cigarettes. Emilio lit up a cigar, like the one Don Avila used to smoke.

Pedrito then said he wanted to show me something, so we stood up and walked away from the house. He explained to me that the two men that were sent to pick Don Avila up from the airport had betrayed them, and that Emilio had all of his men looking throughout Medellin; having his connections search the rest of Colombia for any signs of them. So far, no one was able to find anything.

We notice that the house was barely visible, so we decide to go back. When we reach the house, the boys were inside, and Emilio was waiting for Pedrito with three men by his side.

"Come," Emilio says, gesturing with his hand to Pedrito. "I want to show you something I found." Emilio had a smile on his face, but I noticed that it was very different than any other smiles he'd given before. It was as if Emilio was smiling to himself and not at Pedrito.

"Can Raul come, too?" I heard Pedrito ask. I stop midway up the stairs, proceeding to go into the house. I look back and see Emilio staring at me, almost as if he was thinking about what to answer.

"Sure," Emilio replied shortly. "He can come." Emilio began walking towards the back of the house, where there were three smaller houses that weren't visible from the front of the main house. One of the smaller houses were guarded by two men. One was holding a rifle, the other had a gun tucked inside the waist of his pants.

"Donde estan esos hijo-eh-putas?" (Where are those sons-of-bitches?) Emilio asked once he, Pedrito and I were before the guards.

"Hai dentro patron!" the guardsman with the gun at his waist answered, as he opened the door for us.

We walked into an unfurnished room, yet, it was well lit. In the center of the room, there were two men on the floor on their knees, with their arms raised above their heads; tied up with rope that had been thrown over a beam and secured to a pole. They're shirtless, and it seems as if someone has been beating them badly with a whip—the two men having cuts on their chest and faces. They were bleeding profusely from their wounds.

"These are the ones that sold out your father," Emilio said, pointing to the two men who are still on their knees. "They're responsible for the death of your father. That's Angel, and that's Miguel.

"Pedrito walked up to the two badly beaten men: "Who killed my father?" Neither of the two men answered. Pedrito then forcefully kicked Angel in his stomach. "QUIEN?" (WHO?) Pedrito shouts.

"Pedrito—" I say while taking a step forward. I immediately stopped when I felt a hand rest upon my shoulder firmly. I look back to see that it's Emilio.

"Leave him," Emilio commands. I turn to look at Pedrito, who's now violently shaking Miguel's head, grabbing him by his hair as he continues to yell loudly.

"QUIEN FUE? DIME!" (WHO WAS IT? TELL ME) Pedrito asks and shouts. Moments later, Pedrito looks around, still holding Miguel by his hair. He then let's go of Miguel and walks toward Emilio and I.

The guardsman who let us inside is now standing next to Emilio. Pedrito walks up to him, snatches the gun from his waist, cocks it, and runs back to where Angel and Miguel is. I see that Angel and Miguel's eyes are dilated before Pedrito blocks my view of the two men, now standing in front of them.

"Por f-f-f-avor no-no-no-no me maates!" (P-l-e-a-s-e don't kill me!) Angel begs for his life. "Yo no fui quien le mato." (It wasn't me who killed him."

"Entonce fuiste tu, eh?" Pedrito says, turning the gun to Miguel.

"N-O-O-O-O-O-O-O!" Miguel screams.

An excerpt from **GAMES WOMEN PLAY** by
TONY COLLINS
A GHETTOHEAT® PRODUCTION

A woman always sees a man before he sees her. Then, in a blink of an eye, she completely checks out everything him about him from head-to-toe—without him even knowing what the woman is doing. Even faster than her lightening quick assessment of him, she studies very swiftly, all of his surroundings; including any other woman who is interested in him.

Yes, a woman notices every little personal detail about a man. That's right, not one thing about him escapes her laser-like focus. So, as she studies him, at the same time, the woman makes a complete mental list of the number of turn-ons and turn-offs regarding any or all of his personal details. These turn-ons or turn-off may include: details about his personality, his looks, a man's level of personal grooming and cleanliness, body type, clothing, shoes and accessories, financial status, a man's relationship status, and so on.

However, a woman doesn't just stop at this point, the level of merely making a "check list" of superficial observations about a man. She doesn't stop her analysis of a man at the point that most men would end their analysis of a woman. A woman looks beyond the surface of a man's visible details, when she considers whether or not to pursue him. A woman analysis of a man is more complex.

Not only does a woman make a mental check list of all the personal details that a man possess, but also, she notices how well he maintains his personal details. Yet, a woman doesn't stop even at this point in her study of him. She is still not done putting him under her mental microscope. She takes her analysis of him to an even deeper level.

A woman notices if any of his personal details lacking, and she observes which personal details a man should have, but are completely missing. Why does a woman go through all these levels of observation regarding a man's personal details? Well, a woman makes such an in depth study, because she knows that by analyzing the presence, and/or the absence, and/or the condition of a man's personal details, that these three factors raises questions in

202

her mind about him, making the woman go "Hmmm, I wonder why that is?"

Once she begins to ponder, then her naturally-analytical mind, kicks right into high gear. Instantly, a woman starts trying to figure out what's the most probable answer to each of the questions raised in her mind—from studying a man's personal details; putting two-and-two together.

By taking this approach, and backed by a lifetime of observing men, combined with her training from the "Female Mafia", a woman knows that what she can come up with quite a lot of accurate information about a man. Although she may not always be exactly correct with all of her on-the-spot analysis, and "guesstimates" about him, usually a woman is very accurate with most of her breakdown regarding him.

Even more amazing, and usually to a man's complete bewilderment, a woman's reading of him, using his personal details, can be so on point, that she even figures out things about a man that he was purposely trying to conceal.

So, from studying the presence, the absence, or the condition of a man's personal details, and then "guesstimating" the most probable answers to the questions raised by studying them, a woman gets not only a superficial understanding of him, but also, she gets a deeper insight into who this man really is, and what he is really about; at the core of his being, beyond the image that he is presenting to the world.

Therefore, given this scenario, let's follow along as she studies, analyzes, questions, and then figures out, everything about a man without him even knowing what she is doing; all of this taking place in a blink of an eye.

An excerpt from **LONDON REIGN** by
A. C. BRITT
A GHETTOHEAT® PRODUCTION

Back in Detroit, Mercedes was bragging to her sisters about how good the sex was with London. She was truly falling in love with London, and wanted to do something really special for "him". One night towards the end of the week, Mercedes went over to the *Lawrence House*, and convinced the landlord to let her into London's room.

She had all kinds of decorations and gifts for London, wanting to surprise "him" with when London came home.

"I can't *believe* you're going through all this," Saiel said, before she started blowing up some balloons.

"I know...I can't believe I'm feelin' this nigga this hard. I think I'm just whipped," Mercedes replied.

"From what? ...You two only did it once."

"But London can eat the *fuck* out of some pussy though! That nigga stay havin' me climbin' the wall. You know, I ain't never been in here when London wasn't home. I wonder what he got *goin'* on around here that he doesn't want me to see," Mercedes said, as she began going through London's things.

"Mercedes...don't go through the man's *shit!* You might *find* something you *don't* wanna see...and then what?" Saiel asked.

"This nigga, London keeps talkin' about how there's *shit* I don't know about him anyway, so I *might* as well play detective... He's takin' *too* damn long to tell me." Mercedes then picked up a pile of papers out of a file cabinet, and started flipping through them. "Pay stubs...bills....bills...more bills," Mercedes said to herself.

"Mercedes, you *really* need to stop."

"Perhaps you're right," Mercedes answered, as she put London's papers back and opened his closet door. Saiel then looked in the closet as well.

"Mercedes, why you leave so many *tampons* over here? That's weird."

"...Yeah it is...because those *ain't* mine." Mercedes pulled the box of tampons out the closet, and looked in it to see how many were missing. "I don't even use this kind, must belong to some other bitch." Mercedes then put the tampons back where she found them, yet, Saiel picked up a stack of medical papers that had fallen when Mercedes opened the closet.

Saiel read the contents of the paper, and her mouth practically *dropped* to the floor. Mercedes noticed her sister's reaction, so she immediately walked over to where Saiel was.

"What, Saiel? ...What does it say? What is that?"

"U-m-m-m...doctors' papers,"

"What? London ain't go no disease, do he? Because I don't even know if London used a condom," Mercedes said. Saiel looked at her sister again and shook her head.

"Naw...no disease...and whether London used a condom or not, doesn't matter," Saiel answered, as she gave her sister a traumatized look. "Mercedes...I think you better sit down."

"Why? What that *shit* say?" Mercedes asked anxiously.

"London   ain't...Mercedes,   this   nigga...damn! ...Mercedes...ha...London *ain't* no dude!" Saiel said emotionally; completely shocked.

"WHAT?" Mercedes asked with much confusion.

"London...Mercedes, London is a girl!"

Mercedes could tell by the look in her sister's eyes that she wasn't kidding. Mercedes immediately snatched the papers out of Saiel's hand, and read everything from the name, to the diagnosis of a urinary track infection.

"A girl? ...But I fuckin'...I fucked him! Her...it! We had sex, Saiel, how the *fuck* is London a girl?" Mercedes was hurt at first, but it quickly turned into anger. "THAT'S WHY THAT *MUTHAFUCKA* NEVER WANTED ME TO TOUCH DOWN THERE! ...And why he...she, whatever, didn't want to have sex!

"I am so *fuckin'* stupid, he made me, she made me wear a blindfold. Said she wanted to try somethin' new. I don't understand Saiel, I've seen London's chest, and she ain't got no breasts. I mean, there were nubbs, but I ain't think nothin' of it," Mercedes said as she began to cry.

"Mercedes...sweetie, she had us *all* fooled! London don't *look* like no girl! She doesn't *sound* like no girl, and London *sure as hell*, doesn't *act* like no girl! We had no reason to think otherwise. Sweetie, just leave this *shit* alone and let's go!" Saiel said, taking the items out of her sister's hands while ushering Mercedes to the door.

An excerpt from *SKATE ON!* by
HICKSON
A GHETTOHEAT® PRODUCTION

Quickly exiting the 155th Street train station on *Eighth Avenue,* Shani, walking with her head held down low, decided to cross the street and walk parallel to the *Polo Grounds;* not chancing bumping into her parents. As she approached the corner, Shani contemplated crossing over to *Blimpie's* before walking down the block to the skating rink. She craved for a *Blimpie Burger* with cheese hero, but immediately changed her mind; fearing of ruining the outfit Keisha gave her.

Shani then headed towards *The Rooftop*, feeling overly anxious to meet with her two friends. As she walked down the dark and eerie block, Mo-Mo crept up behind Shani and proceeded to put her in a headlock; throwing Shani off-guard.

"GET OFF OF ME!" Shani pleaded as she squirmed, trying to break free. Already holding Shani with a firm grip, Mo-Mo applied more pressure around her neck.

Trying to defend herself the best way she knew how, Shani reached behind for Mo-Mo's eyes and attempted to scratch her face. Mo-Mo pushed her forward and laughed.

"Yeah, *bitch,* whachu gon' do?" Mo-Mo teased. "SIKE!" Startled, Shani turned around with a surprised expression on her face.

"Mo-Mo, why are you always *playing* so much? You almost scared me half-to-death!" Shani said while panting heavily, trying hard to catch her breath.

Mo-Mo continued to laugh, "Yo, I had ya heart! You almost *shitted* on yaself! I could've put ya ass to sleep, Bee!"

"Mo-Mo, please stop swearing so much," Shani replied, as she smiled and reached out to hug Mo-Mo. Mo-Mo then teasingly tugged at the plunging neckline of Shani's leotard, pulling it down to reveal more of Shani's cleavage.

"Since when you started dressin' like a lil' hoe?"

Shani, quickly removing Mo-Mo's hand from her breasts, became self-conscious of what she was wearing.

"I knew I shouldn't have put this on. Keisha made me wear this. Do I *really* look sleazy?"

Mo-Mo frowned. "Whah? Shani, stop *buggin'!* You look

aiiight. I'm just not used to seein' you dressin' all *sexy* and shit."

Shani then looked towards *Eighth Avenue* to see if Keisha was nearby.

"Mo-Mo, where's Keisha? I thought you two were coming to *The Rooftop* together."

Mo-Mo then pointed across the street, as she loudly chewed and popped on her apple flavored *Super Bubble* gum.

"Yo, see that black *Toyota Corolla* double-parked by *The Rucker?* She in there talkin' to some Dominican *nigga* named, Diego we met earlier. We made that *fool* take us to *Ling Fung Chinese Restaurant* on Broadway. Keisha jerked him for a plate of Lobster Cantonese—I got chicken wings and pork-fried rice."

Shani shook her head and chuckled, "You two are always scheming on some guy."

"And you *know* it! A *bitch* gotta eat, right?!" Mo-Mo asked, before blowing a huge bubble with her gum, playfully plucking Shani on her forehead.

Mo-Mo was a belligerent, lowly-educated, hardcore ghetto-girl who was extremely violent and wild. Known for her southpaw boxing skill and powerful knockout punches, she'd often amused herself by fighting other peoples' battles on the block for sport. That's how Mo-Mo met Shani.

Last January, Sheneeda and Jaiwockateema tried to rob Shani of her *Bonsoir* "B" bag near Building 1. Mo-Mo observed what has happening and had rescued Shani, feverishly pounding both girls over their heads with her glass *Kabangers.*

She didn't even know Shani at the time, but fought for her as if they were childhood cronies. Since then, the two have become close friends—Mo-Mo admiring Shani's intelligence, innocence and sincerity.

In addition to her volatile temper, ill manners and street-bitch antics, Mo-Mo was rough around the edges—literally and figuratively. Eighteen-years-old and having dark, rich, coffee-colored skin, Mo-Mo's complexion was beautiful, even with suffering from the mild case of eczema on her hands—and with her face, full of blemishes and bumps from the excessive fighting, junk food and sodas she'd habitually drank.

Bearing a small scar on her left cheek from being sliced with a box cutter, Mo-Mo proudly endured her battle mark. *"The Deceptinettes"*, a female gang who jumped Mo-Mo inside of *Park West High School's* girls' locker room last year, physically attacked her. Mo-Mo took on the dangerous crew of girls all by herself, winning the brutal brawl, due to her knowing how to fight hard and dirty.

With deep brown eyes, full lips and high cheekbones, she highly resembled an African queen. Mo-Mo wasn't bad looking, she just didn't take care of herself; nor was she ever taught how. Because of this, Mo-Mo was often forsaken for her ignorance by most.

Awkwardly standing knock-kneed and pigeon-toed at five-foot-seven, big boned with an hourglass figure, Mo-Mo was a brick house! Thick and curvaceous with a body that wouldn't quit, she had ample sized forty-two D breasts, shifting wide hips, big legs, with well-toned thighs. Having the largest ass in Harlem, Mo-Mo's behind was humongous—nicely rounded and firm. It automatically became a sideshow attraction whenever she appeared, as everyone, young and old stared in disbelief; amazed at the shape, fullness and size of Mo-Mo's butt. A man once joked about "spanking" Mo-Mo's rear, claiming that when he'd knocked it…her ass knocked him back!

Her hair length was short, in which Mo-Mo wore individual box braids, braiding it herself; having real, human hair extensions. Often, her braids were sloppy and unkempt, having naps and a fuzzy hairline. Mo-Mo's coarse, natural hair grain never matched the soft and silky texture of her extensions, but she always soaked the ends in a pot of scalding, hot water to achieve a wet-and-wavy look.

Mo-Mo never polished her nails or kept them clean, having dirt underneath them regularly. Rarely shaving the hair from under her armpits or bikini line caused Mo-Mo to have a rank, body odor. Someone even left a package at her apartment door one day, filled with a large can of *Right Guard, Nair* and a bottle of *FDS Feminine Deodorant Spray* with a typewritten note attached. It read: *"Aye, Funkbox, clean ya stank pussy and stop puttin' Buckwheat in a headlock—you nasty bitch!"* Mo-Mo assumed it was either a prank from Sheneeda and Jaiwockateema, or Oscardo—still sulking over Mo-Mo kicking his ass six years ago.

She'd now lived alone in the *Polo Grounds,* due to her mother's untimely death six months ago—dying of sclerosis of the liver from her excessive drinking of hard alcohol. Just days after Mo-Mo's mother's death, she'd received a letter from *Social*

Services, stating that they were aware of her mother's passing, her only legal guardian, and that she would receive a visit from a social worker; one who would be instructed to place Mo-Mo in an all-girls group home in East Harlem.

Mo-Mo had begged her other family members to allow her to live with them, but they refused, not wanting to deal with her nasty disposition, constant fighting and barbaric lifestyle. Nor did they wish to support Mo-Mo emotionally or financially, resulting her to rely on public assistance from the welfare office. At that point, Mo-Mo hadn't any relatives whom she can depend upon—she was on her own and had to grow up fast.

Luckily Mo-Mo's eighteenth birthday had arrived a day before she was accosted in the lobby of her building by a male social worker, having the rude investigator from *Social Services* antagonize her with legal documents; indicating that she was to temporarily be in his custody and taken immediately to the group home.

"SUCK A FAT BABY'S ASS!" was what Mo-Mo yelled at the social worker before defiantly slamming the door in his face.

Failing most of her classes, Mo-Mo barely attended school. She was in the tenth grade, but had belonged in the twelfth. Mo-Mo was still a special education student, now having a six-grader's reading and writing level. Her former teachers passed her in school, being totally unconcerned with Mo-Mo's learning disability. Their goal was to pass as many students as possible, in order to avoid being reprimanded by superiors for failing a large number of students. The school system had quotas to meet and didn't receive the needed funds from the government for the following term—if a large amount of students were held back.

Along with other personal issues, Mo-Mo was hot-in-the-ass, fast and promiscuous, having the temperament of a low-class whore. She was a big-time freak, a sex fiend with an insatiable appetite for men with huge dicks—becoming weak at the knees at the sight of a protruding bulge.

Mo-Mo's self esteem and subsidized income was low, but her sex drive was extremely high, having sex with men for cash while soothing her inner pain. She didn't sell her body for money due to desperation and destitute—Mo-Mo did it for the fun of it. She *loved* dick and decided to earn money while doing what Mo-Mo enjoyed the most—getting fucked! She was going to have

209

frivolous sex regardless, *"SO WHY NOT GET PAID FOR IT?"* Mo-Mo often reasoned.

Academically, she was slow, but Mo-Mo was nobody's fool; being street-smart with thick skin. A true survivor, who persevered, by hook-or-crook, Mo-Mo was determined to sustain—by all means necessary.

"AYE, YO, KEISHA, HURRY THE *FUCK* UP!" Mo-Mo beckoned.

"Hold up! I'm comin'!" Keisha replied with irritation in her voice; concluding her conversation with Diego, "My friends are callin' me—I gotta go."

"Can I see you again and get ya digits, mommy?" Diego begged, talking extremely fast with his raspy voice.

"Maybe! And *no* you can't get my number—gimme yours," Keisha snapped.

Diego immediately was attracted to Keisha's good looks, snootiness, nonchalant attitude and bold behavior. He smiled as he wrote his beeper number on the flyer he received for an upcoming party at *Broadway International*—while exiting the Chinese restaurant with Keisha and Mo-Mo an hour earlier.

While handing Keisha the flyer, Diego attempted to wish her goodnight, but Keisha interjected: "Can I get three hundred dollars?" she said, looking straight into Diego's eyes.

"Damn, mommy, what's up? I just met you an *hour* ago and you *askin'* me for money already?"

Keisha paused for emphasis.

"…Are you gon' give it to me or *not?*" Keisha coldly asked, still looking into Diego's eyes—not once she ever blinked.

"Whachu need three hundred for, mommy?"

"First and foremost, my name is *Keisha,* not mommy! And I don't *n-e-e-e-e-e-d* three hundred dollars—I want it!"

Diego sat silently, bewildered and turned on by Keisha's brashness.

"Diego, don't you want me to look cute the next time you see me?" Keisha asked innocently while batting her eyelashes; deceiving Diego with her fake, light-hearted disposition.

"So I'm gonna see you again huh, mommy?" Diego nervously asked, smiling as he pulled out a wad of cash from his pocket. His large bankroll, wrapped in jade-green rubber bands caused Keisha's eyes to widen.

"Uh-huh," she effortlessly replied while staring hard at Diego's money while turning up the volume on his *Benzi* box.

Diego was playing his *DJ Love-Bug Starski* mixed tape and Keisha bobbed her head, rocked her shoulders from side-to-side and rubbed her thumb swiftly against her middle and index finger, while singing to *Money: Dollar Bill, Y'all* by Jimmy Spicer; "Dollar-dollar-dollar-dollar-dollar bill, y'all!"

Diego looked at her with his right eyebrow raised, peeling off money from his bundle. He handed the bills to Keisha and hopelessly gazed into her eyes.

Keisha, who became annoyed with Diego for showing too much of an interest in her so soon, rolled her eyes and retorted harshly, "Gotta...go," as she attempted to reach for the car handle. Before grabbing it, Keisha pulled out a napkin from her brand-new, blue and white *Gucci* bag with the signature G's, wiped her fingerprints off the console and opened the car door with the napkin in her hand.

"Yo, Keisha, why you wipe down my car like that?"

Keisha ignored Diego's question and beckoned to Shani and Mo-Mo, signaling them by waving her five-carat, diamond-adorned right hand in the air, before quickly bringing it down to slap her right thigh.

"Yo, I'm ready, y'all—let's go!"

Keisha then walked around the front of Diego's car and proceeded to cross the street; now eager to enter *The Rooftop*. Shaking his head in disbelief, chuckling, Diego couldn't believe Keisha's sassiness.

"YO, WHEN YOU GON' CALL ME, MOMMY?" Diego yelled out to Keisha from his car window.

Keisha immediately stopped in the middle of the street, causing the flow of traffic to halt. She flung her long hair, looked over her shoulder and tauntingly replied, "As soon as you step-up ya whip, *nigga*. Do I *look* like the type of girl who be *bouncin'* 'round in a dusty-ass 'one-point-eight'?"

Diego froze as Keisha continued to speak.

"You don't even take ya *whip* to the car wash. And stop callin' me 'mommy'!" Keisha concluded, flinging her hair again by sharply turning her head. She then stuck her butt out and switched while crossing the street.

Diego stared long and hard at Keisha's rump as she walked away, noticing how good her behind looked in her skin-tight jeans. He then drove towards Eighth *Avenue,* repeatedly hearing Keisha's last comments over in his head.

Keisha stood at the entrance of the skating rink and observed the huge crowd outside as—Shani and Mo-Mo greeted her.

"It's about time!" Mo-Mo snapped. Keisha ignored her and reached out to hug Shani.

"What's up, college gurrrl?" Keisha asked.

"Hey Keisha! I'm fine. I'm chilling like a villain." Shani replied awkwardly, not use to using slang in her daily dialect.

"Shani, it's *'chillin''* not 'chill-i-n-g'! Why you be always talkin' so *damn* proper anyway? I wonder sometimes, yo, if you *really* from the hood!" Mo-Mo snapped.

As Shani attempted to politely respond back to Mo-Mo, Keisha rudely interjected.

"So, Shani, how's DC?" Keisha asked, cleverly examining her outfit from head-to-toe without Shani realizing she had.

"I like DC so far. I'm very excited about attending *Howard University.* I just need to learn my way around campus," Shani answered. Feeling jealous and left out of the conversation, Mo-Mo interrupted the two.

"Can you two *bitches* learn y'all *muthafuckin'* way inside this skatin' rink?" Mo-Mo snapped before entering *The Rooftop.*

"Mo-Mo be illin'! She *betta* watch her mouth 'cause I'm-not-the-*one!*" Keisha retorted while rocking her neck and waving her right hand in the air.

Shani, experiencing cramps from her period and the stress from sneaking from DC to New York City for the grand opening of *The Rooftop,* shrugged her shoulders to relieve the tension she had felt, as she inhaled a breath of fresh air. Shani then slowly exhaled, and quickly adjusted the plunging neckline of her scoop-neck leotard to conceal her cleavage—as she and Keisha followed inside.

LADY SPEAKS THE TRUTH, VOLUME 1
Essay written by SHA
A GHETTOHEAT® PRODUCTION

Growing up in Urban America isn't easy. Throw in the race, gender and age cards. You walk through life with iron-filled crates shackled to your ankles. How can you climb the ladder of success with so much holding you back?

This isn't about me outlining how to live your life or what's right and wrong—I don't know the answer to that. This is about me asking you to wake up! What's up, Urban America? Have we've become so complacent as to stop our complaining because we've been reassured that everything is new and approved, and comes backed with a money back guarantee if we're not satisfied?

I don't know about you but, I'm not satisfied! I'm not a part of the "walking dead" that rest assured in what they've been spoon-fed, that would've been the easy way out: I like it hard.

I don't think you understand me. As my third-grade teacher put it, I wasn't "born with a silver spoon in my mouth." I was born in Kings County Hospital in Brooklyn, New York. It happened sometime after the birth of "THE MONSTER" (HIV/AIDS) and just before the Crack epidemic hit hard.

Though my father owned a bodega and I attended parochial school, I was far from rich. It wasn't steak and lobster; 34th Street Miracle Christmas' and such. However, what we lacked in finances, we made up for through love and unity.

No money meant a closet filled with out-of-style clothes and ridicule from my peers; it was whatever! I was too focused on school to really give a damn. Then my body decided it wanted to start puberty at nine-years-old. Don't think that made me special, there were other girls in the fifth grade with bangin' bodies.

While they were using what they had to get what they want, I stayed in my books. Of course I wasn't popular with the boys, but everybody knew my name. Rhymes were my reason and Hip Hop saved me from the cruelty of the bullies. Well, at least, some of the time.

Being from BK, my ability to write poetry and to get lyrics from any song off the radio, made me tolerable. My strict Haitian father didn't allow me to hang out after school, go on go-away trips or participate in any of the bullshit that happened in my neighborhood. If it didn't happen on my stoop, I wasn't able to go.

Soon after, I was in Queens and desperately wanted to go back to Brooklyn. I thought I'd be much more popular back "home", but the reality was if I wasn't "doing it", I was wack. I accepted that. I had no choice but to be wack and watch every single move that everybody made.

Then I reached high school. I attended a school that made headlines for acid-throwing, gun-toting, monster-infected students! It was the closest one to my house, so I really didn't have a choice. It was then when I got the fever for the fast life. I wanted to be that chick with the fly dudes that pushed the baddest cars, dipped in jewelry of every caliber.

I started asking around for the fly boys from elementary school. Surely by then, I thought, they had to be on top of the game. Dudes were either in Spofford, just recently released from juvenile detention, dead or strung the fuck out on crack-cocaine. Real talk, a sixteen-year-old junkie is not a joke.

Then I started watching the older dudes. This was the era of *The Sleepwalkers*, *The Lost Boys* and others. My young self got a thrill walking through the neighborhood with the older boys checking for me, because of my over-developed body; that made the girls hate me even more. I was already catching hell because of my hair and swagger. Yet, that was dealt with accordingly. I'm not saying I won every battle, but you damn sure won't be able to call me cara cicatriz (Scarface)!

It was all fun and games until someone got his head blown off in Brookville Park one hot summer night…That brought me to the reality of things. I sat back and started making connections. It didn't take too long to figure out who were the major drug dealers, the minor drug dealers, the wanna-be drug dealers, the stick-up kids, the car thieves and the wankstas (Suckers). Before long, I had them all figured out and knew most of their modus operandi; it was too easy.

For the rest of high school, I met a whole slew of characters. I met guys who were predicate felons at the age of twenty; guys who snapped their fingers and made anything you desired appear like magic. I'll admit, crime life is very enticing! But the end results are not.

I played my cards well, at that time, holding them close to my chest. I was very careful about who I was seen with and where.

Undercover detectives were all over the place all the time. Every other day, somebody was getting locked up, and females were getting caught out there on technicalities.

That right there was what *really* made me think twice about all my moves. I lost count of how many females I've seen get charged with years and decades, just because they were at the wrong place at the wrong time. Damn those RICO and Rockefeller laws! They will get innocent people and first-time offenders caught up in the system every time.

Besides the jail time aspect of a hustler's life, I realized that Uncle Sam makes fun and games out of hustlin'. That's another reason I just observed the business of drugs. Tell me why a black man getting caught with crack rocks in BK will get at least ten years, but a white man getting caught on the island with cocaine will get a much lesser sentence? Doesn't crack come from cocaine? Wake up, Urban America!

Why is it that Caucasians dominate the welfare system, but yet African-Americans and Hispanics are portrayed as being the dominate races in the system? Isn't it strange how families stay stuck in the same situation generation after generation? Your momma had you at sixteen, her momma had her at fifteen and her momma had her at fourteen! Yet, all of you still live in the same project apartment? F.Y.I., the projects, no matter how "luxurious" some may seem, are designed to keep the masses psychologically disabled so we can perpetuate the cycle, over-and-over again.

Uncle Sam put up the projects. Uncle Sam allows drugs to come into the country. Trust that if America really wanted to be drug free, then we damn sure would be! Then what would the DEA do? Do you realize how many federal, state and city jobs would be lost if there wasn't any illegal drugs in America?

Thousands of people would be out of work and the economy would fall apart. The Great Depression wouldn't be able to compare to the economic state of America if drug money wasn't in circulation. Uncle Sam can keep his VESID vouchers and his rehabilitation programs: I know the score.

To my young people of Urban America: hustlin' is what it is. We all do it in one shape or another. For most of us, it's a part of life. Victims of our socio-economic status, we have to do what we have to do; just do it wisely. Know when to hit *HARDER,* know when to ease up. I thank God for that ability. Too many times I've come this close to being state property...I'm free. Wake up and you'll be too.

An excerpt from ***SOME SEXY, ORGASM 1*** by
DRU NOBLE
A GHETTOHEAT® PRODUCTION

BIG BONED

"I need you, Melissa; oh I *love* your body! Let me taste you, mmmph, let me *love* you—just give me some sexy!" Jezebel begged while still squeezing the woman's luscious crescents. Melissa had no hope of resisting this sudden passionate impulse that flooded her.

She felt Jezebel's grip tighten on her, then a finger slowly traced between her curvaceous legs. The unexpected jolt of excitable pleasure caused Melissa to rise on her side, throwing Jezebel off of her. She palmed between her own thighs, trying to silence the rest of the roaring waves threatening to overcome her preciousness.

Jezebel couldn't take her eyes off of Melissa, as she breathed erratically, while Melissa couldn't help but to stare back with conflicting desperation. Melissa's hand reached out and grasped the back of the Native-American woman's neck, as she pulled Jezebel towards her forcefully.

Their lips touch, melded, then opened. Jezebel's tongue dove into Melissa's mouth, finding the versatile muscle was eager to wrestle her own. A groan vibrated down Melissa's throat. Her hand came up, and two fingers strung like guitar strings on Jezebel's upturned beady nipple—first playing with it, then catching Jezebel's hardened nipple between her index and middle fingers; closing it within tight confines.

Jezebel then straddled Melissa, the two women's hands meeting, immediately intertwining before their kissing ended.

"I wanted you since I *first* saw you; I've been wet ever since that moment. You're so *fucking* sexy, Melissa. I *need* you, can I have some sexy? Give it to me," Jezebel said in a low, hushed voice.

The twinkle in her beautiful brown eyes affected Melissa like an intoxicating elixir. Melissa watched on, as Jezebel took her captured hand and began to suck on two fingers with her hot, steamy mouth. Jezebel's checked hollowed, as she continued to close in on Melissa's dainty fingers.

Melissa, voluptuous and womanly, petals became slick, and damp—natural juices now running down towards her rounded rear end.

"I want you, too Jezebel, come get some sexy!" she pledged. Jezebel smiled as Melissa's fingers slid from her mouth, leading them down her body. With her lead, Melissa allowed her hand to enter into Jezebel's bikini. A glimpse of her fine, black pubic hair came into view, as Melissa then felt the lovely grace of Jezebel's vagina.

A soothing hiss breathed out of Jezebel. The moistness of her internal lake coated the fingers that ventures to its intimate space. Melissa then bent her hand so the bikini could come down, and she was grand the delightful vision of where her fingers ventured.

Jezebel's outer labia had opened, as Melissa's fingers split between her middle, like tickling a blooming rose. She tipped her hand up, and used her thumb to peel back the protective skin over Jezebel's engorged clitoris. The pink button revealed itself exclusively, and Melissa used her thumb to caress it; stirring up Jezebel's burning desire.

Melissa had never seen or touched another woman's pearl, but found that she'd loved it completely. Two of her fingers then slipped within Jezebel's hot, oily insides, and the Native-American woman had thrust her hips forward to take all Melissa had to offer.

"You're so *hot* inside; burning up my fingers, baby."

"Just don't stop; *please* don't stop what you're doing," Jezebel instructed. Her hips began to undulate, rocking herself to a sweet bliss. Jezebel rode Melissa's fingers like she would her fiancé's long, pleasure-inducing dick.

Melissa then curled her wet fingers back slightly, as she would if she were touching herself, searching inside for that magical area most women long to discover—the G-spot.

Melissa felt Jezebel's tunnel pulsate, and a shock ran through the humping woman, giving Melissa total satisfaction that she'd found Jezebel's spot; now also realizing that, by her being a woman, she had full advantage to knowing another woman's body, better than any man could.

From the co-author of *CONVICT'S CANDY*

BOY-TOY by
DAMON "AMIN" MEADOWS
A GHETTOHEAT® PRODUCTION

GHETTOHEAT.COM®

An excerpt from *SOME SEXY, ORGASM 2* by
MIKA MILLER
A GHETTOHEAT® PRODUCTION

Oh God, I think I broke my clitoris...or at least fractured it. After eight months of non-stop intense and dedicated masturbation, my fingers have grown tired, my wrist threatens me with the dull twangs of carpal tunnel and, as of lately, there is no climax in sight. It's as if over the last eight months during my lack of satisfying dick, and therefore, subsequent mounting sexual frustration, I have *masturbated* myself into a physical catastrophe. My clitoris just...died. There's no longer a satisfying crescendo of orgasmic waves rushing through my pelvis. Nothing's happening South of the border. Nothing. Nada. Zilch. Not a *fucking* thing!

I flop my head back into the plushness of my Versailles jacquard-woven comforter with golden hues, and bury my head beneath the 1200 thread count, matte-satin finish bed sheets, and pray to *God* that I haven't destroyed the most powerful sexual organ on my body. I should have seen this coming.

Over the past four weeks, it's become increasingly harder-and-harder for me to reach the point of orgasm. I have *exhausted* my stash of pornographic movies, and just about bored myself to death, trying to rely on the secret sexual fantasies that I keep imbedded in the "freak" quadrant of my brain. My pornographic movies and imaginative sexual illusions, have all become doldrum. I mean, who can get off to the same *shit* night-after-night? Certainly not me.

When those efforts failed, I resorted to mechanical assistance. One evening, like a sex-addicted junkie, and in a complete state-of-desperation, I hopped in my silver, convertible *BMW Z4 Roadster*, drove forty-five minutes down Highway 35, until I saw the three, brightly-beaming red, neon letters that I sought, peering at me from the exit near the movie theater in Pluergerville: "XXX".

I parked my "Beamer" in the back of the ex-rated, adult video store, and in an attempt to be "incog-negro", I flipped the hood of my *Azzuré* tracksuit over my head, hid behind my *Oliver Peoples* "Harlot" sunglasses, and tried to nonchalantly mosey my way inside.

An hour later, after consulting with the bubblegum-popping female sales clerk; dressed in a tartan plaid, pleated ultra-mini skirt, and red, thigh-high patent leather, platform lace-up boots, I left the store with a plethora of sex-toy treasures and erotic devices: personal lubricants, battery vibrators, electric vibrators, G spot stimulators and orgasm books.

I even bought the infamous two-hundred dollar vibrator called *The Rabbit,* that I heard mentioned on *Sex in the City.* I had just partakened in an erotic shopping spree, one that would even cause *Kirk Franklin* to blush.

Needless to say that, after I tried all of my treasures (and sometimes even twice) I was still no closer to an orgasmic experience than before. So, when my orgasms began to steadily decline and weaken, and when it seemed that I had to *work* harder to implode, I blamed it on a lack of..."inspiration".

The "clitoral" truth is that, I had become a woman obsessed. What I needed to do was pump my brakes. I needed to take a sebaticle from my not-so-good vibrations. My "pussy problem" was fast becoming a perplexing conundrum.

ghettoheat®

GHETTOHEAT® would like to thank the following for their support with this project:

Model, GIOVANNA HENSON
Make-up Artist, WILLIAM MARSHALL
Hair Stylist, KAT JENNINGS for KAT'S LAIR
Photographer, HOSEA JOHNSON
Graphic Artist, MURPHY HEYLIGER
HARLEMADE

Contacts:
KAT'S LAIR, 346 West 36th Street
New York, NY 10018   Phone: 212.595.8075

HOSEAJOHNSON.COM

HARLEMADE, 174 Lenox Avenue
New York, NY 10026   Phone: 212.987.2500

HARLEMADE.COM

ghettoheat

THE GHETTOHEAT® MOVEMENT

THE GHETTOHEAT® MOVEMENT is a college scholarship fund geared towards young adults within the inner-city, pursuing education and careers in Journalism and Literary Arts.

At GHETTOHEAT®, our mission is to promote literacy worldwide. To learn more about THE GHETTOHEAT® MOVEMENT, or to see how you can get involved, send all inquires to: MOVEMENT@GHETTOHEAT.COM, or log on to GHETTOHEAT.COM

To send comments to MIKA MILLER, send all mail to:

GHETTOHEAT®, LLC
P.O. BOX 2746
NEW YORK, NY 10027

Attention: MIKA MILLER

Or e-mail her at: MIKA@GHETTOHEAT.COM.

Artists interested in having their works reviewed for possible consideration at GHETTOHEAT®, send all materials to:

ghettoheat

P.O. BOX 2746
NEW YORK, NY 10027

Attention: HICKSON

GHETTOHEAT®: THE HOTNESS IN THE STREETS!!!™

ghettoheat®

ORDER FORM

Name_____

Registration #_____(If incarcerated)

Address_____

City_____ State_____ Zip code_____

Phone_____ E-mail_____

Friends/Family E-mail_____

Books are $15.00 each. Send me the following number of copies of:

___ CONVICT'S CANDY   ___ GHETTOHEAT®

___ AND GOD CREATED WOMAN   ___ HARDER

___ SONZ OF DARKNESS   ___ LONDON REIGN

___ GHOST TOWN HUSTLERS   ___ BOY-TOY

___ GAMES WOMEN PLAY   ___ SKATE ON!

___ SOME SEXY, ORGASM 1   ___ HARDER 2

___ AND GOD CREATED WOMAN 2

Please send $4.00 to cover shipping and handling. Add a dollar for each additional book ordered. *Free shipping for convicts.*

Total Enclosed = _____

Please make check or money order payable to GHETTOHEAT®. Send all payments to:

GHETTOHEAT®
P.O. BOX 2746
NEW YORK, NY 10027

GHETTOHEAT®: THE HOTNESS IN THE STREETS!!!™